MAR 25

RECOMMENDED READING

RECOMMENDED READING

♡ ♡ ♡ ♡ ♡ ♡ ♡

PAUL COCCIA

zando young readers

NEW YORK

zando young readers

The characters and events in this book are fictitious. Any similarity to real persons, living or dead, is coincidental and not intended by the author.

Copyright © 2025 by Bittersweet Books, LLC

Zando supports the right to free expression and the value of copyright. The purpose of copyright is to encourage writers and artists to produce the creative works that enrich our culture. Thank you for buying an authorized edition of this book and for complying with copyright laws by not reproducing, scanning, uploading, or distributing this book or any part of it without permission. If you would like permission to use material from the book (other than for brief quotations embodied in reviews), please contact connect@zandoprojects.com.

Zando Young Readers is an imprint of Zando.
zandoprojects.com

First Edition: January 2025

Design by Neuwirth & Associates, Inc.
Cover design by Chris Kwon

The publisher does not have control over and is not responsible for author or other third-party websites (or their content).

Library of Congress Control Number: 2024939963

978-1-63893-149-2 (Hardcover)
978-1-63893-150-8 (ebook)

10 9 8 7 6 5 4 3 2 1
Manufactured in the United States of America

THE SUMMER OF BOBBY

(AKA Bobby Ashton's Plan for the Perfect Summer Before College)

- ✓ Land the Perfect Summer Job

- ✓ Land the freshman liaison gig for Summer Reading Festival

- ♡ Make festival SICKENING (see: Bobby Ashton's Plans for Little Elm's Big Summer Reading Festival)

- ♡ Land the Perfect Boyfriend: TRUMAN

- ♡ Rule over Campus Books' book club (alongside Perfect Boyfriend)

- ✓ Look fabulous every step of the way!

To Julie, Mary, and John

PROLOGUE
Say Anything . . . But That

I should have known better than to put my trust in a blow-up horse. Especially a unicorn, a famously mythical, elusive, and mysterious beast. They're a lot like me. I never should have reasonably expected one to be reined in.

So, when my inflatable rainbow unicorn sails past its mark and my meticulously laid plans instantly go to hell, it shouldn't have come as any surprise. The problem with planning everything down to the second is it only takes one second to throw it all off. Instead of the flash mob parting and several theatre students lifting me out of the fountain by my arms like a glorious treasure to be presented to my love, my rogue steed decides to veer under the curtain of water cascading from the fountain's bottom tier. I am soggy. Treasures do not sog.

I wipe the water out of my eyes, my outfit drenched from my bow tie down to my brand-new *real* fake-crystal-encrusted bedroom loafers. My carefully composed ensemble, meant to highlight and flatter my curvaceous body in an alluring way, instead clings and sticks to my every roll and crevice. There are two big dark spots where my shirt has gone see-through, my nipples on prominent display for anyone who looks. And they are looking. I orchestrated this whole thing so they would.

The dancers no longer twirl, step, and spin. They've missed their cues and keep looking from me to one another. A Calvin Harris remix of Madonna's "True Blue," the song I picked to confess my deepest, undying love for Truman, my Tru, continues to play across Little Elm College's main courtyard from Campus Books' speaker system, a system I took the liberty of hijacking for today's spectacle. Madonna is the only one who hasn't missed a beat.

Desperate to get back on course, I resign myself to paddling. My steed is starting to deflate, his head collapsing into itself. The current sends us arcing around the fountain. I only have one choice, a dismount. My unicorn has other plans. It bucks and rears, the water making everything slippery. My ride dumps me into the fountain.

Surfacing, I catch sight of Truman coming out of Campus Books, a frown on his face. Thankfully, he's the type who would come outside his place of work to see what was going on upon hearing a commotion if only to put a stop to it. I knew he would. My plan relied on it. He's a touch predictable, although I prefer to view him as reliable.

Tru has been the object of my adoration since I managed to land a spot in Little Elm's exclusive book club held at Campus Books. My feelings only strengthened after he gave me clear and unmistakable signs of his interest delivered in my preferred love language, books. He told me since I was a romance reader, I should give the greats a go. Austen. The Brontës. Tolstoy. As if that weren't direct enough, he even recommended poetry. Shakespearean sonnets. Keats. Neruda, which is borderline pornographic. Fact: no man recommends love poems to another guy without an ulterior motive.

And after all my carefully laid plans for the perfect summer and all my assistance in helping the residents of Little Elm find their happy endings over the years, it's high time I nudged my own along and let Truman know the flirtation going on between us is one hundred percent requited. Who better to play my Prince Charming than him? My path to true love is laid out before me and I am willing to traverse it. I dare any person in town to claim they've read as many romance novels as I have or watched and rewatched as many rom-coms. Nobody has the track record or expertise I do.

So, I'd come up with my proclamation-of-love plan like a scene out of one of my favorite movies and gone all grand gesture on steroids while flexing. It had to be a boom box above my head, mambo to a ballad at the end of the summer, running through a traffic jam clogging the streets of New York, meeting at the top of the Empire State Building, kissing in an unexpected torrential downpour. Doesn't my Tru deserve that? And just as important, don't I?

And like a movie, my breath should have caught the moment I saw Truman in his jacket with the suede shoulder patches, arms crossed, chewing his bottom lip, brows furrowed. Except I'm busy coughing up fountain water. He watches me get up, slip on coins underfoot, land on my knees, and indecorously waddle across the fountain until I hoist myself over its edge. Water sloshes onto the cobbles as I get out. The look on Tru's face makes it clear he's worried about me. He cares deeply.

I signal to my best friend, Wanda, to cut the music as I step forward a few feet, bridging the distance between Tru and me, between the fountain and Campus Books. Madonna goes silent. Wanda points at her laptop then holds up both hands and shrugs.

I shake my head, letting her know to keep the cameras we positioned around the courtyard streaming. I need her on tech, not worrying about my rampant aquatic equine.

My former friend and current frenemy, Evie Bosendorfer, is watching too with her usual smug look, her phone, recording every second, clutched in her French-tipped grip. Well, good. Wait until Tru and I move from book club will-they-won't-they duo and ascend to the power couple around Little Elm College in a way that future generations will speak of like the legends we are. Because Tru and me, we're not only moving from friends to lovers, we're also the strongest romance of all, the meant-to-bes, the top-tier evolution of #relationshipgoals.

I clear my throat. A dancer nods, remembering what he's supposed to do, and hands me a rose. I get on one knee.

"Truman," I call across the space between us loud enough that the crowd and cameras can hear me. "Tru, would you do me the great honor of—"

"Bobby, please. Don't," Truman cuts in. "Get up. Let's get you dried off."

He's so perfect, thinking about my well-being and comfort first. But dryness can wait.

I open my mouth to finish my speech, but some guy steps out of the Campus Books doorway and places a hand on Truman's shoulder.

I recognize him from the back cover of the latest it-lit book everyone's talking about. A book I saw Truman carrying around. *The Gondolier's Oarlock*, written by local author Scott Horatio. It's the upcoming book club selection and is rumored to be in contention for the awards circuits.

Scott leans in and asks Truman, "You ok?"

Truman pats Scott's hand and nods. Scott steps back.

I make a mental note to skip the next book club meeting.

Unexpected, but Scott is just one more wrench in my plans. So what if there's another guy? Every relationship has its obstacles and I'm sure I can turn this love triangle in my favor. And no big deal if he's kind of a literary celebrity. I've got choreography.

I flick my dripping hair out of my eyes. "Tru," I continue, jumping ahead in my speech. "Like other great lovers, Dante and Beatrice, Antony and Cleopatra, Zendaya and Tom—"

Truman covers his face with a hand. "Let's not do this here. Let's go inside. Somewhere less public."

But I can't. This is a *public* declaration of my feelings. It needs to be done in front of people. I can feel all eyes on me. The bewilderment of the dancers wondering if they should pick up where they got interrupted is apparent from their faces. Wanda glances from me to the camera feeds. Evie smirks.

I hold the rose out farther, begging, willing him to step forward and take it. My weeks of orchestrating this moment can all work out. My plans for our future happiness together can work out too. He only has to step forward.

"Tru," I repeat.

"Come inside, Bobby." Truman steps back, turns, and begins to walk into Campus Books.

"Truman, Tru, please," I call out.

I know if there's a last chance, a Hail Mary, I need to stop him and do it fast. I get up, my head swinging, eyes darting, searching for something, anything that will get him to pause, to come back to me and take the rose.

I see stones by the base of the fountain and rush over, my loafers and the water making it a deadly scurry. I grab a handful of small stones, thinking of my favorite romance book, *Pebbles Tossed at a Window*. It's the one romance Truman has read at my insistence. Even he said it was *cute*. I spin around and begin tossing pebbles at Campus Books' etched glass front window. I miss but the few that hit are barely audible.

I search the ground again and see a bigger stone, more rock-like than pebble. It probably came from one of the flower beds around the courtyard. But if I want it to work like in the book, I need to commit.

All it takes is one second to throw off the most carefully laid plans and for me to realize that throwing rocks at a window, no matter how romantic it seems in a book or movie, is in reality a terrible idea. It takes a single second more for a pair of bargain loafers and some wet cobblestones to send me reeling, arms flailing, grasping at nothing. I fall backward over the fountain's ledge. The rock sails out of my hand.

I hear a crack. For a moment, silence, then the crashing of breaking glass. A shriek from somewhere. The water surges up around me and yanks me down, my head colliding with something. I flounder, sounds of splashing joining the burbling of the fountain. Some of the dancers grip me by the arms and pull me out. My knees collide hard with the cobblestones. I reach up to my aching head. When I pull my hand back, it's red.

The sun tucks behind the Gothic buildings typical of this part of campus, the last slants of its rays breaking off as the fairy lights draped from buildings, trees, and awnings blink into life above us. One more part of my grand gesture as planned.

The Books' front window which spanned the entire length of the building is no longer there. Staff and customers appear from inside the store, peering out through the now-empty space. Pieces of the shattered window have shot across the cobblestones, dotting the ground like glitter.

Truman does turn back around now, glass crunching and crackling underfoot as he approaches. He crouches near me, head hung, eyes in shadow. He reaches out to touch my head but draws his hand away before he does. Tiny bits of broken glass rest on his shoulders like starlight, so close I could brush them off. He cups his hands and lifts the rose from the cobbles, droplets clinging to it like dew. It's slightly crushed but still fine. He leans forward, lips parted, coming closer, closer.

I can smell his clove cigarettes still lingering on him, mixing with the scent of flowers coming into bloom around the courtyard. The breeze cuts through my wet clothing and chills me. I hold my breath. It's as if everyone here does too, watching, waiting for him to slide his arms around my shivering body and press his lips against mine. I stare into his eyes and will him to close the distance between us. We could still have our happily ever after. I know he feels it too. It would take just one second to tame this rogue, deflated unicorn and make everything right again. Please, Tru. Take it. Take me.

Eyes wide, Truman looks around. He notices the red lights of the cameras, my eyes now reflecting their scarlet glimmer along my bottom lids.

He leans past me and drops the rose in a puddle on the fountain's ledge. With it drops my heart.

"Turn those off. Now," he orders. "Bobby, we need to speak. In private."

RECOMMENDED READING

1

Bobby Ashton vs. the World

"I told you to keep the shades drawn." I shield my eyes as morning's bright sunlight forces its way into the living room. "You know I've taken to bed."

"You're on the couch in the middle of the living room," Cass points out. "Taking to bed is for the sick or infirm."

"Well, I'm ill."

"With what?" She crosses her arms. She's in one of her old blazers. I haven't seen it out from the deep recesses of her closet for years. Usually, they hang, smooshed right up against the stylish clothing I convinced her to buy but she's never once worn.

"The Danish disease," I inform her, sitting up and rearranging my silk kimono-style caftan around me, crossing my legs, and pointing my toe to make my calves look as good as Miss Piggy's. Just because I'm in the throes of despair doesn't mean I'm letting myself go, and moi always aspires to rock a ham hock half as well as Piggy. "Like Hamlet," I clarify when Cass doesn't respond.

"That's not a real thing," she says, twisting her hair up.

"Tell it to Ophelia. Melancholy is too a thing. I checked an online Shakespearean version of WebMD. My humors are unbalanced and my biles are out of sorts." I sigh heavily to punctuate the seriousness of my situation.

"Well, sort them out in the car. We've got that appointment with Dean Perez this morning. We need to limit fallout and mitigate damage."

I yawn. It's cute when Cass tries to sound all adult, especially when she's mixed up the dates. "That's on Tuesday," I inform her.

"It is Tuesday, Bobby."

I scramble for my phone to check. I stare at the screen in disbelief. I never forget what day it is. Another undocumented effect of public humiliation must be missing time.

"Why didn't you wake me up earlier?" I rush to the bathroom, grabbing my toothbrush as I strip down and jump into the shower. The water heats up by the time I'm spitting down the drain.

I'm always on schedule. Or I was. Before everything with Tru. I force those thoughts out of my head, something I've been trying to do with limited success since I shattered Campus Books' window.

I grab the nearest towel, not caring that it doesn't stretch all the way around me. A pair of jeans and a shirt are already laid out on my bed. It's not what I would have chosen but Cass tried her best. I swap out the shirt for a hot-pink polo with sunshine-yellow stitching. Melancholics are known to wear black, but I don't own many dark clothes. They blend in and since this body doesn't, I've made the conscious decision to work with my assets.

"I can't find my purple suede wing tips," I call out.

Cass appears at my bedroom door, my shoes dangling from her hand.

In a flurry, we get into the car. It's good that Cass drives with the same abandon with which she parents. She zips around other vehicles, noses into gaps, and speeds through stretches officers never patrol. Knowing Little Elm this well is one of the benefits of having lived here all our lives. Not that anything in town is far from anywhere else, but Cass can shave precious minutes off any commute.

She clears her throat. "I know you haven't wanted to, but do we need to discuss—"

"No," I cut her off.

She reaches over and squeezes my hand as she swerves lanes without signaling.

"Do me a favor, Mom. Once we're with Dean Perez, let me handle things." I intentionally call her Mom to get her attention.

She wrinkles her nose and nods but doesn't react beyond that. My conception came as a late-in-life surprise for Cass, and she always prided her age and wisdom in not imposing an innate power imbalance on our parent-child relationship via oppressive nomenclature. It sounded super progressive until she let it slip that she simply never wanted to be one of those parents craning her neck when a random kid in a grocery store or playground called out *Mommy*.

The town blurs by until we jerk to a stop in front of Little Elm College's oldest and most stately looking set of buildings that house the dean's offices.

"Here we go," Cass says as we mount the steps into the building, then up the high-gloss mahogany stairs. All the lacquered wood reminds me of Campus Books, the shelves polished to a high sheen and smelling faintly of chemicals laced with lemon. We climb a smaller set of stairs to enter an office where a guy is seated behind three computer screens, glancing from one to another.

"You must be the Ashtons," he says, momentarily looking up. "The dean is waiting. Through the doors to my left."

We go inside. Floor-to-ceiling windows take up the wall behind the dean's desk. Burgundy velvet curtains are drawn back by gold cords with large tassels. Another wall is covered with built-in shelving. Sitting on them are leather-bound books adorned with gilt lettering and various little statues, vases, and photos of previous deans shaking hands with people of note. The desk itself is massive. About twice the length or more of any I've ever seen. A gold filigreed burgundy leather pad is inlaid into it. A banker's lamp and a scrambled Rubik's Cube are perched on the desk's corner. A salt-and-pepper-haired man punching the screen of a cell phone with his finger sits behind the desk.

"Michael," Dean Perez calls out. "I don't know what I'm doing with this thing."

The multiscreen guy, Michael, appears at the doorway. "We'll walk through it again later. Bobby Ashton is here to see you."

"Please sit. The stupid thing is supposed to sync to my computer, but it must take some witchcraft to make it work." Dean Perez places his cell phone into a drawer. "Remind me again, Michael. What's this all about?"

"Campus Books' window. I played the video for you earlier . . . on your phone." Michael's eyes glint as he leaves.

A hard and uncomfortable feeling forms below my rib cage. Even Dean Perez has watched the footage.

"Right. Unfortunate incident," the dean comments.

"It was an accident," I say.

"Clearly. Still, Mr. Ashton, that window was of some importance. The donors are descendants of Little Elm College's most famous alumnus."

"With all due respect," I ask, "who is that?"

"I'm not sure. But it doesn't matter as the family not only donated the window but money for scholarships like the one you were offered. They're not happy paying for the education of students who smash their ancestors' memorials. Unhappy people have ungenerous wallets."

"I can pay for a new window," I say. "I'll work it off. I'll do extra shifts at Campus Books."

Dean Perez grimaces and reaches for the Rubik's Cube. "That's another thing. Campus Books' manager isn't too pleased either. You used your brief time employed there to plan the unauthorized stunt at the fountain. You took over their sound system. And, of course, there was the window. Frankly, it came as a relief when you didn't show up to finish your training and they didn't have to fire you."

"Fire me!" I exclaim, standing up. "I texted them I needed a few personal days for mental health reasons. Anyone could understand that after everything I've been through. They can't fire me. I must have some sort of employee rights. Besides, they need me! I'm the Big Summer Reading Festival's freshman liaison!"

"Were." Dean Perez twists the cube again. "There were concerns about you working with the festival coordinator. You're familiar with Truman, of course. It could all be a bit awkward and uncomfortable. You see, the damage is more complex than a broken window. Lots of factors to consider. There's also the nasty business of the donors asking me to reconsider your scholarship."

I gulp. I need that scholarship. There's no way Cass and I could afford me going to college without it. "They can't do that. Can they?"

"They hold the purse strings," Dean Perez says.

Cass reaches across and places her hand on my forearm, guiding me back into my chair.

"I can fix this," I say. "Give me a chance. I can't be kicked out of college before I even start. I'll think of something. I'll do anything."

Dean Perez puts down the cube.

Except, I can't think of anything I can offer or do at this moment. I'm normally great with a plan. After all, a plan is only a plot put into action. And who reads more than me? But my plan for the Summer of Bobby is unraveling in front of me and I've got nothing. I turn to Cass and give her a pleading look.

She nods before she says, "Surely, Dean Perez, a bit of broken glass isn't worth more than my son's future."

"Surely not, Mrs. Ashton."

"I'm not married." She holds up her left hand and wiggles her fingers. "Feel free to call me Cass."

"Cass Ashton," Dean Perez says slowly. "Why does that sound so familiar?" He pushes a button on a large, old intercom. "Michael? Why do I know Cass Ashton?"

A crackly voice responds, "I couldn't say, sir."

The dean pouts before his face suddenly brightens. "Not *the* Cass Ashton? Famous artist? You were big once!"

"She's still big," I say as if it's my cue. "It's this town that's small." I know Cass will pick up on my *Sunset Boulevard* reference because my fabulous taste in movies stems from her.

"Silent films, Norma," Cass says under her breath. She reaches up and undoes her hair, brown waves cascading down around her. "Why, Dean Perez, I'm flattered you remember me."

"You were a visionary," Dean Perez says. "It's a shame you stopped sculpting."

Cass leans back on one elbow and crosses one leg over the top of the other.

I reach out, giving Cass a sign to cool it. She shrugs me away.

"Keep going and you'll have me blushing." She winks. She *actually* winks. No one winks in real life. It's weird. "Now, back to my son. He showed a youthful lack of forethought. We've all been there. At his age, I was no angel."

Dean Perez chuckles. "Neither was I. And as far as indiscretions go, Bobby meant no harm. No one was hurt."

Except for me but no one seems to be thinking about that.

"This sort of behavior is out of character for Bobby," Cass adds.

I want to butt in and argue that, no, grand gestures are my thing and I have successfully helped many of the residents of Little Elm find love with them. I'd even go so far as to say I'm beloved for my grand gestures. No one else in this town is more versed in romance than me. No one else contrives circumstances where two strangers who should be together meet, say, over produce in a grocery store, and somehow end up in an orchard at sunset while a string quartet happens to be practicing sonatas nearby for an upcoming gig. (You're welcome, Alicia and Rashida.) I am the somehow. I've got the gift, nay, the responsibility, to assist the people of Little Elm, and all my romance novel reading and movie watching have honed my natural talents. The kicker is, like a psychic, I apparently can't use my powers for my own gain.

Dean Perez strokes his beard. "I'm sure Bobby's a good kid. Perhaps we could come to a creative resolution."

"My favorite kind," Cass replies.

"Cass," I hiss. None of this sounds right and I seem to be the only one recognizing the warning signs.

She shushes me and waves a hand dismissively. Rude.

I gulp, waiting to see if the dean hits on my mother right in front of me, as Cass, who is knowingly encouraging the situation, throws her head back and laughs.

"While I can't do much about Bobby's job at Campus Books, I'm certain I can smooth things over with our donors. There was some talk of rescinding his admission offer too, but I'm almost certain that was only bandied around in the heat of the moment."

The feeling inside me pulses at the mention of losing my admission. More than my Summer of Bobby plans could be coming undone. I grip the arms of my chair.

"And you said you were no angel." Cass smiles broadly.

"There's one condition," Dean Perez continues. "I retire at the end of this year. I'd like to gift the college something lasting upon my departure. A statue by famous artist Cass Ashton seems grandiose enough."

"You want a sculpture?" Cass's smile falters. "Dean Perez, I haven't sculpted in forever. The closest I come to art nowadays is my online rare wool store and Bobby is the one who handles all the technical stuff."

Dean Perez waves the Rubik's Cube at Cass. "Surely, this trade is worth your son's future."

Cass clears her throat and sits upright. "Surely."

"And if the sculpture was to be constructed by repurposing the larger pieces of a certain broken window, I'm sure the donors could be convinced the accident was fortuitous. A blessing, even."

"A statue made out of broken glass?" Cass asks.

"A statue made out of the most embarrassing moment," I say.

"If you'd rather we explore other options . . ." Dean Perez's voice trails off.

Cass looks at me. I shake my head but I'm not sure if I'm shaking my agreement or dissent.

She stands, reaching her hand across the desk. "It sounds like a deal I can't possibly refuse."

The feeling below my rib cage solidifies and drops deeper into me.

"Excellent." Dean Perez pushes the button on the speaker. "Michael, have the window remains sent to the Ashton residence."

"Thank you, Dean," Cass says. "Bobby, thank the dean."

I force myself to stand. "Thank you, sir," I mumble, staring down.

"Bobby," Dean Perez says. "You keep your nose clean and focus on your academics. No more schemes. Adolescent crushes will still be there after you graduate. I'd prefer the windows around campus be there after you graduate as well."

It wasn't an adolescent crush though. Tru was the perfect guy. He fit into the plan so perfectly. At least, until I found out he was with someone else and didn't return my affection. I was so sure he did.

"It was an accident," I repeat.

Cass takes me by the arm and leads me out past Michael, through the building, and out to our car.

The shock of the meeting with the dean has worn off by the time I close my door. The feeling below my rib cage has turned hot.

"Celebratory caramel macchiato?" Cass asks as soon as she's in too.

"What even happened back there?" I ask, ignoring the offer of my favorite beverage.

"What?"

"Your *Basic Instinct* schtick. The meeting went off the rails. We were supposed to be doing damage control, not flirting."

"I can't help it if I exude sex appeal. He's an attractive man and I'm a woman in my prime."

"Gross. Not a conversation to be having with your teenage son," I say. "Besides, I don't think anyone's sexual prime is post-menopause."

"What you don't know about women—"

"I'll never need to," I finish for her. "He sounded like he was propositioning you."

"Dean Perez? Unlikely. It was harmless."

"Was agreeing to the statue harmless too?" I ask. "Did you stop to think what it will feel like for me to walk by a permanent fixture immortalizing the most humiliating moment of my life?"

"You're lucky you get to walk by it at all," Cass responds. "I did what I needed to keep you in school. You were the one who looked to me for help. I helped. You can't be upset with me now."

The fiery feeling inside me is burning itself out. "There had to be another way."

"You couldn't think of one." Cass sighs. "I know you had that plan. The Summer of Bobby or whatever. But it didn't include getting your heart broken or losing your job. We needed a new plan. We can't afford to lose that scholarship. You knew getting me involved meant playing a wild card. A bit of harmless flirting and semifamous artist Cass Ashton were the only leverage I had."

As much as I don't want to admit it, she's right. If I expected an orthodox solution, I should have been born to a different parent. All I managed to do was uncheck items from my list. No job. No boyfriend. No festival. Almost no college except for Cass intervening.

She grips the wheel and sighs. "This is not the summer I wanted for you either."

"We're barely covering our expenses as it is," I say. "Everyone's already hired their summer staff. How can we afford school in September and whatever a sculpture is going to cost on top of that?"

Cass bites at a hangnail on her thumb. "I don't know. I'll figure it out."

"But," I begin again.

"I'm the parent."

Cass is good at parenting stuff like taking a kid to watch a movie he's not old enough to get into but is obsessed with the previews of. Or buying ten different kinds of chips for the ultimate taste test. Or driving two hours to a store that stocks larger-sized kids' clothing so her prepubescent son doesn't need to wear a men's small and insisting on splurging on fast food along the way even when said son is sure he should be on a diet. In those ways, she's the perfect parent.

It's the practical stuff like checking grocery store flyers for the best deals or getting oil changes at regularly scheduled intervals where Cass isn't the best at adulting. I don't doubt she could figure things out if she had to, like getting milk at a gas station when she realizes we're out at three in the morning. Or sculpting a statue out of broken glass.

It's my fault we're in this situation at all. I read the signs wrong with Truman. I took a college guy's being nice to me as some sort of interest on his part. The task of fixing the mess I created shouldn't fall on Cass. It's mine to clean up.

By the time we pull into our driveway, I've run through all sorts of scenarios trying to figure out my options. The

Summer of Bobby won't be how I imagined it. But like any diva worth their salt, when one door closes, an opportunity for a comeback opens. No more couches with the shades drawn and Adele on repeat. The only one who can stop me from salvaging the Summer of Bobby is me. I swear, like Miley Cyrus before me, I will buy my own flowers and hold my own hand. I'm ready for my close-up, Little Elm!

Once Cass is out of earshot, I open the contacts on my cell, scroll down, and dial the number of the only guy in town who would do whatever he could for Cass and me without question.

I put on my peppiest voice. "Hi, Uncle Andy. I know, I haven't been down to your store in ages. It's actually why I'm calling. I need a job. Any job. I don't care if it's cleaning up garbage or packing boxes or standing on the corner twirling a sign. I'll take whatever you can offer."

THE SUMMER OF BOBBY

(AKA Bobby Ashton's Plan for the ~~Perfect~~ Summer Before College)

- ✓ Land ~~the Perfect~~ ANY Summer Job

- ♡ ~~Land the freshman liaison gig for Big Summer Reading Festival~~

- ♡ ~~Make festival SICKENING (see: Bobby Ashton's Plans for Little Elm's Big Summer Reading Festival)~~

- ♡ ~~Land the Perfect Boyfriend: TRUMAN~~

- ♡ ~~Rule over Campus Books' book club (alongside Perfect Boyfriend)~~

- ✓ Look fabulous every step of the way! (AT LEAST I STILL GOT THIS)

2

The Shop Around the Corner

On Friday morning I take the bus downtown, past all the crumbling industrial buildings to the old Main Street strip that now has worse-for-wear, run-down shops. Some will be out of business by next year. I know Uncle Andy and the local business association had hoped some developer would come in and an upscale furniture store would open, or a condo complex would go up and revitalize things. So far, no luck.

"Bobby?" I hear from the back of the bus as people get off at the next stop.

I turn my head in time to see two arms envelop me. The owner of the arms pulls back and waggles a ringed finger at me. Tricia, a girl from high school I'd first met weeping in the nurse's office over being dumped by her middle school boyfriend.

"Engaged! Can you believe it?" Tricia asks. "All thanks to you. If you hadn't convinced Mikey to leave me all those secret admirer notes and me to reply, I'd still be crying over Jordan."

"Wow. Congratulations," I say, genuinely surprised. We just graduated high school and while I knew Tricia and Mikey were a perfect pair and feel a swell of pride in them planning the rest of their lives together thanks to yours truly, I also feel a pang of it should be me and Tru planning a future.

Tricia's face darkens and I wonder if she picked up on my it-should-be-me vibe before she says, "I saw the video of you at the fountain. I want to be the first to tell you that guy doesn't deserve you. You can do so much better."

Except Truman's rejection is evidence that I, in fact, cannot. But I'm not about to have a breakdown on a bus right before my first day at my new job. Instead, I reply, "No worries! I'm moving on and moving up."

"That's great! You've already found someone new?"

"Not exactly. I'm focusing on me right now and keeping my options open." Before Tricia can ask me more specific questions about what that entails, I say, "Here's my stop. And seriously, congratulations to you two."

"I'll text you an invite to the engagement party," Tricia calls as I get off the bus.

I cross the street to Corner Books, named, as I've long assumed, because it sits on the corner of the block. Not original but it ensures the location is clear. The bulbs flicker behind half of the wraparound sign. The other half's bulbs have been burnt out for as long as I can remember. It's owned by Cass's oldest friend, my Uncle Andy who isn't actually my blood relative. I normally love a bookstore but this one has slid downhill worse than I remember.

I don't need to look through the windows to picture the mismatched shelves Uncle Andy has rescued over the years from curbs around Little Elm. Some metal, others wood, their paint flaking off. They were probably discarded when students moved out of rental units and Uncle Andy picked them up, brought them here, and gave them a new home.

As most of Corner Books' revenue comes from used textbook sales, used shelves fit the theme. The remainder of its sales comes from books that Campus Books doesn't keep in stock because they're not current best sellers or on any course's syllabus. Campus Books, in fact, never started a buy-back program for textbooks because of how well Corner Books handles the market and because, as rumor has it among Campus Books' employees, dog-eared, dated versions of textbooks don't have the same air of prestige Campus Books prides itself upon and would bring down the overall vibe of the store.

I'm ashamed to admit as soon as I got a spot in book club alongside Truman, I purposely distanced myself and avoided Uncle Andy's store. Corner Books wasn't part of the image I was going for either and it didn't suit my rising brand, even though when I was growing up Uncle Andy kept me supplied with as many books as I could go through. Uncle Andy still comes over with boxes of titles he'd ripped the covers off to send back to publishers and advance copies, neither of which he can sell.

Old habits die hard and thinking of my image, I decided even though Corner Books is in a crappy part of downtown, and the mismatched shelves are as old and used as the books, it doesn't mean I shouldn't look my best. It's on my list, after all.

My mustard-colored corduroy pants match my *Fully Booked* stack of novels T-shirt excellently. I threw on a chunky knit sweater and even wore my thick black plastic-framed glasses, so I'd look extra smart and literary. The glasses aren't prescription, but they do have UV protection. They let people know I'm intelligent and well-read. I mean, I *am* intelligent and well-read. But with the glasses on, anyone can tell from a glance.

And maybe while choosing this outfit I might have indulged in a few fantasies of myself looking attractive as I wandered up and down the aisles of the store, nose in a classic like *Wuthering Heights*. Suddenly, a guy with big zaddy energy like Pedro Pascal swaggers up to me and says those three magic words I've been longing to hear my whole life, "What you reading?" Admittedly, the store I imagined I'd be in was more upmarket and less bargain discount, but I can make it work. This is the way.

Despite how cute I look and my positive can-do outlook, I'm nervous and sweating. For one thing, I barely received any training at Campus Books. As awesome as I look and as forgiving and flattering as a chunky knit on a guy of my build is, it is summer. Fat guys, summer heat, and layers aren't a good combo. Stains are forming under my arms, and I can even feel a trickle going down the small of my back into my butt crack.

My brain jumped past the *summer* part of summer job when Uncle Andy agreed to let me work here not as a sign twirler or garbage collector, but as an actual bookseller. I doubt he needs another employee, but as Cass always says, "Andy would do anything we ask and more. So, be careful what you ask him."

I wonder if I can fan out the sweat stains when two faces appear on the other side of the door. One, I know. Uncle Andy. He's in his usual button-down tucked into a pair of khakis, brown belt matching brown shoes. At dinners over the years, I've offered a few suggestions to jazz up his attire, but Cass's snorting laughter kills any hopes of that. I suppose his dull attire fits the worn-in vibe of Corner Books.

"We didn't mean to startle you," Uncle Andy says with a laugh as he eases open the door and the little bell tied to the top of it tinkles. "Come on in. I don't think you've been here since I hired Corner Books' first employee. Gladys, Bobby. Bobby, Gladys."

I've heard mention of Gladys as this old-school battle-ax, but nothing could have prepared me for her. She glowers at me, looking like a cross between a Chihuahua–Jack Russell mix and Sophia Petrillo from *The Golden Girls* with her tightly wound perm, and isn't subtle as she sizes me up through her thick glasses.

If we're going to work together, we need to get off on the right foot. I decide to give Gladys a big, toothy smile. I've been told I have a great smile. Score one for orthodontia. After her brief stint as a receptionist in a retirement community, Cass insists dental hygiene is an investment in one's future.

Gladys looks from me to Uncle Andy. "How do you turn him off?"

She might as well have slapped the smile off my face.

"Well, that did it," she says.

"Be nice, Gladys," Uncle Andy warns. "You've been complaining about how much work there is. Bobby is here to help you."

"I thought I had been clear. I never said I wanted help. I didn't ask for it and, for the record, I don't need any either. I'm not abnormal in the fact that I love to complain."

"Bobby is here for the summer whether you like it or not."

"I certainly do not," she says. "Is his given name Bobby or Robert? I don't care for silly nicknames as you well know, Andrew."

I've never heard anyone call Uncle Andy "Andrew." Not even Cass. Andy isn't even a nickname. It's a short form.

Uncle Andy laughs again, a bit nervous this time.

Despite setbacks, of which there have been numerous instances, the only way forward is to be an optimist and to see the best in situations and people despite how awful some of them (Gladys) may behave. I even read an online article or two on creating positive, fulfilling work relationships when I was asked to join the Campus Books crew. If Bobby Ashton is anything, it's a team player. The first step for a difficult personality is setting clear boundaries so Gladys and I understand the nature of our future working relationship and, in turn, foster an environment of mutual respect.

"Actually, I prefer Bobby," I say, forcing my smile back onto my face. I hold out my hand. "It's a bit more fun and young. Don't you think?"

Gladys takes a long time blinking as she stares at my hand. "I'm too old to be coming to work for fun. I'll be calling you Robert."

"It's Bobby."

"Robert," she repeats. "If you don't like it, don't answer. It won't bother me one bit. I can only assume your parents took time and care in naming you Robert. It's what I'll be calling you."

"Everyone calls me Bobby. It's what my mom named me," I gently correct after I stop gritting my teeth. "Bobby is cuter. Why don't you try it out and see how you like it?"

"I won't and I don't. Same as I won't be directing customers to poems by Bobby Frost or novels by Bobby Louis Stevenson. It's undignified and childish. Cute is for newborns. You're too long in the tooth for that."

I raise an eyebrow at her. Did Gladys seriously just call me old?

"I don't pay you extra for snark, Gladys," Uncle Andy says.

Gladys places her hands on her hips. "Then consider it a bargain I'm providing it for free. If I'm stuck bringing this one up to speed, I'm going to have my work cut out for me. Come on, Robert. Keep up. A little farther past the entrance won't kill you," she says as she turns and storms through the store. "Your uncle has some books to pick up that were mistakenly delivered across town. It's you and me for the morning." She's quicker than I imagined a woman best described as a withered old bat could ever be.

Uncle Andy leans in. "Don't take what she says to heart. She doesn't mean anything. That's just Gladys being Gladys. You'll be fine once she warms up a little."

"Hurry up, Robert," she calls. "We're not paid to stand around looking moist."

Warm up? A Siberian gulag seems balmy right now and Gladys has managed to get me sweating harder in my cords than the summer heat ever could.

3

Just a Boy Standing in Front of a Boy, Asking Him If He Requires Assistance

Halfway through the morning, drill sergeant Gladys must be running low on crotchetiness or patience. Maybe both. She gives up taking me through the buyback procedure and tells me to do a sweep of the store for customers or shoplifters while she brews herself a cup of herbal tea. From the way she spits out the word *customers*, I don't think there's much difference in her mind between them and shoplifters. Both are likely the same level of nuisance to her.

"Approach people in a friendly manner and offer them assistance," Gladys instructs me. "But don't be so friendly they feel comfortable and want to spend more time in the store. Loitering is a real problem, particularly in bookstores. We want customers to make purchases, and then leave. It's a fine balance."

"Good book reference," I say, hoping some Rohinton Mistry may be what finally warms Gladys to me. Tru was a big fan of Mistry, so naturally, I read it. But he shouldn't get too much credit; it was an international bestseller and I read everything.

She adjusts her glasses. "What was?"

"Never mind." I slump off to the nearest aisle.

It's tempting to browse as I walk around. I run my finger along the spines of the titles. Something about touching a book's spine always strikes me as somewhat intimate and slightly naughty. You don't generally go around touching spines unless maybe you're a chiropractor or pet a lot of dogs and cats. I wonder if the books get the same little thrill from it that I do. I smile and hum to myself quietly, so Gladys won't hear me and tell me I'm off-key.

I turn to head down the last aisle to the back corner where the romances are kept and see a leg stretching out across the floor. My mind jumps ahead of me to someone having fainted and needing an ambulance, then to someone in the romance section getting *romantic*. The Campus Books staff told me rumors about students getting caught doing the deed in the library. I brace myself as much as I can and head in.

What I'm not ready to find is a guy reading. Just reading. Head down, nose in a book. Maybe it was too obvious a conclusion to seem plausible, because it's not nearly as exciting as busting a heist, being the hero in a medical drama, or stumbling upon a couple giving a go at Othello's beast with two backs.

The owner of the long leg has his other one bent and is resting his chin on his knee. The book he's immersed in is balanced on the toe of his white sneaker. His hair is short along the back and sides and tousled on top, a little bit longer, highlighted blond. From the way the streaks lie, I can tell they're from the sun, not a salon. He's got on a white tee and a pair of light-wash jeans with the cuffs rolled up, no socks. I can see a glimpse of chest hair over his neckline and notice he's got a fair amount of fine, almost translucent hair covering his arms.

His skin almost glows with a faint golden undertone everywhere it is exposed. Like his hair, it must have decided to drink sunshine.

I don't know how I missed him coming in, there was only one other customer, a girl around my age named Mya who works at the coffee shop down the street and brings Gladys her daily scone. He must have snuck in when Gladys showed me where to stack returns in the back room because there's no way I wouldn't have noticed this guy. I stand there, staring at him, not sure what my next move is.

He reaches out and delicately turns a page. Even more gently he blinks, his eyelashes moving like the wings of a dragonfly at rest. One corner of his mouth shifts up almost imperceptibly. Not a full smile but he's obviously enjoying whatever it is he's reading. I can't see the cover or title.

I half turn to go back down the aisle, figuring I'll return and clear my throat or sneeze to be sure he hears me coming. But I don't get a chance because he looks up.

He blinks that dragonfly blink again, his eyes coming into focus as if he's just woken up. I open my mouth to say something but stop myself when he snaps the book shut. He pulls his other leg up, leans into his knees, and sandwiches the book between his thighs and chest, completely hidden from view.

I narrow my eyes. Whatever is going on, it's fishy.

"May I help you?" I ask in a pointed tone. It's only now that I wonder what I'm supposed to do if I did find a shoplifter.

He swallows and squeezes his lips together. He leans forward even more so he can look past me down the aisle.

"I'm good. Uh. Can I help you?" he asks like he's the one employed here.

"I'm good too," I say, my mind racing. The guy is fitter than I am and could take me. He could be concealing a weapon. I could very well be in mortal danger, and I'm not trained to stop a dangerous criminal. What would I even do? Scream for help? Try to tackle him? Get into a fistfight? I might get in a good slap or two but that's it.

We continue to stare at each other.

"You sure?" he asks, with a tilt of his head.

I put my hands on my hips and blurt, "I'm trying to figure out if you're planning to burgle."

The guy laughs, leaning back. It's enough that I can see the title of the book. *The Silver Devil*, one of the rippingest bodice rippers out there. Not what a sun-soaked would-be frat boy should be reading. Even if I'm not dealing with a shoplifter, my initial instincts may not be completely off. This guy could still be a low-level perv.

"I'm not going to steal. Cross my heart." And he does. He crosses his heart, like a Boy Scout, before he checks the time on his phone resting on the ground beside him. "It's later than I thought. I'll get out of your way." He stands and scans the aisle for a way out. There is none except to go past me.

But the aisle is narrow. And I am not.

He realizes this when we end up squished only a few inches apart. His cheeks are spotty and red under his golden tan. His blue-gray eyes are like ice over a puddle. He's still clutching the book to his chest.

"Is it any good?" I ask. When he continues to stare into my eyes without responding, I add, "The book."

He looks down. "It's not the sort of thing I normally read."

"It's exactly the sort of thing I normally read," I admit, surprising myself. Being fat and Cass's kid, I'm all for being who you are and letting your personal brand of freak flag fly. But this guy is a stranger and admitting to reading romances to him is kind of like telling him what cut of underwear I prefer.

He moves as if to step away, but his back is against a set of steel shelves that would look more at home in a garage stocked with power tools than housing romance novels.

"I could make a few recommendations," I offer. "To get you started. Since I know the area well."

"No, that's ok."

"It's no problem. Seriously. It's my favorite thing."

"Making recommendations or books?"

"Both."

He holds up *The Silver Devil*. "I was giving something different a try. I'm not sure it's for me."

"That one might have been a lot to start with," I say. "There's more variety within the genre nowadays."

He hesitates, then says, "No offense, but I'm not sold on romance. The relationships portrayed in these books are problematic. They're not realistic or attainable."

"Problematic relationships are completely attainable."

He laughs. "Touché. So, you're an expert?"

I shrug and can't help but smile. "I know a few things."

"About love?"

"About romance."

"What's the difference?" He runs a hand through his hair.

I smell laundry detergent and grapefruit shampoo and the kind of inexpensive aftershave fathers might wear gathered in an auditorium on parent council night. I study his face. He looks slightly amused, the smile on his face stretching from his lips through his cheeks and into his eyes.

"Everything." I pause. "And nothing."

"I should call you Casanova then."

Not wanting to give away too much without knowing a little about this stranger, I shrug again. "Depends. What should I call you?"

He grins. "I'm new here."

"That's not what I meant."

"I know. I really do need to go." He turns and strides toward the front of the store.

I follow. "Did you want to steal that?" I point to the book he's still carrying.

"Oh right. I don't think so. Like I said, it's not really my thing." He holds the book out.

I pull it toward me. The cover, a half-naked woman in the arms of a stern, rakish man, is dated and the pages are yellowed but otherwise, it's in perfect condition. He hasn't let go of the book. Our fingers graze on the spine and I feel a tingle.

"Robert?" I hear Gladys's sharp voice from behind me.

The guy jerks his hand back from *The Silver Devil* as if he received an electric shock.

"If he's ready to cash out, I better do it. You don't know how to work our machine," Gladys says as she comes up beside me. "Give that here."

The guy's eyes go wide. I know that look. It's the look of being caught. The look of embarrassment. A look I've received my entire life. A lot of people can be judgy about a lot of things including liking romances, and *The Silver Devil* leans toward salacious and scandalous. That doesn't make reading it something to be ashamed of. There's a world of difference between a guilty pleasure and feeling like you're doing something wrong.

It's not like this guy and I know each other. It's not like I have a reason other than I've been in his shoes, feeling like someone is judging me for what I like to read, or how extra I am, or how fat, or how I've messed up. Those feelings suck and I don't want someone else feeling that way if I can help it. Especially not because of some book.

With one quick motion, I hide *The Silver Devil* behind my back.

Gladys fixes me in her glare. "I don't much care for what it is you're playing at. Hand it over."

I position myself so Gladys can't reach around my body and make a grab for the book. In those few seconds, the guy is out the door, the little bell jingling.

"Not even noon and you already lost your first sale," Gladys says with an eye roll.

I stare after the guy. Maybe it's the devil in my hands spurring me on, but I can't stand thinking of him without a little romance in his life even if his first venture into it was more tawdry than happily ever after.

"I'll be right back," I say and hurry out the door before Gladys can object. My thighs rub together as I run up the block, the material of my pants heating up and swishing loudly making me sound like an oversize corduroy grasshopper.

"Hey," I call. "Hold up."

The guy stops when he sees me.

I pant as I hold out the book. "Here."

He doesn't move to take it. "I don't normally—"

"You said already. I don't normally run in the heat. Consider it a welcome gift, new here."

He extends his hand slowly to take the book from me. "Do you normally give guys you just met gifts?"

"It's a day for not normally."

"Maybe I'll catch you around, Casanova," he says. "Or is it Robert?"

"Bobby. And it's not a big town."

He holds the book up. "Thanks, Bobby." The sun gathers on his shoulders and the top of his head, outlining him.

"And I should call you?" I ask.

"New here," he says before he turns, sunlight sparkling off his lashes and in his eyes. He grins back at me over his shoulder as he walks away. "Luke."

He turns the corner before I head back inside Corner Books.

Gladys is waiting, tapping her foot. "What sort of nonsense was that? We're a store, not a library. You can't be giving things away for free."

I slide my wallet out of my back pocket, thinking of Luke absorbed in the book and knowing it belonged with him. Whatever the damage is, it's worth it.

4

Walking on Broken Glass

Uncle Andy insists on driving me home after we've locked up for the day. Although I told him he didn't have to, I'm grateful not to be on the bus. The humidity built up over the day is lingering, and my cute outfit feels damp and uncomfortable. I'm also grateful that he's content drumming on the steering wheel and happy singing the wrong lyrics to the Bee Gees and Billy Idol instead of discussing my first day.

We pull into the driveway to find Cass and my best friend, Wanda Lee, sitting on the steps to our porch in front of what looks like dozens of party-sized pizza boxes. Wanda and I grew up together after our moms bonded during prenatal class as the two misfits, my mom the oldest and hers the youngest, and Wanda's mom moved in upstairs shortly before Wanda's birth.

Cass calls across the front yard, "How are my working men?"

"Exhausticated," I say. "What's all this? Did we get a delivery of pizzas that should have gone to a tailgate?"

Cass grabs a handful of her maxi dress as she stands and ties it into a knot.

I catch Uncle Andy sneaking a look at her calves.

"We got the glass delivery today," Cass says. "I insisted the pieces be put in shallow boxes to avoid further breakage. Now we've got to move them into my studio." Cass gives a playful squeeze to Andy's bicep. "Good thing Bobby brought the muscle."

Uncle Andy squares his shoulders and flexes under Cass's touch. She goes from a squeeze to a pinch.

"How about a beer?" Cass asks.

"I'll split one with you," he replies. "I'm driving."

"Always so safe. You know where they are," Cass says, motioning into the house.

I say to my mom, "We don't have a studio."

"Yet," Cass replies.

Wanda turns off her game. "The living room is the only space big enough. I made her wait for you."

Thank you, I silently mouth to Wanda. I can only imagine the mess I'd have come home to if my bestie hadn't had my back.

I go inside and walk around our living room, considering it from different angles and imagining where furniture, the containers of wool and shipping envelopes, and the pizza boxes of glass will be arranged to leave Cass enough open space to work.

"Don't block the flow," Cass directs from the doorway to the kitchen, where Uncle Andy stands behind her, sharing the beer. "Or the natural light." Cass begins squinting through her thumbs and pointer fingers arranged into a rectangle as if that will help.

There's got to be a multiverse variant of me out there bossing a crew around on one of those house-flipping reality TV shows.

After a few minutes, my brain has made sense of where everything currently is and where it needs to go, and I've laid out the new floor plan in my mind. I give instructions on where to set up Cass's weird yarns, stuff like camel and yak hair she imports and sells for a few hundred dollars per lot. I don't know what people use the yarn for, but customers pay top dollar, so it needs to remain a priority. With Cass needing time to sculpt, I'll have to pick up the slack for the online wool store, Watch Me Unravel, between my shifts at Corner Books.

"Moving all these books is going to take a lot of time," Uncle Andy says. "I have experience."

He's right. We have so many books, they're stacked up along the walls and Cass started using them as the base of furniture. The coffee table in the center of the room is made entirely of coffee table books with a piece of glass laid on top.

"No, it won't," Cass says, pushing Uncle Andy back. "C'mon, Wanda. Grab one end of the table. We'll slide it over by the window."

Cass and Wanda push the table. Nothing topples over. The books don't even shift. Miraculously not a single book falls out of place. The table slides along the living room floor.

Cass straightens up and brushes off her hands.

"I know you fancy yourself some kind of superwoman, Cass, but how did you do that?" Uncle Andy asks.

"You've seen my art before," Cass says. "You heard my reviews. *Ashton's statues spit in the eye of gravity and dare it to undo their beauty.* It's all about internal supports and hidden casters. You didn't think I haphazardly stacked all these books without thinking how I'd move them later, did you?"

"I did," I admit. "You could have told me so we could have cleaned under there."

"Why do you think I didn't?" Cass asks.

"You really need to patent these designs," I say. "We could be rich. You could make kits so people could assemble their own coffee tables. We could sell them to IKEA. Tell her, Uncle Andy. It's a good plan."

Cass speaks before Uncle Andy has a chance to agree with me. "Commercialism killed my art once. I won't let it do it again. Let's get all that glass in here," she says.

Cass starts singing Annie Lennox, adding an extra *walking on* before she gets to the *broken glass* part as we move the boxes into the house. It's kind of insensitive but there isn't a better song for this moment I can think of.

Wanda's shirt rides up as she's passing me the last of the boxes and I notice the colored lines snaking up her torso.

"You finished your tattoo," I remark.

Wanda smiles as she hikes up the legs of her shorts so I can see the purple old-school video game controller. It's a testament to her favorite pastime-turned-source-of-extra-income since Wanda's streaming has taken off recently and she's been smart enough to monetize it. The controller's wires go up her thigh and side, then under her bra, twisting around peonies and hibiscuses.

"My oejobumo are pissed at Mom. They couldn't believe their daughter allowed me to bring dishonor on our ancestors and potentially all of Korea."

"I'm impressed. I thought your mom had wrapped Korea up already with the teen pregnancy thing," I say as I inspect Wanda's ink. I guess Wanda's grandparents don't know Ms. Lee has a peony tattoo on the back of her shoulder or that Wanda did this without her mom's permission. Since turning eighteen, Wanda's taken steps to go from indoor kid behind a computer screen to woman ready to take the world head-on.

Wanda is the product of a classic star-crossed-lovers romance right out of *Romeo and Juliet*, the Baz Luhrmann version. Instead of death by miscommunication, it ended with a long-lost father and the birth of my best friend. Wanda's dad's parents blamed her mom for leading their son astray and moved states to give her dad a fresh start.

"I should aim higher and try to dishonor all of Asia," Wanda says. "But Korea isn't a bad start."

The living room looks more functional, bright, and open than it did a week ago when it was my den of depression. I wouldn't want a permanent art studio in the middle of our house, but this setup will get the job done.

As I stack the last box, I catch sight of Wanda, Andy, and Cass behind me. Some of the sadness I've felt since what happened with Truman lifts. Everything fell apart except for them. They're still here for me, like they've always been, even if it means moving heavy boxes filled with broken glass. Their willingness to do unpaid, physically demanding labor shows how much they care.

Cass interrupts my thoughts. "I haven't even thought about dinner," she says.

"I ordered us something," Uncle Andy says, holding up his phone. "Wanda, there's lots for your mom and you too. If she's working late, you can take some upstairs for her."

"What are we having?" I ask, impressed at Uncle Andy's forethought.

"Thai," he says. My mom opens her mouth but before she can speak, he adds, "From the place on the other side of town you prefer. Cilantro on the side because you can't stand it. Spicy for you, mild for Bobby. Kids, would you mind setting the table?"

"You know me so well," Cass says.

Wanda and I head to the kitchen, saying everything that's going through our heads with one look. It's not a new realization, but something both Wanda and I have felt for a long time. Cass and Uncle Andy make sense together. There's such obvious chemistry between them and harmless, low-level flirting of the highest will-they-won't-they variety. But I haven't quite figured out how to move forward their friends-to-lovers plot.

"At what point does their glacial pace kill all hope?" I ask.

"Stay out of it," Wanda warns.

I sigh. "I know."

It's not that I don't want to help Cass and Andy, but the right time and the right plan have never appeared. At least not yet. Even Cupid needs help, and I'm a catalyst, not a bystander. But after misreading things with Truman, now is not the time for me to get another love connection wrong.

Still, the smile Cass gives Uncle Andy when he pulls out one of the chairs at our kitchen table for her is different from any smile she gives anyone else.

"Stay out of it," Wanda whispers as she reaches across me for the mango salad.

"I know," I repeat.

I can't risk it going wrong for Cass and Andy. The stakes are too high. If I push them together and it doesn't work out, it could mean Uncle Andy is out of our lives.

But the smile he returns has always been reserved solely for her. Cass holds his eyes for a second before sharply looking away, her cheeks coloring.

5

Show Me the Money

"I'm asking you to work a cash register, not perform open-heart surgery," Gladys says. "I told Andrew you weren't ready. I knew it was too soon. I'm going to show you one last time. Try paying attention for a change."

Gladys hammers through her instructions again as she jabs at the ancient register. It isn't far from something you'd imagine seeing in a museum or a saloon. I have a pad with notes scribbled down but they're nearly incomprehensible. I own a cell phone. It's not like I don't know how to use technology. I really don't understand how Corner Books can survive with such an old machine that works counterintuitively to every other device on the planet, a comment that could apply to the register or Gladys. The old machine and the old employee must have made a pact to hate on the new guy.

"D'ya got it yet?" Gladys asks. "Those shipments in the back need unpacking. I can't stand here all day until this simple task sinks through your skull."

I don't *got* it. But I'm not about to admit that to old Gladbag as I've nicknamed her.

"Of course. But are you sure you should be moving around boxes?" I ask, hoping she'll take me up on the unspoken offer for me to do the unboxing. "I mean, they might be too heavy for you."

"Man the cash," Gladys commands and stomps away.

Since I started, Gladys has been the one to train me. Uncle Andy works in the back office, only coming onto the floor when needed. Mainly I've been told to focus on stocking shelves and keeping the place tidy. Several times a day, Gladbag presents me with used textbooks and makes me assess their quality for buybacks and resales. When she told me I'm a harsher judge of the condition people keep their books in than she is, I figured I'd finally impressed her with something. I've watched the door a lot, waiting for customers to appear. According to Uncle Andy, things pick up closer to the start of the school year.

I might have also hoped that Luke would reappear, but no luck. Not that I expect him to show up again. But meeting him was the most exciting part of working here so far.

But if he did show up, then what? I crossed Truman's name off my Summer of Bobby list, so there's an opening. But my gaydar didn't go off with Luke despite my being intrigued by him. On top of that, Luke made it clear that romance isn't his thing. He's probably busy with guys like him and activities like ultimate frisbee or hacky sack. Clearly, I'm not versed in what straight college guys do together, but I don't think I'm far off. He's not thinking about the fat gay guy who works at the used bookstore who gave the new guy in town a book.

Unbidden, Dean Perez's warning about keeping my nose clean and staying away from boys comes back to me. One more reason I should forget Luke.

The bell above the door tinkles and I see Mya's caramel spiral curls bouncing in. "I've got Gladys's scone and your macchiato," Mya says.

"I could use the caffeine." I reach out and take a swig from the paper cup.

"Long day?"

I nod, not daring to bad-mouth Gladys in case she overhears.

Mya leans across the counter. "She's not all bad. I'm not even supposed to deliver, but Gladys has been tipping me with graphic novels. How can I say no?"

"DC, Marvel, or non-franchise?" I ask.

"I'm not an amateur. Hit me with a deeper cut," Mya says.

"I've got a few recommendations," I say, ready to find Mya's next perfect read.

"Next time. I've got to get back," Mya says before she goes.

I find a stool tucked under the counter and pull it out. The leatherette has peeled back in one area, exposing the compressed foam underneath. It's not the most comfortable and it's kind of small for a thick guy like me, but it's better than standing. I pull out my Summer of Bobby list from my pocket. First item: a job. I've got one but it's far from perfect. I make notes on how to make the best of Corner Books.

First hurdle: Gladbag.

Second, if I'm being honest with myself: me. I'm not exactly nailing my role as a star employee. I can't work the register and there don't seem to be enough customers to justify my working here.

Third, and it's a big one with a lot of appendices and notes in the margin: Corner Books lacks the refined style that screams *Summer of Bobby*. If Uncle Andy sprang for a new sign and some new décor, shelves that matched, and a curtained area to hide the worse-for-wear used books, then maybe I'd have an enviable job at a cool store. Maybe we'd be able to get customers to stay and browse. But every time I bring it up to Uncle Andy, he tells me we'll talk about it later or that Corner Books can't afford my taste.

I'm adding to my notes when I hear someone clear their throat. I jump. When I look up, for some reason I expect to see Luke.

The person opposite me is not Luke. But it is a guy. I'd guess he is about ten years older than me. He moves his head and his hair sways across his forehead before it hangs back in his eyes. He smiles and even though one tooth is noticeably crooked, it's kind of cute.

The guy tilts his head and his crooked-tooth half smile and swishy bangs have pulled me in. If this were a period romance, I'd have a marabou fan and bat alluring eyelids at him while music swells and we'd spend the evening making eyes at each other across a crowded ballroom. He did materialize as I was pondering my man problems, after all.

"Hey," he says.

I slip off the stool. "Hey. Can I do something for you?"

He reaches into his pocket and pulls out a twenty-dollar bill. "I need change for the meter. Mind helping me out?"

"For sure!" I begin to push buttons on the keyboard. The dumb register doesn't even have a touch screen. The monitor keeps flashing with options. I keep hitting buttons. I don't know how I do it, but the cash drawer pops open. I narrowly avoid it smacking into my belly.

"Quick reflexes." He places the twenty down on the counter but keeps his hand on top of it.

I feel my lips pull up. Why, my good sir, are you being forward with me? Never before has a guy complimented my reflexes. I'm almost certain this is a meet-cute. The type of story we can tell our grandchildren.

I grab four fives from the till.

Our hands brush as I count the bills out. His hands are rough and rugged. I'm not sure if a hand can feel swarthy but if it could, his would.

"Five. Ten. Fifteen. There's twenty," I say.

He reaches for the pile and lifts one five-dollar bill. "Do you mind giving me some coins?"

"Right!" I say a little too enthusiastically. Meters don't take paper cash. I should have thought of that.

He slides the rest of the bills into his pocket.

Our hands touch again as I drop the coins into his hand. So, *so* swarthy.

"Don't forget your five," he says, holding out the bill.

"I nearly did. Thanks."

"Later."

"Hope so," I say, realizing as it comes out of my mouth it's kind of desperate, but the guy is already heading out the door.

I go to put the five into its slot and it dawns on me, I never took the twenty. I check and double-check, making sure it didn't fall onto the floor. I move the stool and crouch to peer under the counter. I can't find it. I counted the money out right on top of it. He must have pocketed it without realizing.

I race around the counter and out the door. The little bell rings.

I stare one way down the block and then the other, but the guy is nowhere in sight.

Good sir seen across a ball straight out of a historical romance, my fat ass. That was no meet-cute. He's a charlatan! A swindler! He ripped me off!

I stomp over to the nearest trash can and give it a kick. Then another and another and another. All I accomplish is making my foot sore.

As I gingerly trudge back into Corner Books, shoulders stooped, I try to remind myself it's only a couple of bucks.

Except, it's not. It's knowing I'm a sucker. It's knowing I believed, even if only for a brief instance, some random guy could walk into Corner Books and see me and like me. Love at first sight and all that. I remember Dean Perez's warning about boys.

The worry that every time I ever feel something for a guy it will end badly creeps into my mind. I know that sort of feeling isn't helpful. It doesn't get a comeback accomplished. It can only make me feel bad for myself, cause a relapse into my Danish disease. Normally my defenses are higher, and I can push a feeling like that down, ignore it. I need to be the peppy, helpful, bookish, fat, and confident gay guy around Little Elm if I'm going to salvage the Summer of Bobby. I don't have time for being some foolish romantic loser who no guy likes. Maybe Luke was right, love and romance aren't the answers to every issue.

Gladys is waiting for me inside. "You never, ever, ever leave the cash drawer open. Never mind leaving the store unattended. I'd ask what you were thinking, but were you thinking?"

"I was scammed," I mutter. "I'm the victim of a crime."

Her eyes soften from a piercing gaze to a scowl. "What happened?"

I tell her, rambling on about the guy's crooked tooth and swarthy hands and how I thought he was flirting with me. She listens without any comments until I'm done.

"You're a victim of your own stupidity," she says once I've finished.

"I'm not stupid."

"I didn't say you were, so stop acting like it. If it were up to me, I'd fire you. Too bad I can't. Nepotism got you this job. Nepotism will make sure you keep it despite your screw-ups."

"Nepotism didn't do anything for me. Andy isn't even my uncle."

"Whatever, Robert. Take it up with your not-Uncle Andrew when he gets back in. Better he hears it from you than from me."

I already feel like crap without Gladys's mean comments. That guy took advantage of me, but I *did* mess up. One more notch on the bedpost of the Summer of Suck. I can feel my biles going haywire.

But Gladys doesn't lessen her onslaught. "I obviously didn't train you well enough even though a high-achieving chimp could have understood the job. I'll handle the cash. You go over to those shelves on that wall," she says, pointing. "Make sure no books slipped behind the others and that everything is in alphabetical order by author surname."

I nod.

"Do you know the alphabet, or do you need me to teach you the song?" Gladys asks.

I purse my lips. "I know the song."

"Good. Get to it already."

I spend the rest of the afternoon rewinding and replaying everything that happened over the last few weeks. The more I think and the further I go back in my memories, the worse I feel. First, Truman. Then this crooked-toothed crook. Dean Perez was right. I'm not exactly great at picking love interests. Where guys and I are involved, I should get me to a nunnery.

I'm not sure what to say to Uncle Andy except for the truth and that he shouldn't have been so quick to hire me. Maybe I'm not cut out for the nine-to-five grind. Retail must be built for people named Gladys and Robert, not for chubby bookworms named Bobby who convince themselves some guy is going to come through the door to woo him and loses money instead.

It's clear: this is not where I'm meant to be. I'm supposed to be at Campus Books. I'm supposed to be walking amidst the high-gloss polished floorboards. Between the mahogany shelves. Conversing in a corner with the book club crew over what next month's pick should be. Poring over the Reading Festival plans while a certain someone leans close and whispers something in my ear, a suggestion of more poetry for me to discover. But they're just baseless dreams.

I'm brought out of my reverie by Gladys sniping at someone that is not me. It's the first time in a week. I walk to the end of the stacks and poke my head out.

"You're not being very helpful," a woman in yoga gear says. She has a tight ponytail high on her head. She glistens, which is almost the same as being sweaty, except attractive. "The book went viral last week. It's all about finding pleasure."

Gladys screws up her face like she sucked on a lemon. "We don't sell books like that. You might try a different type of store. There's one a few blocks over."

Now the woman screws up her nose. I'm sure I too look equally disturbed.

"No. Not like that. Everyday pleasures. Like the cereal made from berries and coconut water," the woman explains.

The cereal! I know exactly the book she's looking for!

I race through the stacks. The bell above the door tinkles. I find the self-help section and scan the spines. Ah-ha! I pluck a book from its spot, a small jolt shooting through my fingers. I charge to the front of the store.

"If she isn't clear on some substantial and identifiable details," Gladys says to Uncle Andy, who has returned, "I can't help her. I don't have a crystal ball or the power to read minds. I certainly wouldn't be working here if I did."

"I've got it!" I call, waving the book in the air.

The woman beams as I hold it out to her. As she reaches for it, I notice she rubs her thumb across her ring finger.

There's a band of white, shiny skin that isn't tanned like the rest of her hand.

"This is it!" she says.

"Lizzo was eating the cereal on TikTok, and the foodies went nuts for it. I knew exactly what you were talking about as soon as you said berries and coconut water. I can't imagine it tastes anything like cereal. Personally, I'm a Lucky Charms fan. Love a rainbow marshmallow." I turn to Uncle Andy. "It's our only copy. We should order more. It's supposed to be the hot-girl-summer self-improvement read."

"Let me ring you up," Uncle Andy offers. "Good job, Bobby."

"Are you new?" the woman asks me.

"I started last week," I answer.

"Don't finish ringing me up yet," she says to Uncle Andy. She turns to me. "Besides Lucky Charms and Lizzo, what else do you recommend?"

Uncle Andy looks from the woman to me, "You got this, Bobby?"

I look at the three adults standing there watching me and nod, my biles settling themselves. "I got this," I say. "This way."

"I'm Cindy," the woman says as she follows me down one of the aisles. I glance back and see her absentmindedly rubbing the spot on her finger with her thumb again as she looks at the shelves we pass.

"Did you lose your ring, Cindy?" I ask.

She stops and stares down at her thumb pressed against her ring finger. "No," she says, drawing out the word. "My husband."

I turn around and can hear my mom in the back of my head chiding me for what I'm about to ask, even though Cass herself would have opened her big mouth too. Some people call it nosy. I call it curious. "Like, lost . . . to another woman?"

Cindy bursts out laughing. When she's done, she wipes tears from the edges of her eyes. "Gosh. No. High blood pressure."

I swallow hard, knowing I stepped in it. "Shit. Sorry."

"Don't worry," Cindy says still laughing. "It's the sort of thing he would have asked. He had zero tact too."

I want to tell her I have some tact, but . . . maybe I don't. I'm not exactly the type to shrink into the wallpaper.

Cindy continues, "But he made up for that with loyalty. I only recently stopped wearing my ring. It's awkward trying to date when you're still wearing your wedding band.

"How about a yoga book?" Cindy asks, reaching for a nearby title, her thumb still tucked tight against her ring finger.

Things come into focus in my mind. The yoga clothes. The cereal. Self-improvement books. Dating. She's ready to put herself back out there. The wounded widow finding love again is a romance staple. Cindy is a slam dunk. I will help her learn to love again just like I'm sure her dead husband would want her to.

But the way her thumb keeps going toward the ring that is no longer there makes me hesitate. I can't say why, but Luke's words come back to me again. Maybe Cindy needs a different solution.

But then, what do I recommend?

I suddenly remember a book I read at the end of middle school. The author happened to be passing through Little Elm during the festival, and I convinced Cass to buy me a copy after hearing him speak. I know it won't be as easy a sell as the yoga book or a romancing-the-widow novel, but something tells me this book might be a better fit.

"Follow me," I say.

We go to Fiction: J–M. I stroke along the spines of the books looking for the one I hope is there. Fortunately, we have a copy of *All My Friends Are Superheroes* by Andrew Kaufman. Uncle Andy really does listen when I tell him to stock a book. It's about a man without any superpowers whose wife has been ordered to forget him by her superhero ex, and he needs to convince her to remember their time together before she moves on and he loses her forever. It's not exactly a romance.

As I touch the spine to pull it off the shelf, it almost tingles in my grasp before I hand the slim book to Cindy. I feel like even though Cindy expects herself to move on, much like the characters in the novel, she might not be ready. I know barreling through, pretending as if the pain isn't there doesn't get rid of it. The yucky stuff sticks around and waits until your defenses are low before showing itself. Healing takes its own time, whether the reason behind it is hypertension or rogue unicorns and broken windows.

She holds the book back out for me. "I don't know."

"Trust me. This is the one for you." I know from the way she's finally stopped fiddling with her ring finger, it's what she needs.

THE SUMMER OF BOBBY

(AKA Bobby Ashton's Plan for the ~~Perfect~~ Summer Before College)

♥ ✓ ~~Land the Perfect ANY Summer Job:~~
   Corner Books

♥ Play nice with Gladys
   (NEXT TO IMPOSSIBLE)

♥ Become a star employee
   (GETTING THERE!)

♥ Overhaul Corner Books' image

♥ ~~Land the freshman liaison gig for Big Summer Reading Festival~~

♥ ~~Make festival SICKENING (see: Bobby Ashton's Plans for Little Elm's Big Summer Reading Festival)~~

♡ ~~Land the Perfect Boyfriend: TRUMAN~~

♡ No boys like Dean Perez warned
    (especially guys who swindle you)

♡ ~~Rule over Campus Books' book club~~
    ~~(alongside Perfect Boyfriend)~~

✓ Look fabulous every step of the way!
  (NATURALLY)

6

He's All That

An hour before closing on Friday, Uncle Andy emerges from the back and comes over to the register, where Gladys is trying to teach me to run the end-of-day sales reports.

"Bobby, my office." He taps the corner of the counter before he walks away, not looking to see if I follow him.

I shrug at Gladys in a *what's up* motion. She smiles for the first time since I started working here. It leaves me unsettled.

Never having been in his office, I am surprised when I follow Uncle Andy into what could more accurately be called a cupboard, stacked high with boxes. Wedged into the corner is one of those rolling buckets with the mop leaning against the wall. Andy's desk is also composed of boxes. A laptop perches on them. He takes a seat in a folding lawn chair and motions for me to unfold a second. I have to sidle into the room and barely manage to get the other chair unfolded before I plop into it, hoping the latticed nylon straps don't give out.

Uncle Andy holds out an envelope. "This is for the time you've spent here."

I stare at the plain white envelope in Uncle Andy's outstretched hand. Something doesn't feel right. I reach out tentatively.

"Is this?" I ask, not daring to finish the sentence. I explained the crooked tooth guy to Uncle Andy and thought after the success with Cindy, everything was ok.

"Your paycheck," Uncle Andy says.

"My final one?" I brace myself for the answer.

Uncle Andy frowns. "Are you quitting?"

"No. Are you firing me?"

"Why would you think that?"

I rub my hands on the tops of my knees but don't say anything. We both know why.

"You're doing fine."

"I lost money," I say, thinking of my Summer of Bobby comeback plans. "I can't get the POS to work. Gladys isn't exactly enamored with Robert. She likes Bobby even less." I realize too late that giving reasons why Uncle Andy should fire me may not be the best move.

"You're learning," Uncle Andy says. "It's going to take some time. As for the guy, it's like I told you: he took advantage of you. Even more experienced retail staff get tricked. I asked you back here to see how you're doing. I should have checked in with you sooner."

I relax a little, but not enough to trust the lawn chair beneath me.

"Seeing you with that customer," Uncle Andy says.

"Cindy."

"See. There you go. Cindy," he says. "You've always had something extra about you. You've got a knack, Bobby."

Normally when I've been called extra, it hasn't been a good thing. A lot of times, it's come before large.

"I know this isn't your dream job and you've made it clear Corner Books could use quite a bit of sprucing," he continues.

Feeling very seen, I open my mouth to contextualize, but Uncle Andy holds up a hand.

"You're already a good addition here, and I'd like to hear your ideas for new directions Corner Books could take. I want more Cindys in the store. You're the one to do it."

I clap my hands and lean forward. The chair, stuck onto me, pulls with me. "If you're serious, I'm great at coming up with plans."

"I'm serious," Uncle Andy says. "And I know you are. Get some suggestions together this weekend and we'll discuss."

"Gladys is going to hate them."

"I'll take care of Gladys. We'll talk on Monday. Now get to the post office before it closes. I saw the huge bag of mail you came in with. Cass's yarns must be selling well."

I nod. "The fashion magazines say angora is going to be big this fall, and we found some forgotten skeins when rearranging the living room. I sent out a mass email with a code for free shipping with minimum purchase."

"A knack. Go on now," Uncle Andy says.

I push on the handles of my chair hard to dislodge myself, then maneuver out of the office, collect my things, and head out the door. Gladys doesn't even look up from the register or say goodbye.

I hustle the two blocks to the post office and make it there just as Mae, the clerk, turns the sign to *closed*. But once Mae notices me, she unlocks the door.

"Come on in, Bobby, sweetie."

"But you've already closed for the weekend."

"Not for the boy who convinced my husband to reenact the *Ghost* pottery scene. I can fudge the time on the computer and get those into the next shipment."

"The pottery is still working out well for you, I take it?" I say.

Mae smiles as she scans through my packages. "We've thrown a lot of clay and don't have a single damn vase to show for it."

After paying for postage on all my parcels, I hurry out so Mae can close shop. I'm not fully paying attention as I wave over my shoulder and step onto the sidewalk.

"Woah, Casanova," I hear.

I spin to find a shirtless Luke nearly on top of me.

"I almost ran you over. You shot out of there fast," he says. "Did you just burgle the joint?"

"You ok, sweetie?" Mae asks with a dirty look in Luke's direction.

"All good. Lock up and go start up that wheel," I reply.

"I guess you two are friends," Luke says.

"It's a small town." I make a show of dusting myself off. "Why aren't you wearing a shirt?"

"I was running. It clears my head and helps me figure out where everything is in Little Elm," Luke answers matter-of-factly while he searches the ground. "I didn't knock your glasses off. Did I?"

Without thinking, I answer, "I don't wear glasses."

Luke furrows his brow. "I saw you wearing them when we met."

"Those? Oh. They're fake."

Luke pulls a white T-shirt from where it's tucked into the back of his shorts and uses it to wipe his face before he puts it on. "Why would you wear fake glasses? Do you have some sort of Superman Clark Kent thing going on?"

I shrug. "To make me look smarter."

"Aren't you smart?"

"Yes. Well, most of the time." But I don't need to clarify that to someone I've met only once.

"And you think a pair of glasses is what makes others recognize your intelligence?"

I feel my cheeks heat up. "When you say it like that, it sounds dumb."

Luke makes this expression like he's shrugging his eyebrows back at me.

I huff, a warning that Luke should drop the issue as it's leaving me feeling called out and prickly. "It's not as ridiculous as it sounds. People judge the first thing they see. It's natural. Like your Superman Clark Kent dichotomy."

"When you effortlessly drop a word like *dichotomy* into everyday conversation, people are going to figure out quickly you're smart."

"Maybe, but people judge books by their covers all the time. It's why publishers put so much time and money into designing them." I do a quick scan of Luke and notice the beads of sweat dotting his skin.

"A good cover won't keep you turning the pages. I'm more interested in content than cover treatment."

I shake my head. "The cover helps get the book into readers' hands. It gives the content a shot. Those glasses are one way of controlling perception. Put them on and people will think you're smart. Take them off and add a great haircut, and you're a hottie people start noticing. It doesn't matter how talented or creative or beautiful you are inside—only that people can see it. You eat with your eyes first."

Luke laughs. "Aren't you mixing metaphors? Are we talking about books or food?"

"It's all the same."

Luke shrugs his eyebrows again. "I don't see what's wrong with how you look."

Nothing. Nothing's wrong with how I look. I don't know how to make him understand that I know putting on glasses to look smart is asinine, but it allows me at least some control over how I present to the world.

Luke waits for me to say something but when all I do is look away from him, he asks, "So, you wear glasses to correct other people's vision?"

I cross my arms. "You're making fun of me now."

His lips turn up almost imperceptibly like when I found him reading. "A little bit. It's just clothes."

"But you can take off your clothes," I say, registering Luke's eyebrows shooting up. I point at my shirt. The front says *Masc* in cursive script adorned with curlicues in the middle of an explosion of blooming flowers. "I can't take off who I am. I can't take off this body and hang it in the closet and put on a new one."

"Why would you want to?" Luke asks without a second's pause.

The innocence in his tone makes me roll my eyes. He knows exactly why. He can't possibly miss I'm fat and that informs everything that follows after it. I've accepted it and the body I live in. I even like my body most of the time. But it doesn't mean I'm immune to the realities I wasn't built to fit into. My clothes aren't just about control; they're my armor. I cross my arms across my floral *Masc* tee and don't reply.

Luke catches my eye roll and says in a somber tone, "I meant, even if you could, I wouldn't want you to put on a different body to make some random person's life easier. It's yours. It's you. You wouldn't be all of who you are without it."

I look down. I want to hold what he says and wear it like a crest. But I know despite all my self-acceptance and body positivity, if given the chance to swap out my body, I'd probably take it and I'd see the switch as an upgrade. I try to keep those admissions buried because acknowledging them is like accepting there's something wrong with how I was made. I'm too stubborn or, perhaps, unwilling to cede that ground.

"You wouldn't understand. You look like that." I motion at him.

He scrunches up his face. "Like what?"

Perhaps I should say sorry because I'm unintentionally borderline insulting his body, but instead I barrel on. "Like a frat guy about to pledge and get with sorority Bambi."

Luke's face relaxes and he runs a hand through his hair. "So that's what you thought of me?" I catch the whiff of grapefruit and aftershave again, musky in the summer heat. "You want to know my first impression of you? You were inquisitive. And intuitive. And showed me kindness and generosity. I didn't need a pair of glasses to see those things."

My shoulders lower. I hadn't realized they were hunched, prepared for some sort of heated retort from Luke. Makes me think I really should have apologized when given the chance. "Thanks," I mutter. "But those aren't physical."

"No. They're not."

When I don't respond, Luke says, "I like arguing with you." He pulls out his phone and unlocks it before he hands it to me. "Give me your number. I said I'd meet my roommate at the coffee shop down the block before I ran home. I want to continue this another time."

"Arguing?"

"Having my point of view challenged."

I program my number into his phone and hand it back to him. "I could use a macchiato."

"Let me buy you one as a thank-you."

"For the book?" I ask.

"For being argumentative."

"I'm not—" I begin but catch Luke's smirk. "Fine. But only because Mya's working, and she makes the best macchiatos."

We enter the shop and I'm surprised to hear, "You brought Bobby?"

Luke looks from me to the speaker, a guy named Jerome I went to high school with but don't know well. I catch Mya out of the corner of my eye and give a small wave.

"How did you know to bring the big gun?" Jerome asks Luke.

"What are you talking about, man?" Luke asks.

Jerome looks at Luke like he's stupid. "Everyone in Little Elm knows Bobby is the guru of love. If anyone can help me get Mya's attention, it's him. He even knows her."

I shake my head. "My skills have been on the fritz as of late."

"You've got to help me," Jerome pleads. "Please. It doesn't have to be some epic thing. I don't need a balcony or a sunrise or white doves."

"Casanova?" Luke raises his eyebrow.

I frown in response. "You don't *not* need those things for a *grand* gesture." I catch sight of Mya again smiling at the three of us. Her eyes linger on Jerome through the steam a second longer than on Luke or me.

Maybe Jerome and Mya are exactly what I need to get my matchmaking powers back. An easy practice coupling to build me up again.

"Do you read graphic novels?" I ask Jerome.

"Do comic books count? I'm big into the MCU."

Close enough. "Come by Corner Books next week. I've got some recommended reading before you're ready to make a move with Mya."

Jerome reaches one arm around me and claps me on the back. "Whatever you say."

"Your usual, Bobby," Mya calls. "On the house."

I collect my drink, and Luke follows me outside.

"I don't think you should get involved with Jerome and Mya," Luke says once the coffee shop's door is closed.

"I think I know what I'm doing."

"That's what I'm worried about. He's one of my roommates, and I don't need to be in the middle of some drama."

"Then don't get involved." I take a sip of my macchiato. It's perfect. "I can't guarantee they're soulmates, but I've helped people like Jerome and Mya hundreds of times."

Luke seems as if he's about to say something but then looks back at Jerome through the coffee shop window. "Nothing I say will make you reconsider. Will it?"

I take another sip.

"Then I'll help you," Luke says.

I nearly spit out my macchiato. "I don't need help. This is child's play."

"Jerome and Mya aren't toys," Luke says. "Someone needs to keep their eye on you."

A bus pulls to a stop across the street and the driver, Andre, nods in my direction.

"Another person you helped?" Luke asks. "I don't think I realized how small a town Little Elm is. That's my ride. I can't keep Bambi and the other sorority chicks waiting." Luke starts jogging across the street.

"Wait. You're not running back?" I call, hoping Luke forgets the frat boy comment sometime soon, but I don't think he will, and I'll have to find a way to smooth it over—especially since we'll be helping Jerome and Mya together.

Luke doesn't turn or reply. The bus pulls away with a mechanical exhale.

I haven't taken a step when my phone dings.

Luke: *Didn't need to clear my head anymore. You gave me some things worth thinking about. See you at the next kegger. I can introduce you to Bambi.*

I type my reply and hit send.

Me: *Like I'd ever be caught at a frat party.*

7

Makeover Scene

Luke leaves me on read and I'm not about to be the one to text him first. Besides, I have Corner Books to think about. But shaking our conversation about my fake glasses from my head proves more difficult than I imagined. It's next to impossible as I start planning my outfit for my presentation to Uncle Andy.

I pull out a selection of short-sleeved button-ups in pastel colors. If there are any hesitations from Uncle Andy, pastels will help calm his worries. My summer plans and Corner Books' future are riding on my ideas to improve the store's image. And while Luke may see past first appearances, shoppers don't. Corner Books needs not so much a makeover, but a full facelift.

As I refine my ideas to make Corner Books more like Campus Books, I can see how far they are apart. The gap between them may as well be an ocean wide. Corner Books looks nothing like Little Elm College's bookstore. It's like the difference between me and Luke. But Luke didn't see a problem with how I looked.

What if there's not a problem with how Corner Books looks either?

Uncle Andy's store is unique. It has a certain character and charm. Instead of overhauling the store, we need customers to take a second, deeper look to notice the qualities that make Corner Books the cool, less snobby destination for Little Elm's readers. As I settle on a baby-chick-yellow shirt, I throw out my initial notes. I stay up late rewriting. If this works, I have not only checked another box under summer job but maybe even found my dream job despite not being the best at it yet and my snarky co-worker.

The only issue left is drawing in customers. I pick up my phone. "Wanda, I've got questions about how you get your viewers. Is now a good time to come up?"

It's late Monday afternoon before Uncle Andy and I connect. I decide to consider the extra time a gift to rehearse what I'm going to say between Gladys's drilling me on the old cash register. By the time Uncle Andy calls me from the back, I've got the hang of straightforward sales but returns and exchanges are a work in progress with processing buybacks still beyond me.

"My office?" Uncle Andy asks.

I remember the folding lawn chairs and the tight squeeze. "How about we start outside?" I suggest and head toward the front door.

We're no sooner out the door than the florist across the street, Mr. Fumagalli, pokes his head out of his offices. "When do you think they'll start hanging the banners for the festival, Andy?"

"Any day now," Uncle Andy replies.

"How's your wife?" I ask.

Mr. Fumagalli beams. "She still puts every bloom I've ever touched to shame and jokes that she's the only woman in town I never give flowers to."

But it's only a joke as Mr. Fumagalli has never needed Bobby Ashton. Every day, he chooses the most beautiful bloom from his shipment and brings it home to his wife. He doesn't need a single pointer.

Mr. Fumagalli returns inside, and Uncle Andy and I stand on the sidewalk staring up. I shield my eyes and point. "Some of my suggestions are easy fixes. Superficial but they'll make a big impact. Like the sign," I say.

"I know. We should replace it. It's old."

"It's retro." I decided last night to keep our conversation focused on the positives of Corner Books. Looking at the positives of crappy situations is so on brand for me right now. "It needs a good wash and some new bulbs. If you've got a ladder, I'm sure we can do it ourselves."

Uncle Andy frowns.

"Isn't there a ladder?" I ask.

"We have one. But do you know how to do that? We should probably hire a professional."

"It's changing a light bulb. I'm sure I'm butch enough." I flex my arm like Rosie the Riveter. "Cass and I have been doing small repairs around the duplex for years. You can learn to do anything with the right online tutorial."

Uncle Andy bites his bottom lip. "I'll let you in on a secret, Bobby. But you need to promise not to tell Cass."

I try not to nod too enthusiastically. I love a secret.

Uncle Andy says, "I'm not a fan of heights."

"I'll climb the ladder," I assure him. "I won't look down if that helps."

"I'll imagine you falling instead of me."

We hear someone cough from nearby and turn our heads to find Gladys listening in from the store's entrance. "I'll hold the ladder."

I eye her skeptically. "Without trying to knock me off?"

"Don't flatter yourself. You're not worth the conviction."

We go back into the store. I point out that all our tables are currently reserved for used textbooks. Both Gladys and Uncle Andy agree moving the tables to the front of the store and stocking them with new releases so customers see them first is a better sales strategy.

I hammer through more minor suggestions until the phone rings. Gladys answers and snipes at a customer who asks her to check if a book is in stock.

"That's another thing," I say as Gladys stomps down one of the aisles, the store's phone in hand.

"I'm not replacing Gladys," Uncle Andy replies. "She's already warned me her attitude is not up for discussion."

I shake my head. "I didn't dream that big. The sales system. It's outdated. And before you tell me that we can't get a new one, it's too expensive, hear me out." I take a deep breath. "Corner Books has no online presence. Even if you don't want to commit to a new system, we should have a basic website. People my age prefer online to phone calls."

Uncle Andy nods. "I'll think about it."

While I don't think Corner Books is going to close shop anytime soon, I can't imagine there's a huge profit margin waiting in reserve. I already knew coming in I'd need to let some larger items go. I shift focus to other smaller fixes like the old stool behind the register or safety rugs we could fix, replace, or clean.

As we wrap up our conversation, I say, "The shelves."

Uncle Andy sighs. "I knew you'd go after my shelves."

"They work," I say with a smile. "I've got to admit, at first all I saw was mismatched, used junk. Then I looked again. You've got that nothing-matches-so-everything-matches style going on. We could even distress a few to give them a reclaimed look. Gladys would be a pro at beating them with metal chains."

"You joke," Gladys deadpans, appearing from the stacks.

"Let's consider the story we want to tell," I say, slowly turning as I point features of Corner Books out. "The exposed brick wall is awesome. So is the old tin ceiling, even with the missing pieces. We could tie it all together with something like a statement color. We could paint a couple of shelves or bring in chairs and throw cushions. We'll go bright and bold."

"Perhaps sour apple or chartreuse," Gladys suggests.

Certainly not what I'd choose, but I'm surprised Gladys isn't shooting me down, and even more because her color choices aren't awful.

"If we glitz our image up a bit, we'd go from the place where students schlep downtown to buy affordable textbooks to a place where people want to shop. We could entice a broader range of readers into becoming regulars. You see how certain crowds turn up in big numbers for the fantasy, sci-fi, horror, and romance talks at the Big Summer Reading Festival. Campus Books isn't catering to their preferred tastes outside the festival. Why can't we? Why can't we be their destination for a bookstore? We'll even start holding exclusive readings and signings. That's how we afford that new point-of-sale system. It's the snowball effect." Wanda gave me some more specific pointers to attracting an audience, but image is paramount.

"What if the snowball never gets going?" Uncle Andy asks.

"If we don't increase sales, we stop at painting the shelves. If they do, baby steps forward. I know I'm prone to big plans, but the beauty of this one is we can pull the plug at any stage."

Uncle Andy is quiet as he squints and turns slowly like I did in my living room to picture it as Cass's studio. I wait for him to say something.

"Do we hate floor lamps?" he finally asks.

"We love floor lamps," I say, placing a hand on his shoulder. "If you see a coat rack or umbrella stand, throw it in the back of your truck."

Uncle Andy is silent for a moment again before he says, "I've always wanted this to be more of a place authors would want to visit." He pauses. "I'm impressed with your ideas but even more with your restraint, Bobby. I have to be honest; I worried about your knack a little after we spoke."

I let my hand drop from Uncle Andy's shoulder.

He continues, "I was prepared for you to tell me everything you could see wrong with my store. Every crack in the wall and dog-eared page. Instead, you saw all the potential."

Thinking of Luke, I say, "Corner Books has good content. All it needs is an updated cover."

8

Love Grinch

I pull out my phone near closing time.

Me: *You owe me a coffee.*

Almost instantly my phone dings.

Luke: *I make good on my debts. Look up.*

Luke enters Corner Books with Jerome on his heels, a carrier tray of drinks in his hand.

"You wore a shirt this time," I say.

Luke places the carrier on the counter. "The sorority babes like me better without it, but I already cleared my head with a run earlier."

"Shouldn't it be empty by now?"

"Still ticked off at me? Is that why you haven't texted?"

"I'm not ticked off. I texted you right now," I say. "You were the one who left me on read after our last encounter."

"That's how it works? One for one?" Luke asks.

Jerome cuts in. "Not to sound ungrateful, but can you two bicker later? I really need that Bobby Ashton Midas touch."

"We weren't bickering," we say in unison.

"And Midas didn't end well," Luke adds before I can.

I give Luke an appreciative smile.

"I know you're magic," Jerome says to me. "But Mya's in the coffee shop right now. Shouldn't we be over there instead of in a bookstore?"

"Oh, padawan," I say, pulling a stack of graphic novels from behind the counter that includes *Scott Pilgrim*, *Heartstopper*, and *Saga*. "Research. Mya is into graphic novels."

Luke grabs *Saga* from the stack and starts flipping through. "This is what she's into?" he asks, eyes getting wide. "This graphic novel is . . . graphic."

I almost blurt out what Luke was reading when we first met but Jerome is here. "It's an epic, doomed romance set in a warring galaxy."

"It's a bunch of naked humans with animal parts and TV heads."

"Let me see," Jerome says, taking the book from Luke and settling himself in the nearest chair.

"What's your plan? To have Jerome strip down and glue a pair of ram horns to his head?" Luke asks.

"If that's what's necessary, yes. I'm giving them common ground." I take my macchiato from the tray. "I owe you a thank-you."

"I owed you a coffee."

"For our last conversation."

Luke raises an eyebrow and I notice his lips move into that hidden smile he makes. "Are you ready to admit I was right about the glasses?"

"Not a chance, but it did make me think about Corner Books in a new way. It's got a lot more going for it than I first saw."

"Those glasses of yours are skewing your perception. You're not good at seeing past first impressions." Before I can tell Luke he's wrong, he says, "I thought about our conversation too and where you were coming from. It opened my eyes. Want to do the same by explaining to me your obsession with matchmaking and romance, Casanova?"

I take the lid off my cup and swirl the contents around. "There are all the obvious reasons like loving love or escapism or living vicariously or beating the odds and finding true love against all obstacles. And whether it is in a movie or TV show or in a book, romance is something my mom and I share." I stop for a minute to gather my thoughts. "I guess I like the feeling of connection that romance brings. We all want to be connected. We all want to be loved."

"Humans are social animals."

"That's clinical."

Luke seems to study my face before he says, "Casanova, don't you think it's potentially damaging to buy in to a belief system that is flawed?"

"Finding true love isn't flawed," I scoff.

"If it's the only end goal, it's limiting. Out of all the billions of people in the world, you're meant to be with just one? Well, there go the polyamorous, the aromantics, and the asexuals. What happens if you don't find that person? Or if it goes wrong? And it goes wrong a lot. You have to admit, the way people act in these stories is diagnosable."

Like I don't know that. I put down my macchiato, which has suddenly started coating my tongue in a saccharine way, and cross my arms.

Luke must notice because he runs a hand through his hair and says, "I'm probably not the romantic type. I don't get why people can't be clear and direct. I can't even sit through those old Tom Hanks and Meg Ryan movies. Those two idiots really do deserve each other."

My jaw drops.

Luke sees *Heartstopper* and keeps going. "Another one I couldn't get through. Everyone I know thought it was so cute, but it was a lot of manufactured drama." Luke finally notices my face. "What?"

"Nothing," I splutter. "Except you're the only person I know who hates love. Seriously, who hurt you?"

"I don't hate love. I just don't like emotional manipulation. It's the same reason I don't watch horror movies."

"You don't *love* love," I say. "Let me guess. You heckle at weddings too."

"I don't go to weddings if I can avoid them, but heckling might make them more bearable."

"It wasn't a suggestion." I push Luke's arm. The muscle is firm. He barely budges. "Besides ruining weddings, what do you do for entertainment? Action movies?"

"Right. You're still on the frat boy thing," Luke says. "I watch documentaries. Real ones. No reality TV."

"No one likes documentaries. People only watch them to sound smart later. They're the film version of reading a textbook. Your girlfriend must be one lucky girl."

"I'm single."

"Because you're a love Grinch. You've got a rinky-dink little heart."

"Ouch, Casanova. Your boyfriend must have his hands full with you."

I suck on my bottom lip.

Luke glances at me. "Playing the field is legit too," he says quickly. "I assumed the local romance expert must be off the market."

I release my bottom lip. "I'm on the market. Not for lack of trying."

"Why do you need to try?"

"Because romance requires vision but also work and effort and I don't trust it will happen for me if I don't make it," I say simply and truthfully.

"Now who is a love Grinch? Why does it need to be some big effort? Can't being with someone be as easy and natural as breathing?"

"Now who is the Casanova?"

I startle, having forgotten it's not just Luke and I, when Jerome says, "This book is amazing. I didn't know comics could be like this. There are more. Right?"

"I told you so," I say to Luke. "You know how the Reading Festival has a bunch of opening acts?"

"Are you serious?" Luke asks.

Jerome looks at Luke as if he's speaking another language. "It's called Little Elm's *Big* Summer Reading Festival. How else do we get people pumped for the big event but through a bunch of smaller ones?"

I can see from Luke's expression he's trying to figure out if we're kidding or not. Little Elm takes its literature very seriously.

"Despite me being vocal about the Comic Arts events, they were cut from this year's pre-festival programming due to budgeting."

"But they were so popular," Jerome says.

"I know. Which is why Corner Books is going to host its own book club and feature a graphic novel. How do you feel about horns?"

Jerome looks at me askance. "Horns?"

"It was all Luke's idea."

9

Three Coins in a Fountain

I wipe my forehead across the back of my arm as I step off the bottom rung. Corner Books' sign still needs a good scrub, but it's fully lit and fixing it was almost as easy as screwing in a light bulb. Between getting Jerome ready for the Comic Arts weekend and fixing up Corner Books, it's been a hectic week.

"Light it up, Gladys," I say as my feet hit the sidewalk, and she heads inside to turn the power back on.

A bus stops across the street, and I hear, "Don't you check your phone? We've got to go."

Wanda checks both ways as she darts across the street. Uncle Andy and Gladys step out of the store as the sign flickers to life.

"Not while I'm on a ladder," I say. "Is everything ok?"

"The Baroness," Wanda pants. "She just announced a pop-up signing here in Little Elm. You've got to be there."

The Baroness von Snatched. My favorite author of all time who wrote my absolute favorite book, *Pebbles Tossed at a Window*. I knew she had a book coming out, a new direction for her career with a saucy romance, but she's infamous for not being seen often in public for years and never appears out of drag.

"Where?" I ask.

Wanda hesitates before she says, "Don't freak out. It's at Campus Books."

The Baroness von Snatched may be the only person who can make me desperately want to go back to the scene of my humiliation and the store that fired me. But I can't just walk out of Corner Books on a whim. I'm in the middle of a shift.

"I'm working."

"Debatable," Gladys says.

"Tell him he has to go," Wanda says to Uncle Andy. "You were the one who got him hooked on her."

It's true. Uncle Andy gave me *Pebbles* without knowing it was my preteen heart's come-to-Jesus moment. Except Jesus was a drag queen who retired from the club scene and became a cozy romance author. *Pebbles* with its gay heartthrobs in a sweet first-love story gave me all the feels. Still does.

And the Baroness is the icing on my rainbow confetti cake. She's mystique personified. A legend in the romance world as she's managed to keep her alter ego completely hidden from the larger world, a feat in the time of everything being documented on social media. With a hiatus and a new direction, it makes sense she's stepping back into the limelight to promote her newest.

Uncle Andy says, "Don't think I don't know. I remember being harassed into joining a Little Elm's Baroness fan club."

"You're a few years late on your dues," I say.

"I'm sure I am. You saw this on social media, Wanda? I don't think you had social media on your list of suggestions, Bobby."

"I was saving it for our next conversation. I didn't want to scare you right out of the gate."

Uncle Andy nods. "Smart. If you're serious about holding events here, you need to go. Consider this research. I want you to report back with everything Campus Books does successfully and how we can do as well or better. That is, assuming Gladys can live without her sparring partner for an afternoon."

"As if he's a match," Gladys says. She looks at Wanda's shiny, white PVC catsuit, an outfit I know Wanda bought to stream in because it shows off her curves and ups her stream views. I suspect Wanda left midbroadcast.

While this isn't something Wanda would normally wear around Little Elm, especially in the summer, she's rocking it and I'm here for it.

Gladys is not. "What the heck are you supposed to be?" she asks. "A tube of family-sized toothpaste?"

Wanda looks shocked before bursting out into laughter. "You described her perfectly," she says to me. "She doesn't miss a single shot. Grab your stuff, Bobby. Let's go."

I look at Uncle Andy. "You're sure?"

"Scope out the competition. As your boss, I expect details." Uncle Andy places his hand on my shoulder.

"I'll call an Uber," Wanda says.

Uncle Andy quietly slips some cash out of his pocket into my hand before he releases his grip on my shoulder. "Get yourself a signed book."

"I can't buy it there. Not with your money. They're the competition. You said so yourself."

"I'm your uncle. And before you point out I'm not, I'm your boss too. Take it. That's an order."

I tuck the bills into my pocket.

Wanda ducks into the car that pulls up to the curb. Once I'm in, she pushes the backpack she's carrying toward me. "I knew you'd want to get your books signed. Cass let me into your room."

The rest of the trip goes by in silence. I rest the bag on my lap, dropping my phone, Uncle Andy's money, and my wallet inside. Staring out the window, I bounce my leg.

Wanda places a hand on my knee to stop me. "It will be fine." She fishes around in her purse for a tube of lipstick and begins to reapply. "You want some?"

"I'm good."

We exit the car.

I stop, take a deep breath, and ask the question lurking in the back of my mind. "You don't think he'll be there. Do you?"

And if Truman is there, then what? Do I pretend he doesn't exist? Do I say hello and pretend everything is fine, never been better? Do I turn up the charm so he knows the good thing he missed out on? Can I commit to any of these roles in an outfit that is nowhere near Princess Diana's little black revenge dress?

Wanda takes my hand. "Truman was always a snob about anything that doesn't drip with *literary merit*." She says the last two words in an upper-crusty voice. "What if he is here? Around Little Elm, this campus is Rome. All roads lead here. Unless you move, you're going to run into him."

She's right. I can only avoid Truman for so long. If Little Elm College is Rome, the apex of the empire is the fateful fountain. I've avoided coming back for as long as I can. A comeback means I've got to come back.

Wanda links her arm through mine as we march down the promenade. I force myself to hold my head high. My first public appearance at Campus Books won't be without good posture.

"I know you said you wanted to put it behind you and bring back the Summer of Bobby like nothing happened, but we can talk about it, you know. Like really talk about it," Wanda says.

I can't even think about having that conversation. I know it's overdue. I tell Wanda everything. But how do I ask her to lend a sympathetic ear when she asked over and over if the grand gesture for Truman was a good idea? She tried to warn me, and I ignored her. And she still helped me despite her intuition. She must think I'm so naive.

"Things wouldn't be this way if I had listened to you," I mutter as we walk up the cobblestones.

Wanda squeezes my hand. "You know I wish I had been wrong. It wasn't enough that I told you. You had to find out yourself."

I squeeze her hand back. "You're a good friend."

"I know."

As best friends, we both know we'll talk about what happened with Tru more, but not right now.

When we reach the fountain, it burbles like the day everything went awry. Its waters are clean and clear with only a few stray coins snug against its tiles.

"One of the maintenance staff must have gathered up all the loose change," I comment.

"I heard they can make a mess of the motors and spray nozzles."

"What do you think they do with the money?"

"Maybe repair the fountain. I know other places donate the money. I guess they figure all those wishes are a pay-it-forward kind of deal." Wanda reaches into her purse. She pulls out two pennies. She hands me one. "Let's make wishes. You love doing that. You never know what will come true."

"This fountain hasn't exactly been lucky for me in the granting department."

"We've been doing it all wrong." Wanda spins us around. "You need to toss it over your shoulder, like they do in Rome." She holds her coin for a second then throws it over her right shoulder. We hear a plunk.

I hold the penny back out for Wanda. "A different fountain. Not this one."

"Keep it," she says. "You never know when you might need a wish or a bit of good luck."

I ask, "What did you wish for?"

"If I tell you, is it still going to come true?"

I give it a few seconds' thought before I answer. "I think the whole confidentiality clause only applies to birthday candles. But best to keep it to yourself in case."

"Do you think that's where that *penny for your thoughts* saying comes from?"

"Probably not." I slip the coin into my pocket. I'll save it for when I have something important to wish for.

"In Rome, you're supposed to throw three coins. One for a safe return. Two to find love. Three to be loved back."

Maybe if I had been thrown into the fountain once more, things would have worked out differently. As we cross the threshold into Campus Books, I wonder if I made a mistake by not throwing the penny in my pocket over my shoulder, especially if it would have helped with a safe return.

10

Mamma Mia, Here We Go Again

Stepping into Campus Books feels like coming home. A sense of comfort doesn't wash over me so much as absorb me into it. The smell of books and lemony wood polish that keeps the mahogany shelves, rails, walls, and floors at a high-gloss sheen surrounds me as soon as I'm through the doors. The sounds of chitchat and patrons. It's an everyday paradise unto itself. This is a place books deserve to be. It's a place I thought I did too.

The staff ushers customers into a lineup that snakes through the stacks, past the registers to a signing table set up on a small platform. The table is piled with *By Midnight's Stroke*, the latest release by the Baroness von Snatched, current mother of the House of von Snatched.

As we take our place in line, I run my fingertips along the spines of the books on the shelves we pass.

Wanda and I score prime spots in the line beside the path to the signing table. The Baroness will need to pass right by us. We high-five.

I take in everything going on and mentally make notes. Corner Books is nowhere near this level. At least, not yet. There are about eight staff members, none of them Tru, keeping the customers flowing properly into lines or using handheld devices to cash them out. There are no posters, perhaps due to the sudden nature of the signing, but plenty of books are stacked around the store being rung up quickly. I grab one from a nearby table.

You can feel the anticipation crackling through everyone, the crowd getting pumped for the Baroness to arrive. It's infectious and only part of that is because of the guest of honor. The other part is everyone here is excited to celebrate a singular thing, the birth of a new book.

"See," Wanda says. "No one is paying attention to you."

"As long as it stays that way."

The crowd gasps. I turn toward the entrance and see a silhouette striking a pose outlined in the doorframe.

The Baroness steps inside. Her chestnut wig is teased and back-combed so it stands at least a foot off her head under a wide-brimmed hat adorned with feathers and a veil. There must be an enormous amount of spray in her hair because not a single strand dares move out of place. She makes a show of removing a pair of rhinestone cat-eye sunglasses and folding the arms. Her lipstick matches her harlot-red skirt suit perfectly. The plushest fur, dark as night, is draped over one shoulder, tails hanging to her knee.

She places her sunglasses inside her handbag before she undoes a button on her jacket to reveal a bustier encrusted with stones that match the jewelry dripping from her ears, neck, lapels, wrists, and fingers even though she's wearing black gloves. Who wears rings over a glove? A baroness. She holds out her handbag for one of the assistants who trails behind her. Another one steps forward to place an ostrich-feather pen in her outstretched hand.

"She has arrived!" the Baroness shouts across the store.

The crowd erupts into cheers and adulation. Someone whistles from way in the back. Others quickly follow suit and begin hooting.

"She is life," I squeal, leaning into Wanda.

The Baroness stands on the steps leading into the store, legs spread in a power stance, balancing on the thinnest, highest spiked heels imaginable. She places both hands on her hips, her jacket creating a ruffled bustle behind her.

"I think we can do a touch better with that entrance," she says. "Let me get myself ready." She cups each of her breasts and pushes them up with a devilish wink. The crowd cheers and whistles all over again. "Maestro, cue the music, and don't skimp on the octane." Like that, she's out the door again. Her entourage positions themselves, heads down, in a V-shape in front of the doorway.

A fanfare sounds from the loudspeaker. The Baroness struts back into a mashup of Cher with Kim Petras. Icons. Stepping dramatically foot over foot as she advances, body swaying, lip-synch flawless, she parades into the store as if on a catwalk.

The crowd reacts twice as loudly as before. They jump up and down. Others snap photos. Some are screaming, "I love you!"

The Baroness stops to pose, holding out her hand adorned by her massive, sparkling rings or thrusting her hip and elongating an arm.

As she passes us, Wanda has her phone at the ready.

The Baroness stops and leans past her assistants between us. I stand there holding the backpack, the zipper undone, all the Baroness's novels on display.

"My, my," she says. "Someone likes to read. I bet you have a massive"—she pauses and winks a heavily shadowed lid at me—"vocabulary."

I can feel myself blush. I want to come up with something witty to say back, but I know I won't top her. She is in her element.

The Baroness snatches Wanda's phone and snaps selfies with the two of us in the background. She gives pout, smile, duck lips, raised eyebrow, smirk, head tilt, shot after shot. For the final two pics, she leans in and plants a kiss on my cheek then Wanda's. I look over at Wanda to see big red lips marking her cheek.

"Tuck that away now, gorgeous. Trust me, you'll want to keep those," the Baroness says.

Wanda grabs my arm. "You undersold how incredibly fabulous she is!"

I stand on tiptoe, snapping more photos, swept up with the rest of the crowd. "She is the moment! She's every moment!"

We all watch, entranced, as the Baroness continues her way through the crowd, brushing her feather pen over audience members and taking more photos until she reaches her table. She smooths her outfit as she sits, then kicks her legs high in the air, and ever so slowly makes a show of fanning them to cross them. Her assistants place bottled water around her and begin opening books to the title page.

"Take that away," the Baroness tells the nearest one. "Be a doll and get me the kind that effervesces." The assistant goes running off in search of sparkling water as the Baroness continues, "Now that I'm sufficiently prepared, unleash my beautiful beasts upon me. Come, my pretties."

The lineup moves slowly but there isn't one complaint. Everyone is excitedly whispering to one another. The Baroness calls only a couple of people over at a time for what she refers to as an audience with her, greeting each reader and speaking to them while she signs, not rushing at all. You can tell she knows she's there for them, answering questions, mugging for more photos, listening to their favorite parts of her books, or how her words affected them. This is as much about her putting on a show as it is about her readers' experience meeting her. And she knows it.

Wanda and I inch closer to the front of the line. We're only a few people from being called up when I catch sight of them. Two guys are standing apart, on the next floor up that overlooks the store. One is leaning forward, hands clasped in front of him. I can tell exactly who he is. I'd know him anywhere but especially across a crowded bookstore.

I freeze, glued to the spot, not moving or saying or doing anything. The line moves forward.

Wanda tells me something. I don't catch it. Someone coughs behind us. I lock eyes with him and know he's seen me too. He shouldn't be here. He can't be. He's not scheduled.

Wanda follows my gaze. "Oh, crap. Truman."

My bag of books drops to the floor.

11

You Had Me at What the Hell

Customers in the crowd turn to see what's holding up the line. There is no one left in line in front of Wanda and me.

"It's going to be ok," Wanda says as she crouches down to gather the backpack.

"Come on, buddy," one of the Baroness's assistants says as he steps forward. "There are people waiting. Don't take all day."

I hear murmuring around me and that feeling of people turning to stare that's become all too familiar lately.

Wanda grabs my arm. She tries to nudge me forward.

"I know him," I hear from the crowd and turn my head. "He's the guy from that epic fail video. The broken window guy."

A murmur begins in the crowd, and I pick out familiar faces among the strangers. Residents of Little Elm. People

I've helped matchmake staring back at me with looks of sympathy, the same as Truman before he dropped the rose on the fountain's edge. It's worse than derision.

Out of the corner of my vision, I see the Baroness wave to one of the staff who leans in so she can whisper in their ear. The staff member starts coming toward me. Wanda eases me forward, but my eyes are now focused on Tru. Behind him is Scott, his boyfriend. I know they see me. Tru walks toward the nearby stairs and descends, looking from the steps in front of him to me and back. I can make out the look on his face, the way his brows bend toward the bridge of the nose, his eyes all intense. He's in his nice-guy mode and if he launches into that in front of everyone, they'll see me as poor, unwanted, unloved Bobby Ashton, the chubby gay who helps everyone else find love but gets his own heart broken.

I can taste the fountain water again. I can almost gag and spit it out. I can hear the glass crack, then shatter as it hits the pavement and the water crashes around me.

The Baroness is standing now. "Darling, are you all right?"

I manage to shake my head, eyes still on Truman. My face burns and my heart is beating as if it's in my ears. He's moving through the crowd, dodging people. Getting closer. The faces of the crowd heighten with concern.

I can't be their pitiable loser. Not again.

"I'm so sorry," I say to Wanda and the Baroness. I don't think about what I'm doing. Something inside me says *go*. I dart out of the line toward the exit.

"Bobby, stop," Truman calls out over the noise of the crowd.

I knock the end cap of a shelf. The display collapses. Books scatter around my feet. People step from the crowd, arms outstretched, ready to steady me but they don't make it in time.

I stumble over the mess and out the door.

The fountain looms in front of me, spraying water. The cobbles are hard and uneven under my feet.

I duck into an alley between the buildings, not daring to walk down the promenade, not risking Tru's chasing after me. It's the type of thing he'd do. That's one of the reasons I fell for him.

I crouch beside a dumpster to catch my breath. Elbows on my knees, head in my hands, I force myself to inhale and exhale slowly, carefully, regaining control. My heart is still knocking through my ears like it's trying to escape. There's no way I can reframe running away from Truman and knocking over a display of books as a comeback.

Someone grabs me. "Are you ok?"

I scream and swat at the person before I see who it is.

Luke's blue eyes are clouded with gray and concern.

"Luke?" I ask. "What the hell? Are you everywhere now?"

He's crouched down too, holding on to my shoulder even though I smacked him. "Hello to you too. Are you going to slap me again?"

"Are you going to sneak up on me again?" I counter. I can feel a trickle of sweat run down from my temple. "There are no laws in Little Elm against wearing a shirt when you run, you know."

Luke lets go of me and pulls his tee on over his head. "Nipple chafing," he says as if that's all the explanation required. "Are you ok?"

"I'm fine." I stand up and begin patting my pockets, searching for my phone and wallet. When I don't find them, I remember I put them into the backpack. The backpack that is now with Wanda inside Campus Books. I can't go back to retrieve it. I've got no way home but to walk.

"You're not fine," Luke says. "What's going on?"

I walk toward the end of the alley, away from the main part of campus. Luke's long legs keep up with my quick pace with no effort.

"Why did you ask if you already knew the answer?"

"What would you do if you saw a guy you knew bent over beside a dumpster? You wouldn't stop to check on him?"

I make sure there's no one around before I step out onto the sidewalk. My pulse is no longer racing. I plan a route for the quietest way home where I'll see the fewest familiar faces. "I'd figure he wants to be alone." I start walking again.

Luke falls in line beside me.

I stop. He stops too.

"I'm seriously fine," I say. "You don't need to follow me."

"Who says I'm following you? My apartment happens to be in the direction you're going. We can walk alone. Together."

Luke picks up speed and gets ahead of me. I take a few steps to catch up. He doesn't push for more conversation. He doesn't ask me what happened to lead me to hiding behind a dumpster. I know I wouldn't be so uninquisitive if there was a mystery walking along beside me. I'd get to the bottom of it. But it's nice not having to discuss the whole long story.

There's something extra nice about Luke still getting to know Little Elm's Bobby Ashton. And even if I'm not one hundred percent certain, I would bet Luke doesn't know about me and Truman. I've got a clean slate with him, and it makes walking with him in silence easier. It's a comfortable quiet.

We match our paces, walking in companionable silence until we reach a bunch of houses designed for boarders and dormers with each floor meant for a different resident, stretching taller than the average house.

"This is me," Luke says with a nod at the nearest building, an old elm tree rising above us.

"Where do you set up the keg to do handstands?" I say under my breath, but loud enough Luke can hear me.

"Want to come in and watch a documentary on the dark underworld of tickling?" he asks, ignoring me. "You might feel better about whatever went down or at least laugh along."

"You can't honestly think that will help."

"I've also got one on competitive professional chicken fanciers."

"As enticing as those sound, I'll take a rain check."

"Suit yourself." Luke moves up the concrete steps toward the building. "Bobby?"

"Yeah?"

"Tomorrow will be better."

"How do you know?"

He stands on the path above me. "I should have brought it up the other day, but you were already calling me a love Grinch. My parents have had three divorces between them and are both on to their latest partners. Nothing got ugly or nasty, but people who had said they were sticking around signed some papers and took off. There were days when I felt like hiding behind a dumpster too."

I watch the clouds reflect in Luke's eyes and we hold each other's gaze until he blinks his dragonfly-wing lashes.

"I'm still going to call you a love Grinch," I say.

"Sounds fair, Casanova," he says. "The good stuff and the bad, everything passes. I promise, tomorrow will be better."

"How can you promise that?"

"Being a realist doesn't mean I'm not an optimist." He walks to his front door, then disappears inside.

I shove my hands in my pockets and find the penny for a safe return. Maybe Luke's right. Perhaps tomorrow will be better.

12

A Star Is Born

My feet are sore by the time I get through the front door and kick off my shoes.

"Bobby?" Cass calls from the living room. "We're in here."

I enter our living room turned art studio to find Cass, papers fanned out in front of her, showing off her concept design sketches to Uncle Andy.

"Kinetic and gravity-defying, but interactive," she says as she grips his arm and points to a set of drawings. "They're sure to keep Bobby in college."

"They're unbelievable, Cass. Really," Uncle Andy says.

"I made Cajun stew." Cass squats to gather up her sketches. "And Wanda dropped off your backpack. She's in a stream now but wants to hang out later." Cass starts humming Annie Lennox. *Walking on, walking on, walking on* . . .

I see my backpack on a kitchen chair and grab my wallet and phone. There is a missed call and texts, all from Wanda.

Uncle Andy removes the lid from the pot and stirs. "Don't worry. I doctored it. How was the launch?"

I don't want to lie to Uncle Andy, so I decide to leave out the part where my lizard brain went into overdrive, and I ran. "Amazing," I say and jump into details of how fabulous the Baroness was. I've since been thinking about how I'd organize a similar event at Corner Books. "I'm going to get her into your store one day."

"Baby steps. We're not ready to host anyone of that magnitude."

"Yet."

"Yet," Uncle Andy agrees, ladling out stew. "Let's see how your graphic novel book club goes."

Cass joins us and upon her first taste proclaims, "I told you the spiciness would mellow out as it cooked."

Uncle Andy's eyes crinkle as he smiles at me.

After dinner and a shower, I head upstairs to Wanda's in my pajamas with *By Midnight's Stroke* in hand. I borrow a pair of Hello Kitty slippers from the front hall and drop Ms. Lee's dinner beside their rice cooker on the kitchen counter before heading back to Wanda's bedroom.

"Sims?" I place a container of the stew beside Wanda and flop onto the chair she placed off-camera for me so even if she's streaming, we can hang out. I know she's not broadcasting because of her sloppy bun and old sweatshirt.

"A bunch of new mods released a couple of hours ago. It's hilarious."

"Playing solo?"

"With an online friend."

"Anyone I know?"

"Not really. We're still getting to know each other."

I peek over her shoulder and see the player's handle, chickn_backflip, hovering over their character.

Before I settle in to read, I ask, "How did the Baroness react?"

Wanda leaves her character going to the washroom. "She did the splits."

"You're making that up."

Wanda fixes me with a stare. "She climbed onto the table, let out this holler, then jumped into the air and landed in the splits. Everyone forgot about you. She said to tell you she's had her share of guy trouble and hopes she'll meet you again. What was it she said? The course of true love . . ."

"Never did run smooth," I finish. "I can't believe I missed it." But hearing the Baroness's message to me somehow makes my feet hurt a little less.

"It wouldn't have happened if you hadn't run," Wanda says.

"I didn't plan to. My brain was telling me to get out of there. My legs followed orders."

"At least it was only a few books you crashed into this time," Wanda says. "Truman told me he's not going to stop texting to check on you even if you don't answer."

"I'm trying to move on and salvage this summer. Dean Perez told me explicitly no guys."

"Don't let that become your excuse not to deal with the Truman stuff." Wanda's character begins DJ'ing and soon her house is filled with partying Sims.

"My comeback can't involve me looking back."

As much as I want to read *By Midnight's Stroke*, Wanda and I are overdue for a talk. I spill my guts about Truman and the Summer of Bobby and my plans to turn it around.

Wanda listens, occasionally checking her screen to reply to chickn_backflip. When I'm done, she says matter-of-factly, "Plans can change."

"They can still work with some adjustments."

"There's nothing wrong with starting over. Doing something new. It keeps things fresh."

"I hear you, Wan," I say. "But it's my summer. I can't just walk away from it."

"No. Running is more your style."

I launch one of Wanda's Sailor Moon pillows at her.

She settles into her game, and I start to read.

I must fall asleep because I wake up to Wanda's mom telling her to turn off the games and get some rest. Ms. Lee covers me with a blanket and kisses her fingertips and plants them to Wanda's forehead then does the same to mine before she leaves the room.

Ms. Lee drops me off for my shift at Corner Books the next day. I see Gladys arguing with a customer through the front windows and I'm barely through the door when I hear my name. Cindy comes at me, wrapping her arms around me and pulling me into a hug.

"I had to come down here. I was skeptical, I admit it," Cindy says, releasing me. "Your pick was exactly what I needed."

I look down and see Cindy's wedding band back on her finger. "That's awesome."

"I've been telling everyone. Everyone," Cindy continues. "They've got to come down to Corner Books to meet the Book Whisperer. It's what I've been calling you."

"I've called him a few things too," Gladys says.

Cindy shoots daggers at Gladys. "Anyway, I've got yoga soon and my instructor has been having an awful time getting Campus Books to keep his recommended titles on hand. Is that something Corner Books could do?"

In my periphery, I see Uncle Andy approaching us. "Great to see you again, Cindy. Absolutely, we can. Send him in."

"Perfection," Cindy says. "I'll bring him in with the girls from class in a few hours. You'll be here, right, Bobby? I want them to meet you and you've got to see our yoga instructor. When they advertise hot yoga, they mean him. I may not be in the headspace for someone new, but looking is no commitment."

I laugh. "I'll be here."

Cindy stops on her way past the register and picks up a flyer from the counter. "You're hosting a book club? I know there's the one at Campus Books, but you have to apply and apparently no one gets in. A couple of my girlfriends have been on the waitlist for years."

I wrinkle my nose at the mention of Campus Books' book club. I heard all about the waitlist, first as rumors when I applied and later when Campus Books' managers and the longstanding club members discussed applications and how people scored. It was a joke that most of the applicants were so far down the list because of their score they'd be dead before they were ever invited.

At the time, I felt proud I'd ranked high enough to be asked in on probation before being made a full member. My being chosen for book club was the final nail in the coffin for my friendship with Evie Bosendorfer, whose application was rejected. Remembering this and how I thought nothing of it at the time, I feel ashamed for thinking I was above anyone when I probably only made it in due to the spot the club held for high schoolers.

When I brought up the idea of hosting Corner Books' own book club, the first thing I got rid of was a selection process. As long as people are respectful of the store and each other, everyone is welcome.

"It's a new thing we're trying out," I say. "If you know anyone who would be interested, take some flyers for them."

"I know a lot of people," Cindy says.

"Take the entire stack. We can print more." I put all the flyers into a paper bag and hand it to Cindy.

"I'll make sure these get distributed," Cindy says, sliding the bag onto her arm.

Gladys studies Cindy before she asks, "What are your feelings about chartreuse?"

Cindy turns her head, considering. "That would really pop with a touch of neon violet."

"I told you." Gladys points a knobbly finger at me. "Her taste isn't as bad as I imagined. Cindy, was it?"

Cindy turns back to me. "See you in a bit, Bobby."

I smile. The Summer of Bobby is back stronger than ever. Luke was right. Today *is* better.

13

Nobody Puts Bobby in a Corner

Cindy returns as she promised. The yoga teacher is indeed hot (also as she promised), and her friends are excited to discover a "cool little book spot with a whole lot of charm" as one of Cindy's fellow yoginis puts it. They even seem to get a kick out of Gladys and her "no BS, boss babe attitude." By the time they leave, I've made about a dozen suggestions, sold twice as many books, and Uncle Andy is bragging about how good our daily sales figures are.

Over the next few days, Uncle Andy and I order cans of paint to be picked up on the weekend and scope out used furniture stores in the area. All the while, I group text Jerome and Luke. Plans for Corner Books' first book club and Jerome's grand gesture are whipping through my mind and being discarded or adapted just as quickly, partly because Luke is a wet blanket.

It might be that we went with chartreuse as the accent color, but I've noticed a difference in Gladys too. It's not like there's a one-eighty. She isn't pleasant. She still shoots zingers my way, and being the bigger person, something I have (with resentment) decided to be, I ignore them. But she is less barbed. Her insults seem to lack their usual edge.

I know I'm not imagining Gladys softening when she tells me on Saturday morning, "I see your sense of appropriate work attire has marginally improved, Robert. Your outfit doesn't completely offend me today." That's almost a compliment coming from her.

I know what she's referring to. "My T-shirt last week didn't deserve a dress code violation." I remove Gladys's handwritten chastisement from between the pages of the book I'm in the middle of reading and wave it at her. The tee in question had a drawing of Jane Austen lifting the hem of her skirt and showing some ankle.

"She was working a stripper pole, and a crowd of men were leering and offering her cash. One was in the midst of making it rain."

I'm slow to think of a comeback because I'm surprised she knows that term.

"Your fashion need not be crass and humorless, not to mention potentially blasphemous," she says.

I roll my eyes. Today's shirt, *I Like Big Books and I Cannot Lie* with a copy of *Moby-Dick* under it, must have flown over her head. She pushes the returns cart of books for reshelving down one of the aisles.

"What's up with Gladys?" Uncle Andy says quietly. "You haven't been slipping antidepressants into her tea like your mom suggested, have you?"

"If I had them and she didn't watch her mug like a hawk, I would have."

"Have you noticed she's reading when she's in the stacks? It must be something she doesn't want us to know about because whenever she catches me coming, she finds a way to hide the book."

"You don't think she's some sort of secret agent, do you?" I ask. "No one would suspect her."

"No. This has got to be personal. I've worked with her for years and know nothing about her outside of this store."

"I bet I can figure it out," I whisper back.

"How much?"

I consider for a second. "If you find out what she's up to before I do, I'll agree you can purchase those hideous beanbag chairs you saw at the thrift store with the condition you spring for them to be professionally cleaned. If I win, I want full control of the music in-store for one week." Nothing that plays over the store's speakers has been current for decades and while I respect the classics, I also really want to see Gladys's face when Megan Thee Stallion plays.

"Deal." Uncle Andy holds out his hand.

I shake knowing I must be victorious because the beanbag chairs are heinous, and one had a stain of unknown origins. Besides, they throw off the aesthetic we're going for. Uncle Andy doesn't stand a chance against my resolve.

Gladys wheels her cart out from between the shelves and eyes us suspiciously. "You two look guilty. Save yourself some time and tell me what you did now."

I toss my head a little as I laugh and say as coolly as I can, "I was suggesting a new initiative where we all personally recommend three books every month."

"Great idea. Love it," Uncle Andy quickly agrees.

Gladys bumps her cart into Uncle Andy as she passes. She begins loading more books onto the cart. "Hate it. I don't intend on taking on any more work. Especially not in my private time."

Uncle Andy places a hand on Gladys's shoulder. "What goes on in that private life of yours anyway, Gladys?" He winks at me. He must think he's so smooth.

Gladys smacks Uncle Andy's hand away. "Mind your manners, Andrew. And your beeswax. What I do outside this store is none of your business. I trust you to remember that in the future."

Uncle Andy rubs the back of his hand as he returns to his office.

As soon as Gladys pushes her cart to the far end of the store, I hurry into the aisle she was in moments before and begin searching for clues. Not only will winning this bet give me bragging rights and musical control for a week, but I would also finally have something on Gladys.

I start at the bottom shelves and start examining. I run my fingers over the spines, but nothing is standing out or setting my instincts off. I rise out of my crouching position and keep investigating but there's nothing unusual. Not a single thing is out of place. Gladys's organization is so good it would be easy to pick out anything that doesn't belong.

While I admire her attention to minute detail, it also means she knows how to cover her tracks.

I slip into the next aisle. Gladys is one more over. I peer through the gaps between the books and shelves. She's reading bent over the cart. I can't get a clear view of the book in her hands. But she hasn't noticed me yet so I'm good. If I had a higher vantage point, I might be able to see what the book is.

I put a foot onto the bottom shelf. It seems stable enough when I put a little pressure on it. No sagging, no creaks. No bend in the middle. I use it to step up, clinging to a higher shelf. The vantage point is no better. I shift some books to the side and push my head through the gap.

Gladys is no longer bent over. She's nowhere in sight. I crane my neck and can almost make out the back cover of the book she was reading sitting on top of the others, but no luck.

I pull my head out. I wonder if I stepped up one more shelf if I could discover the secret and win the bet with Uncle Andy. I grip higher up and lift my foot again, putting some weight on the second shelf. It bows under the pressure.

"What in blazes are you doing?" Gladys barks from behind me.

I give a small shriek and stumble back onto the floor, hands jerking up to clutch at my chest. "Are you trying to kill me?"

"I don't need to. You're going to kill yourself. I really shouldn't have to tell you this, Robert, but you never, ever climb the shelves. If that comes crashing down on you, it's going to send every other shelf over like a set of dominos and you'll get pinned underneath. Considering your reputation for accidents, you can thank me for saving your life and never do anything like that again."

My heart is still beating hard as I lower my hands. "I'm not about to thank you for sneaking up behind me and scaring me."

"That's rich coming from you. You were spying on me."

"I was not," I lie.

Gladys taps her foot. "Then what were you up to?"

"Practicing for shoplifters?" Even as I say it, I find it hard to believe.

"Baloney. Don't you have enough to worry about in your own life without needing to stick your nose into some old lady's business?"

I decide to try a different tactic, the direct approach. "Uncle Andy and I know you're up to something."

"What if I am? That's my concern. Not yours. This may be hard for you but butt out."

The bell attached to the front door rings.

Thinking fast, I say, "You help that customer and I'll finish shelving."

"Nice try," Gladys says. "I'm not falling for it."

Knowing I'm beat, I round the corner to see none other than my mortal nemesis, Evie Bosendorfer, the off-brand Bobby two-point-no as Wanda and I call her. She looks around the store, nose up in the air as she silently judges.

"So, this where the great Bobby Ashton ended up. Slumming it down in this precious little shop."

"What is it you want, Evie?" I ask. I know I'm being rude, but I can tell Evie rehearsed her opening and I'm not interested in playing at her games.

Gladys's cart whines from down one of the aisles. Gladys calls, "We ask how we can help, not 'What is it you want.' I shouldn't have to remind you."

"Actually, I came to thank you. I have some good news to share," Evie says. "After all, without you, I wouldn't be where you want to be."

I try impersonating Gladys as I glare at Evie. "Speak clearly."

Evie goes over to the counter and leans against it with one elbow, raising her hand to rest her chin on it. "After all these years, looks like I've finally one-upped you."

"That's still a cliché."

Evie is another example of me reading people wrong. Another blind spot in my prescience. We became friends when we started high school. Wanda was always polite but distant with Evie, something I attributed to Wanda being most comfortable with people online and not IRL. I, however, was flattered by Evie wanting to hang around me, wanting to like the things I did, and to try out for every club and volunteer for the same committees. Only when Evie was trying to edge me out of a spot in Little Elm's book club did I realize I was dealing with a *Fatal Attraction* bunny boiler.

It killed her when she was waitlisted for book club. Then I got my admission to Little Elm College, my scholarship, the job at Campus Books, and the honor of being Little Elm's Big Summer Reading Festival's freshman liaison. Evie thought she was my competition, but I knew I was above her and one step ahead of her the entire time.

Until I wasn't.

Evie places her Chanel pocketbook on the counter. There's no way she could afford so much as a Chanel button. I'm certain even from this distance it's a knockoff by the way the gold is flaking off the hardware. "You probably thought cozying up to Truman would get you whatever you wanted. But we all saw how that worked out for you." Evie exaggerates a pout.

I cross my arms. "What is it you want, Evie?" I ask again.

"I told you. To thank you. Without your clumsy proposal, I wouldn't have been asked to be the festival's freshman liaison. I know how much you wanted that position."

Evie knows how to make her words sting. I can feel them prickling along my arms and making the hair stand. Why did it have to be Evie they asked to replace me? Why couldn't anyone else have muscled her out?

"Do your fact-checking and don't be so smug." Gladys stands at my elbow, her glower focused full force on Evie.

"Pardon me?" Evie asks.

"What's the saying? Oh yeah. Check your receipts. He had the job. They wanted him first. You're second fiddle. The standby. Plan B. They settled for you when things didn't work out with him. Don't try to rewrite history. You'll always be the second choice."

Gladys is right. I will always be who they asked first. I didn't expect that reminder would come from Gladbag.

Evie picks up her purse and stops leaning on the counter. "Well," she says. "I don't know if I see it that way."

Gladys shrugs. "Then see it the wrong way. That's your problem."

Evie wrinkles her nose.

"Are you going to buy something, or did you come in for the abundance of free air?" Gladys asks.

Evie replies with a rather loud sniff and gathers her pocketbook. I'll give this to Evie; she always knows when she's beaten and when to take off.

When I lost the festival position, I tried to convince myself it wasn't a huge deal and it didn't matter as much as I thought. It was free work I didn't need to do anymore. But around Little Elm, the festival is big. If it had gone off perfectly, all the praise and accolades would have been mine. At the same time, if it wasn't as good as previous years, no one would ever forget. I'd been planning this summer's festival since before I got into book club—the same way some people plan their dream wedding. I even had a dedicated online drive for all my documents. After my mortification at the fountain, I haven't been able to look at any of it. Not even to delete it. It was another thing I decided to put behind me.

I pull out my Summer of Bobby list and add a new item under the Big Summer Reading Festival.

I take a few deep breaths before I walk over to the aisle where Gladys has resumed stocking shelves. A diagram of a motorcycle's engine reflects in the thick lenses of her glasses as I approach. Gladys slams the book in front of her shut and shoves it under some other books. I don't have time to make sense of Gladys and a motorcycle. They don't go together whatsoever. This new intel only makes whatever's going on with her more mysterious because I now truly have no clue what she's up to.

"I owe you a thank-you," I blurt out before I lose my nerve.

"You were floundering." Gladys turns back to the trolley. "It was pathetic. I felt bad for you."

First the compliment on my shirt, and now her pity. All of Gladys's attention is going to go to my head. "Well, thanks. You were sort of amazing."

She shoves the cart in front of her as she walks away. "No. I *was* amazing. I'm not unaware of that fact."

THE SUMMER OF BOBBY

(AKA Bobby Ashton's Plan for the ~~Perfect~~ Summer Before College)

- ✅ Summer job: Corner Books
- ♡ Play nice with Gladys
- ♡ Become a star employee
- ♡ ~~Overhaul~~ Spruce up Corner Books' image
- ♡ ~~Land the freshman liaison gig for Big Summer Reading Festival~~
- ✅ Hope Evie tanks Big Summer Reading Festival
- ♡ ~~Make festival SICKENING (see: Bobby Ashton's Plans for Little Elm's Big Summer Reading Festival)~~
- ♡ ~~Land the Perfect Boyfriend: TRUMAN~~

- ✓ No boys like Dean Perez warned
- ♡ Matchmake Jerome and Mya; and
  - ♡ Restore my matchmaking mojo
- ♡ Rule over ~~Campus Books'~~ CORNER BOOKS' book club
- ✓ Look fabulous every step of the way!

14

Ugh! As If!

"I can't believe Gladys took on Evie for you," Wanda says as we reach the outer perimeter of campus. "I mean, I can believe Gladys was kicking ass and taking names. She's a stone-cold assassin. But you always made it sound like she doesn't like you."

"She doesn't," I say, covering my eyes and looking at the grounds beyond the sports fields. The banners Mr. Fumagalli was asking about are starting to pop up around town. "I think she might equally dislike everyone and Evie made herself an easy target."

"Got to give it to Gladys, she shoots to kill." Wanda stops at the edge of a field. "Thanks for walking me. If you want to take off, I can find the coding labs myself."

"It's your first day," I reply. I didn't love waking up to walk Wanda here, but she would have done the same if I needed moral support. Even if she isn't saying it, I can tell by the way she keeps readjusting her backpack straps that she is nervous. Although Wanda's streams are bringing in decent revenue, she needed a steadier source of income before college, and remote jobs are scarce around Little Elm. Despite how good she is with the people she knows, the daily face-to-face interactions are going to stretch Wanda's comfort zone. "You're going to be awesome. Besides, I've got to get used to being on campus again. I can't run every time I'm here."

"It's too early for Truman to be around," Wanda says, addressing my real concern. "What are you going to do before Corner Books opens?"

"Finally get the last of the painting done. It feels like we've been redecorating forever, and it's only been a couple of days. There are a lot of final touches to get done before Corner Books' first book club."

We cross under a huge banner announcing the dates of the festival, the morning heat strong but not unbearable. I wonder if it's a field or a pitch. I'm not sporty but I know there's some sort of difference. Maybe it depends on what sport is being played on it at the time.

"I'm supposed to meet the rest of the day camp counselors outside the Athletic Center," Wanda says, checking her email for the sixth time.

We approach the building but don't see anyone around. I try one of the doors nearest us. It doesn't open.

"Hey, Casanova." Luke strides across the field toward us wearing a tank top, shorts, and backward baseball cap. "You have to go around to the front of the building."

"Casanova?" Wanda asks.

"Don't ask," I mumble. Wanda is trying to catch my eye and wants to know who the guy I'm talking to is. "What are you doing here?" I ask Luke.

"I'm one of the college's lifeguards for the summer," Luke says. "I thought I told you."

I shake my head. Most of our communication has been via text and that's mostly revolved around my plans for Corner Books' book club.

Luke holds out a hand for Wanda to shake. "I'm Luke."

She fist-bumps him instead. "I've heard about you. Wanda here."

"Really dumb question," he says. "I think I know you. Lt_GlittrB0mb?"

Wanda smiles. "Good eye."

"No way. Your stream helped me get through *Venomwood II* big-time. I almost didn't recognize you out of costume."

"Kind of the point," Wanda says.

"Gotcha. I'll keep your lieutenant rank under wraps with the other staff."

Wanda's shoulders relax and she lets go of her backpack straps. "It's cool. I'm trying to put myself out there more. If they find out, they find out. It might help build the fanbase."

"Is that why you've been streaming with chickn_backflip lately? To piggyback on each other's fans?"

Wanda blushes. She never blushes. "No. We play well together. That's all."

"You two are freaky in sync."

My romance senses are tingling and I'm about to grill Wanda about who this chickn_backflip is, but she cuts me off.

"Let's get moving. I don't want to be late on my first day."

"Are you sticking around?" Luke asks me as we walk. "I could get you a pass for the pool."

Wanda coughs and snorts as she tries not to laugh. "Bobby? He doesn't swim. He likes to lounge or work on his tan or swish around deck in a caftan."

Since Luke is watching us, I tilt my head and smile, pretending to be amused Wanda told him all that.

Luke scratches his head. "That's too bad. The outdoor pool isn't really for sunbathing and the indoor pool is mostly used for laps."

The lifeguarding job must be why Luke appeared in Little Elm at the beginning of the summer instead of closer to September like students normally do.

We reach the front of the building and Luke asks, "Will you be around after we finish up? I know we text, but I was thinking we could hang out. I don't know anyone besides my roommates yet, and you could show me where this town's good pizza place is."

"There isn't one," I say. "The pizza sitch in Little Elm is tragic."

"You have to go about thirty minutes out of town to PizZaZa Gabor's for the good stuff," Wanda adds. "But you need a car."

"Ah. Ok. I guess pizza isn't an option." Luke shuffles from foot to foot before pointing at the double doors to the Athletic Center. "We should get inside."

Wanda grabs my arm. "I'll be in in a minute."

She smacks my arm once Luke is out of sight.

"Ow!" I say. "Why'd you do that?"

Wanda raises both eyebrows. "Where do I start? How about, why didn't you tell me about meeting a guy?"

I raise my hands in an *I don't know* kind of way. "I did tell you. And he's not a guy. He's Luke."

"You didn't mention the nickname."

"Because it's silly." I don't mention my nickname for Luke.

"You two have been texting. A lot."

"About Jerome and Mya." I know I glossed over a lot of details about Luke with Wanda, mostly saying he's a guy who's new in town. I'm not even sure Luke and I are friends yet, so it's always felt premature to share a lot about him. Seeing my chance, I redirect the conversation. "You and chickn_backflip have been gaming together. A lot."

Wanda laughs. "Nice try. That's not the same. We're just gaming."

"And we're just texting."

"For a guy who eats, sleeps, and breathes romance, you're so dense sometimes. Luke was feeling you out."

I burst out laughing. "I don't think so."

"He asked you to hang out."

I shake a finger back and forth between us. "No. He asked *us*. It was a group hang."

"Because you're not giving him the green light. It was insurance against you rejecting him. If you said no, he wouldn't lose face."

"I didn't reject him. And he's not into guys. He told me so."

"You're sure?"

I open my mouth in mock indignation. "You know how finely tuned my gaydar is. I always know which movies stars are queer."

"That doesn't prove anything. You think every celebrity is queer."

"Because they are. Give it time and all will be revealed. Ok. You want proof? He's a sunbaked jock who games and basically admitted to me he's into sorority girls named Bambi. His name is Luke. Not Luca. Not Lucas. Plain. Old. Luke. Even if he decided to dip a toe into the sparkly end of the pool, I'm no himbro. I'm the deep end of fabulous you cannonball into or get away from the splash zone. Unless he's some self-hating closeted chubby chaser, a guy like Luke would never look twice at a guy like me."

"That's all crap. You're amazing."

I suck on my bottom lip and think about Luke saying he didn't see anything wrong with how I looked and the things he first noticed about me.

"You saw us standing together," I say. "We don't go together."

"Not looking like Truman didn't stop you from pursuing him hard," Wanda says, reading my subtext again.

"Tru is gay, and we have books in common. Luke is a love Grinch. He doesn't like anything romantic, not even weddings. We are vastly different people."

"Love Grinch? Do you not hear yourself?" Wanda rubs her hand across her face. "You were wrong about Truman."

"All the more reason I'm not making the same mistakes with Luke," I say with what I hope is finality. I know I have a history of creating fantasies around people, whether it's

Evie or Truman or that guy who stole the twenty from me. The only difference with Luke is I caught myself before I fell full speed down the rabbit hole like I did with the others. Luke has no romantic interest in me or anyone else I know of. Even if my judgment lapsed, Luke isn't someone to have a crush on. He's a documentary-watching wedding heckler who doesn't love love. There's zero chance of reciprocation.

"Luke isn't Truman. You said so yourself," Wanda says.

"Exactly. Stop seeing things between us that aren't there."

Wanda throws up her hands as she walks into the building. "Boys!" she exclaims. "I can't believe how clueless you all are."

15

About a Bench

My week fills up with preparation for Corner Books' first book club, but Mya was reluctant to commit. Luke was the one who came up with the brilliant plan to order snacks from the coffee shop and request that Mya deliver them. For a nonromantic, he isn't the worst at benevolent conniving.

By Friday afternoon, I've finished cleaning the store and arranging then rearranging the chairs for this evening's club. I eye the vacuum again. I've run it three times but a fourth couldn't hurt.

Gladys darts over and stands in front of it. "I've got one nerve left and you're jumping all over it."

"I need things to go exactly according to my plans. I know I redid the seating, but maybe—"

"No!" Gladys exclaims loud enough that Uncle Andy comes out from the back. "Andrew. You need to do something.

He's stressing out and it's getting to me. Neither of you want to deal with a stressed Gladys."

Uncle Andy unplugs the vacuum and wraps the cord around it. "Bobby," he says gently.

I throw my hands up. "Fine. I won't vacuum or rearrange the chairs. If tonight ends up sucking, it won't be because of me."

Uncle Andy walks down one of the aisles and comes back with a copy of *Pebbles*. He holds it out for me to take. "Take this and go for a walk. Get something to eat. Don't come back before six. Everything is under control."

"But what if—"

"You're going for a walk," Uncle Andy repeats.

"Fine. Whatever." I take the book and a final look around the store as Uncle Andy guides me to the door and out onto the sidewalk.

"Everything is under control. It will all work out great. See you at six," he says.

My walk starts as a stomp as I mentally go over every item I checked off on my list for tonight.

"Everything is under control," I mutter to myself. "It will all work out great." Famous last words.

I tuck *Pebbles* into my back pocket and text Luke.

Me: *Got banned from Corner Books until tonight.*

I'm surprised my phone lights up right away.

Luke: *What did you do now?*

Me: *Nothing! Can you meet me and go over the Jerome and Mya plan one more time?*

Luke: *I'm on break. Meet me on campus.*

I put away my phone. I now have a destination at least and the walk to campus will kill some time and burn off some of my chaotic energy.

I'm going to text Luke to ask him where he is once I near the Athletic Center, but I hear a familiar voice nearby before I get the chance. Evie.

"The Big Summer Reading Festival is going to be *the* event of the year," I hear her tell someone. "You're new here but it's a big deal and I'm the one in charge."

I duck behind a tree to eavesdrop more. Who is Evie lying to and trying to impress?

Luke, a book tucked under his arm, is standing beside Evie. She tosses her hair and laughs at whatever it is he says. I can't hear his part of the conversation, but I see Evie fake a pout before he turns and walks away. Evie heads in the other direction.

Luke is coming right at me. I can't have him discover me eavesdropping, but there's nowhere to hide.

Luke looks over his shoulder as he rounds the tree. I try to circle around the trunk but he's coming too fast. I hold out a hand to stop him from crashing into me. We collide anyway. His arms shoot up around me, keeping me from falling backward. For a second, it's like we're hugging. My cheek presses against the firmness of his chest. He smells even better up close. I look up at his golden face and hair and into his eyes. He does that blink of his and the slight smile. His arms tighten around me for a second and the hair on my arms stands on end.

He parts his lips. "Bobby?" he asks. "What do you do? Lurk around Little Elm, waiting for people to trip over you?"

I shove him in the chest, and he steps back. "What do you do? Barrel around town nearly knocking me over?" I bend to retrieve his fallen book.

Luke smooths his hair back. "Sorry. I should pay more attention to where I'm going."

"I can't blame you. I've wanted to get away from Evie before too."

"She's"—he pauses and searches for a word—"driven."

"That's a nice way to say *pushy*." I hand him *The Silver Devil*.

"Thanks," he says, adjusting the bookmark between the pages. "I'm not a fast reader. You probably are."

"A little bit."

Luke scratches his arm. "Were you listening in on my conversation with Evie?"

"I would never," I scoff.

"The lady doth protest," Luke says. "I guess you heard her telling me how jealous you are of her getting the festival job."

"What else did she say?"

"Nothing except the Reading Festival is like Christmas. I figured she was exaggerating. But the banners and posters appearing around town are a lot."

"The festival is Little Elm's biggest event of the year. How did you not know about it when you applied to go to school here?"

"I came for the business program."

"Wanda's doing business and programming. Now that her streaming is gaining popularity, she wants to make a go at a job she loves."

"She's smart. She's good with people when she warms up."

"Wanda's good at boundaries."

"Is that where you two diverge?"

"Hardy-har-har," I say.

Luke grabs my hand and the hairs on my arm stand on edge again.

"I know you want to talk but I need to show you. I found this awesome bench. It's my favorite on campus."

"You've got a favorite bench?"

"Don't you?"

"No one has a favorite bench."

Luke grins. "Then wait until you try this beauty out. I won't be the only one to have fallen for it."

"Sure. I've always got time to fall in love," I say. I feel myself go red before I add, "With a bench."

Luke leads me to a bricked-in arch set in the side of an older campus building. The masonry forms a ledge on top of which someone placed some weathered boards. The wood is worn and hardly seems like intentional seating.

"This is it? I hate to break it to you, but this isn't a bench. It's a half-assed ledge."

Luke laughs. "No way. Someone put those there on purpose for people to sit on. It's a bench."

"Ledge."

"Be quiet and sit." Luke stands in front of me and places both hands on my shoulders. It takes him almost no force to give me a little push that makes my knees give way. I have just enough time to pull *Pebbles* from my back pocket. As I sit, I feel the cool bricks against my back. The sunlight pours through the foliage, dancing back and forth across me as the leaves sway in the breeze. The wood may be old but it's soft and comfortable and easy to settle in. It's not a spacious area. When Luke sits beside me, his knee almost presses against mine.

"Tell me it's not your new favorite bench now," he says.

"Fine," I concede. "It's my new favorite bench despite it being a ledge only because I've never had a favorite bench." In all honesty, I probably would have walked by here a hundred times and never noticed it. If things had gone as planned for me and college, I probably would have been in too much of a rush to get to book club or see Truman to slow down enough to notice it.

Luke stretches and his shirt rides up. There's a line of hair that goes down from his belly button under the waistband of his swim shorts. I look away as he leans back and makes himself comfortable against the bricks.

"There's a spot like this back home behind the old city hall where the bricks are always cool even on the hottest days," he says. "And this shack where a guy feeds all the feral cats in the area."

"You're a cat person?" I ask.

"I like them but prefer a big dog. I never had one though. I'm allergic. My skin gets splotchy from petting them and petting cats gives me a rash."

"That's a severe reaction. My mom, Cass, isn't a pet person. It's a shock she managed to raise a kid."

"You don't mind living with her and not going away?"

"Not really. Little Elm is great and Cass isn't your typical mother. Plus, college is expensive. Was it a big deal for you to move here?"

"I'm used to going between different households because of all the divorces," Luke says. "I don't think moving here from North Maple I was prepared for how small-town a small town can be."

"For example?"

Luke laughs. "The Reading Festival. Everyone knowing one another. The meddling in other people's business."

"I don't meddle."

"You do meddle. And you've sucked me into it too. I'm an accessory to your crime."

"Or a sidekick to my heroism," I counter.

"Or a fool who should know better." Then Luke points at *Pebbles* and asks the most perfect question a guy could ask me while sitting on a ledge under the shade of the elms. "Want to tell me about that?" He closes his eyes and leans his head back, ready to listen, his face pointing toward the sky. He swallows. The muscles of his throat move, his Adam's apple bobs. There's a tiny bit of stubble across his jawline.

So, I tell him about the Baroness and tease the plot of the book. How the two boys never quite seem to be in the same place at the same time to make it work. How the odds are stacked against them. How all seems lost.

Luke pulls his knee near me up and hugs it to his chest as he listens. His lips pull up in an almost-unnoticeable smile.

"It's just so satisfying," I finish. "It's exactly how love should be."

Luke opens his eyes. "I forgot you're a Casanova. You must have fallen in love a lot."

"With every turn of the page."

We sit in silence, the wind lifting and blowing the heat away from our bodies and the bricks cool on our backs.

After a while, I ask, "What do you like about *The Silver Devil*?"

"The passion. The intensity. There's something primal, a sense of if I don't have you, I'll go mad. I don't believe that's what love's like, though."

"How would you know? Have you fallen in love a lot?"

"Did you forget? You said it yourself, I'm a love Grinch. I'm immune to love."

"Maybe you haven't given the right one a chance." I place my copy of *Pebbles* on the bench between us. Hesitantly, I reach out to take Luke's hand. I put it on top of the book. My fingers stay on his for only a second before I yank my hand away, as if shocked by static.

"You should read that," I say. "See if your inner cynic changes his mind."

"I'm a realist, not a cynic." Luke lifts his hand off the book. "This is your favorite. What if I hate it? I don't want to ruin it for you."

"You won't. Trust me like I trusted you with this bench. Even if it is a ledge."

"Fine. I'll try to read it fast."

I shake my head. "Take your time with it. Certain things need to be savored."

The sun sways across Luke's face, over his eyes, nose, lips, cheeks, brow. He doesn't glow gold. He's just a guy sitting on a bench in the shade. I'm just the guy sitting beside him.

Luke places *Pebbles* on top of *Devil*, gripping both in his large hand. "My next shift at the pool starts soon."

"I've still got time to kill. I'll walk you."

We don't say much except about the weather on the short trip. When we get to the doors of the Athletic Center, a minibus pulls up.

The driver opens the doors and calls down the steps. "Sorry. Sorry. We're running behind. It's been a day."

"Don't worry," Luke answers. "I'm early. I'll get them going."

"You really are a lifesaver, Luke," the driver says. She moves aside to let Luke onto the bus.

"Luke!" several voices call as he ascends the steps.

In a matter of minutes, Luke returns and assists a line of senior citizens off the bus toward the Athletic Center. He tells each person how great they're looking as he offers them his arm when they reach the bottom step.

The last to descend is someone I know.

"Bobby!" Mr. Martinez calls, waving me over. "I heard you were working here."

"Not exactly. I'm downtown at Corner Books," I say and quickly change subjects to Mr. Martinez's partner. "How's Mr. Shah?"

Mr. Martinez grips my hand with both of his. "Playing poker back at the seniors' residence. He's a terrible bluffer but he has fun."

I start to laugh.

Mr. Martinez says to Luke, "I lived on the same block as Ravi for twenty years, never even knowing he was there. And this one"—he motions to me—"spends five minutes with us at a garage sale and convinces us to take a private cooking class together when we both checked out the bakeware. We saw an old casserole dish and he saw a partnership. Next thing we know, he's got us signed up for cooking classes together. Another do-gooder."

"Food is a primal love language," I say.

Mr. Martinez falls behind the other seniors. "Go on ahead. Start without me."

Luke heads inside while I hold open a door for Mr. Martinez, who is slowly ascending the stairs.

Mr. Martinez points inside with his cane. "Your instincts are right hanging around that Luke. I know he's not looking for any sort of recognition, but it's not everyone who gives up their time for a bunch of seniors to do water aerobics."

I can't help myself and need to know more. "How did that happen?"

"Our old lifeguard graduated. We only get pool time if a lifeguard volunteers to open the pool for us and supervise. Luke was the only one of the new hires who offered. Stick with him. You don't want one like that to slip away."

"It's not like that between us. Neither of us are looking for love," I say, knowing that I crossed off a boyfriend from my Summer of Bobby list.

"I wasn't looking either when you introduced me to Ravi. My only regret is how much time I spent without him when he was right under my nose. Don't waste your time. Luke is one of the good ones." Mr. Martinez winks at me before he pulls himself up tall and struts into the building.

16

How Bobby Got His Groove Back

Corner Books' book club consists of a broad range of people. Some, like the woman with the shaved head, leather vest, and tattoos are more unexpected than others. Another woman in sweats tells me she's a housewife and nothing in any book can be more graphic than childbirth. I take her word for it and don't clarify that's not the meaning of *graphic novel*.

Cindy slips in but only stays long enough to compliment the décor and turnout.

Mya is setting up coffee and pastries when Luke comes up beside me and whispers in my ear, "We have a problem."

He takes me by the arm and leads me to the back, where Jerome is struggling to get on a pair of furry pants way too small for him.

"They sent a kid's costume," Jerome says.

I grab the packaging and turn it over in my hands. "No. I confirmed with Little Elm's costume store before they dropped off. We were supposed to get a D&D-style quester. This is a faun. Where are the horns?"

Jerome slides a headband on with two pink goat horns that bobble.

"You were supposed to be dressed like a character from the book to ask Mya out in that loosely sounding ye olden time English. You're going to look ridiculous without the proper horns."

"He was going to look ridiculous anyway." Luke pulls out his phone. "Call the costume store and have them drop off something more appropriate."

"They're closed," I say.

"Can't you get ahold of someone? I thought you knew everyone in town."

"If I did, don't you think I'd be calling already?" I start to pace.

"How does Little Elm even keep a costume store alive?" Luke asks.

"We have a very active LARP community. And that's not a question for right now."

Luke quietly asks Jerome, "Is this another thing I ask you if it's for real and you say yes and I don't believe you but then I Google it and you're right?"

"Why would I make it up?" I snap. "Do I seem like I'm in a joking mood?"

Jerome grabs me by the shoulders. "Dude. Pull yourself together. Mya's out there. I need your magic. What's the plan B?"

But I don't have a plan B. I've always been right when it comes to romance. Or I was. Then I got thrown off. I start to breathe heavily. I can't be wrong again.

"Toss me your car keys," Luke commands Jerome. Luke spins me to face him. "Stall Mya."

"But I don't have another plan," I say.

"You've got me." Luke snatches Jerome's keys out of the air without turning away from me. "I've got an idea." He pivots me toward the front of Corner Books and gives me a small push before he leaves, pulling Jerome through the back door.

I take a deep breath and plaster a smile onto my face. "Mya!" I call across the crowded store. She's heading toward the front door with Uncle Andy. "The food looks amazing!"

Mya shrugs. "It's only cake and cookies."

"Stay for the meeting," I say as I reach her. "You'd add a lot to the conversation."

Mya fluffs her tight spiral curls. "Another time. I'm beat after my shift. You can tell me about it over your next macchiato."

"Are you sure because—"

"Let the girl go home," Uncle Andy cuts in. He hands Mya a white envelope. "There's extra in there as a token of thanks."

"I really think you'd enjoy the evening . . ." I begin again, but Mya is already halfway out the door.

Mya steps out onto the sidewalk and I hurry after her, ignoring Uncle Andy asking me where I'm going and reminding me the book club starts any minute.

I stop just outside of Corner Books. Jerome is under the festival banners and buntings decorating the street, playing the opening cords of A-ha's "Take On Me."

Mya stops as Jerome plays. Her expression turns from exhaustion to something soft as she watches him. Her gaze doesn't leave his as she taps her foot to the beat.

When he's done, Mya claps with the rest of the crowd that has come outside from Corner Books to listen to the impromptu wordless serenade.

Luke steps to Mya's side from wherever he was watching and whispers something in her ear. She walks toward Jerome and speaks to him. I can't hear what they're saying, but when Mya hands Jerome her phone, I gasp, clasping my hands together, and then clap. The crowd joins in.

"Book club time," Luke says, opening Corner Books' door wide. "Let's get the conversation going."

The crowd reenters the store.

Jerome reaches Luke as I do.

"We're going out next week." Jerome beams. "I knew bringing Bobby into the game would work out." He claps Luke and I on our shoulders. "I'm going to put my guitar back in the trunk of my car, then join the book club. I'll need something to talk about on our date."

Before Luke heads back inside, I grab his forearm. "Why that song?"

Luke shrugs with his eyebrows. "The music video with the comic panels. It's all I could think of."

I keep my hand on his arm. "I have to know. What did you say to Mya?"

"The truth. My roommate likes her and he's been too shy to let her know before tonight."

I smack his bicep. "What is wrong with you? No one is ever direct about their feelings. Your amateur move could have blown the whole thing."

"I know," Luke says. "Serenades are the worst. Imagine having to stand there awkwardly pretending you're not wishing it would end already. I should have thought it out better, but Mya seemed to like it."

I shake my head. "Serenades are romantic."

"They're torture. Like being musically waterboarded."

I groan. "At least your bad attitude didn't stop you from being a decent sidekick, love Grinch."

"Damn straight," Luke says. "Good thing I decided to keep my eye on you. I pulled your ass out of the fire tonight."

I shove Luke in front of me into Corner Books. Not as I planned, but I daresay my groove is on its way back.

17

Eternal Sunshine of the Not Spotless House

After the success of Corner Books' first book club, Gladys stations herself at the register, ringing up the last customers, while Uncle Andy, Luke, and I tidy up chairs. Finally, Gladys accompanies the final attendee, the tattooed woman, to the door and surprises Uncle Andy and me when she wishes the woman a good night and tells her to return soon.

The bell above the door jingles. Without looking up, I say, "Sorry, we're closed."

Cass is standing there, leaning into Uncle Andy. Wanda is behind her.

"We came to congratulate you," Cass says. "The store is fantastic. Bobby's got my eye for design. I love how you retained the character of the space."

Gladys clears her throat. She's positioned herself again by the register with two large plastic tote bags. "If you don't need me any longer, I'll see you in the morning, Andrew. Make sure to lock up properly."

"Andrew?" Cass asks. "I haven't heard anyone call you that since your mother caught us hitchhiking to New York when we were fifteen."

"You hitchhiked to New York?" I ask. "At fifteen? Do you know how dangerous that is?"

"Calm down. We never made it. Andy's mom was the only car to pass us and even she didn't stop."

Luke leans in and whispers, "I think you got more than her eye. Your mom is cool."

"I picked up PizZaZa Gabor's. It's keeping warm back at the house," Cass says and holds up her car keys. "Who's riding with me?"

Uncle Andy plucks the keys out of Cass's hand. "Why don't you ride with me and let the kids take your car? No one is a more cautious driver than Bobby."

Uncle Andy tosses me Cass's keyring. I fumble but Luke closes his hands over mine, so I don't miss the throw.

"I've got them," I say.

Luke lets go.

As we leave the store and Uncle Andy and Cass hang back to lock the store up properly, Wanda darts for Cass's car and calls, "Not shotgun."

I start up the car and check my blind spot before pulling out. Wanda begins talking about some new anime show on Netflix with Luke. I'm glad she's carrying the conversation because while I know I'm a good driver, I'm not very experienced and tend to play it safe. As a result, we pull into the driveway long after Uncle Andy and Cass have arrived.

I leave Wanda to show Luke into the house, hurrying ahead of them to make sure our home is presentable. For all I know, Cass could have left our underwear drying on the backs of the kitchen chairs or something equally awful.

"Where's the emergency?" Cass asks as I barrel from room to room.

I do a sweep of the main floor, closing bedroom doors, checking the bathroom, making sure the toilet is flushed, and end up in the living room. It's a disaster. Glass is strewn across the floor, along with Cass's sketches, a measuring tape, and various tools.

I go to close the door but find Luke standing there. He steps inside before I can do anything and walks around the perimeter of the room, taking in everything. He stares up at the stacks of books running up the walls, the majority with their covers ripped off, then at our worn furniture shoved up tight into the area by the windows, the disarray of Cass's art strewn over the floor, the boxes of yarn. It isn't just letting Luke into our home and knowing it's a mess but his getting a good look into our life that leaves me feeling so exposed.

"This is where you live?" Luke asks.

I nod and wait for whatever Luke is going to say next.

He looks up the wall nearest him at the books. "You read all these?"

I swallow. "A lot of them."

Luke turns and keeps peering around. "My mom has always kept whatever house we lived in like Martha Stewart was going to show up any second for a photo shoot. Your house looks like you actually live in it. The coffee table is awesome."

"My mom designed it," I say. I let out the breath I didn't know I was holding. "It's normally our living room but it's doubling as Cass's studio for now."

Luke crouches, elbows on his knees, to give a closer look at Cass's mess. "I've never been in an artist's studio. Your family and your home are so cool."

"We're eating," Cass calls from the kitchen.

Luke straightens up and we join the others. Wanda hands us pieces of paper towel with slices of pizza on them.

I sit between Wanda and Luke.

"To Bobby and Andy," Cass says, lifting her glass. "And to Corner Books."

We all raise our glasses and cheer before starting to eat. Cass offers Andy a swig of her beer, but he declines.

Luke puts down his pizza. "Are you Bobby's father's brother?" he asks.

"We're not related," Cass answers before Uncle Andy has a chance.

"My dad is French," I add. "Parisian to be specific."

"Don't start with all that again," Cass warns.

I grin, knowing that's my cue to tell the story. "Cass had this big show in Paris. She was the toast of the town. Across the gallery, a man sees her and knows he'd give anything to be with the brilliant woman who created such beauty."

"You're laying it on a bit thick," Cass interjects. "It was nothing like that."

"One night of passion and they parted ways, never to see each other again. She returns to Little Elm and nine months later, a son is born."

"You can spare the embellishments next time you tell it," Cass says, taking another slice out of the box for herself and one for Uncle Andy.

"Then you aren't a couple?" Luke asks.

Uncle Andy shakes his head. "We had one bad date in high school."

I look at Cass. "I didn't know this."

"I did," Wanda says around a mouthful of pizza. "Cass told my mom Andy stood her up."

"Why didn't you tell me?"

Wanda shrugs. "Because I know how not to spread gossip."

Uncle Andy turns in his seat to face Cass. "I didn't stand you up. My car wouldn't start. By the time I got there, you were out with some other guy."

"I don't want to rehash this," Cass says. "Water under the bridge." She gives Uncle Andy the smile she reserves for him only.

His eyes flash. "That wasn't how it was, Cass Ashton, and you know it."

It's only a second and if you didn't know Uncle Andy, you'd think it was anger. I've seen Uncle Andy argue on the phone with distributors and this look isn't anger. But there is heat behind his eyes. Something fiery. That's passion, the same kind you see in the eyes of a roguish man on the cover of a romance novel.

My mom gives the smallest, slyest smile and bats her eyes at Andy. I notice her arm move and know she's patting his leg below the table, but his eyes remained locked on hers.

Oblivious to what we were just privy, Luke takes another slice. We all stop to watch him as he turns it around and starts eating the crust first.

"What's wrong?" he asks around the pizza crust in his mouth as we all stare.

"Do you always eat pizza like that?" I ask.

Luke shrugs. "Usually. I like the pointy end most, so I eat it last."

"The tip is the best part," I agree.

"That's what they all say when all they've had is the tip," Cass says and begins to laugh maniacally.

"Mom!"

I glance at Luke, whose cheeks have gone red, but notice a tiny smile.

"Lighten up, Bobby. Just because you're gay doesn't mean you're the only one allowed to throw around innuendo. You don't have a monopoly on quick wit and some double entendre."

․․․

Uncle Andy offers to drop Luke off when it gets late.

I slip on my shoes and step outside. Cass chats with Luke while watching Wanda climb upstairs.

My mind wandered after dinner to Mr. Shah and Mr. Martinez and how they lived so close to each other. They were right there all that time and if I hadn't followed my instincts and pushed them together, they'd have missed out on a lifetime together. They waited too long as it is. Then I think of all those other couples I've helped. And tonight's success with Jerome and Mya.

Meanwhile, right in front of me are Cass and Uncle Andy. I can't stand picturing either of them on the seniors' bus going to aquafit alone. I can't wimp out anymore when it comes to the two people I care about most.

I make a mental note to add to my Summer of Bobby list: *Mom and Uncle Andy.* I don't know how I'm going to do it, but by the end of the summer I'll find out if that spark in Uncle Andy's eyes will ignite a flame or burn itself out. Too much time has been wasted already when they could have been happy together. But now that I know they felt it once too and the opportunity was lost, I'll help them reclaim it. Wherever the road leads, it's time we all know.

I watch, standing on the porch beside my mom, as Luke and Uncle Andy pull away.

"I like that boy," Cass says. "We should have him back."

THE SUMMER OF BOBBY

(AKA Bobby Ashton's Plan for the ~~Perfect~~ Summer Before College)

- ✅ Summer job: Corner Books
- ♡ Play nice with Gladys
- ♡ Become a star employee
- ✅ Spruce up Corner Books' image
- ✅ Hope Evie tanks Big Summer Reading Festival
- ♡ ~~Land the Perfect Boyfriend: TRUMAN~~
- ✅ No boys like Dean Perez warned

- ✓ Matchmake Jerome and Mya; and
- ✓ Restore my matchmaking mojo
- ✓ Make Corner Books' book club a big hit
- ♡ Cass and Uncle Andy

18

Homewrecker

"I texted Luke to join us when he's done," Wanda says as she slides into a booth at Elm Dogs.

Like Queen Clarisse Renaldi of Genovia, I make it a point never to slide but I make an exception here. Booths are one of those unknowns. Their tables might be bolted to the floor, making it difficult to get in or out of. Or the table might push into one's belly creating a tabletop muffin top. Or the table does move and moving it makes a noise so sitting down becomes this awkward spectacle.

But Elm Dogs has the perfect booths because whoever installed them cared less about fitting in one extra table and more about spacious, comfortable seating for all shapes, sizes, and abilities with tables that aren't stuck to the ground or walls.

Wanda's thumbs fly across her phone's screen. She smiles when she hits send.

"Who are you texting?" I ask.

"No one." Wanda types out another message, smiling.

"Is it chickn_backflip?" I ask. Wanda doesn't answer so I keep talking. "C'mon. What's going on? You can tell me."

"I could but I won't. It's none of your business," Wanda answers. "He's a guy I'm getting to know and I don't want to talk anymore about it."

Before I can ask more questions, Wanda waves over to the cash. Mr. Papadopoulos, the owner, holds back our server and comes over to our table himself.

"Bobby, my favorite customer!" He grips my face with both hands and plants a kiss on each of my cheeks.

"I beg pardon?" I say. "Since when?"

People from other tables are staring. That's when I notice Luke standing near the entrance watching me get kissed.

"Since my son dumped his girlfriend because of you."

I look around nervously. Luke isn't coming any closer.

"Mr. Papadopoulos, I'm not even sure I know your son. I don't go around breaking guys up with their girlfriends."

"He tells me, he meets this sweet, smart gay boy at Corner Books. I knew he was talking about you. Next thing, he's breaking up with his girlfriend. You've changed the direction of my son's life."

I slink down in the booth. "I really don't know what you're talking about."

"The book you recommended," Mr. Papadopoulos says. "He reads it and realizes how awful his lousy girlfriend is. Now he's left her and is going back to college. From now on, you eat here free. Maria, get the Book Whisperer the Coney Island dog and fries on the house." Mr. Papadopoulos claps a hand onto my shoulder. I sink a little more. "You put him back on the right path. Our family owes you a debt of gratitude."

As Mr. Papadopoulos clears off and diners return to their meals, Luke slides into the booth beside Wanda.

He grins at me, holding back a laugh. "Wow, Casanova. Homewrecking now?"

"I don't even remember his son or the book I sold him," I admit. "We've had so many customers recently."

"Free food is free food," Wanda says.

Luke reaches over me to grab a menu from the holder behind the condiment squeeze bottles and I smell his scent.

"Sorry it took me so long to get here. Evie was inviting me to some party next weekend. It's going to be in the field behind the AC," Luke says.

"Athletic Center," Wanda translates for me.

"They have firepits and there's supposed to be a marshmallow roast. My roommates and I are going to go. You should come too. Starts after sundown."

Wanda says, "Next weekend? We'll . . ."

"See," I finish, kicking Wanda under the table so she knows to stop.

Luke says, "I'm going to the bathroom. If the server comes back order me the New York–style turkey dog."

Once Luke leaves, Wanda asks, "Why did you stop me from saying it was your birthday?"

"I don't know. I don't want to make a big deal out of it."

"But you love your birthday."

That's true. Normally, I plan an entire day of rom-com movies and snacks. Both the really trashy kind you don't normally consume because they're pure garbage. As kids,

Wanda and I inevitably threw up before cake was even served and the movies had finished. "I've had enough of being the center of attention lately. I don't need our first real college party turning into my birthday party. I'd rather keep it on the down-low."

"Are you maturing in your ripe old age?" Wanda's phone goes off. She smiles as she texts back.

"At least tell me if you like what you're getting to know," I say.

Wanda keeps texting and smiling. "I wouldn't be spending time getting to know him if I didn't like what I was discovering. I'm not that girl. But I'm asking you seriously to leave it alone, Bobby."

"Leave what alone?"

"You know what. I don't want you asking me a lot of questions and I especially don't want you interfering. This is my business. I'll handle it how I want. Got it?"

Whenever Wanda's had a secret in the past, I'm the first person she's told. Whatever's going on with this guy must be pretty serious. While I want to be the type of friend who is supportive of his bestie's personal growth and boundaries, no one knows more about love than I. Who just finished getting thanked for improving a total stranger's life? Why even have a gay best friend? Wanda's not wanting my help is borderline insulting.

"I want you to promise to stay out of this and let me handle things however I decide best," Wanda says, staring me down.

"A promise made under duress doesn't stand in a court of law."

"Promise," she says again.

"Tell me a little more about him and I'll promise. Is it serious?"

"It's serious enough I need you to promise. Promise, Bobby."

I'm about to concede when Luke returns, and our server arrives with the biggest order of loaded fries I've ever seen.

Mr. Papadopoulos comes to our booth again. "You are truly a godsend." He begins clapping and the other diners in the restaurant join in.

I sink down in the booth again. They only stop when I give a little wave.

Wanda doesn't clap. She purses her lips and continues to give me the stare.

I'll let Wanda handle things herself like she asked. For now, anyway. But if it comes to the point where she needs a godsend, I at least won't have to break a promise to be hers. If I can add Cass and Andy to my list, I can just as easily add Wanda and chickn_backflip.

19

About Damn Time

"Want to come up?" Wanda asks as we walk up our driveway.

"I should probably sleep in a real bed tonight," I say. Part of me thinks Wanda may benefit from some alone time with chickn_backflip. Despite her not trusting me, I still want what's best for her. "Besides, I need to talk to Cass about the party."

"I can't imagine she'd say no."

"I'm not sure. We've spent the last seventeen birthdays together. I think she loves the movies and vomit fest as much as we do. It's our special thing and I am her only child."

"For the record, I don't love throwing up. Your mom is a bad influence. She encouraged me to eat all that candy every year I got sick."

"Me too. I wonder if having me when she was older left her without the energy to parent like the other moms."

"Cass is just cooler than other parents," Wanda says. "I'm heading up."

I stand outside and wait for Wanda's signal, flicking the lights on and off four times to let me know everything is ok upstairs. We made up the routine when Wanda was old enough to sleep upstairs on her own when her mom worked nightshifts. Even though we're too old for monsters to be hiding under our beds, I always wait, and Wanda always flicks the lights.

When I go inside, Cass calls, "Keep your shoes on."

"What's going on?"

Cass lifts the visor of the face shield she's wearing. "I've been watching stained glass tutorials online. Fascinating. I don't know why I didn't try it before. Careful though. The slivers from cutting glass get everywhere."

I grab our broom and begin sweeping and decide to cut to the chase. "About my birthday."

Cass lowers her visor and snaps a piece of glass in half cleanly. "I think I got the hang of this. What are you planning to get sick on for your eighteenth?"

"I thought we could keep it simple. A small family dinner, you, me, Uncle Andy, and Wanda, followed by me going to a party."

"A party?" Cass puts down the glass she's scoring and lifts her visor again.

I keep sweeping. "A college party. On campus. With Wanda. Luke will be there too."

Cass takes off her work gloves. "A bunch of minors at an afterhours college party?"

I stop sweeping. "There's nothing to worry about. I'm very mature and responsible."

"That's exactly what I am worried about," Cass says. "You're a fuddy-duddy."

"I am not."

"Oh yes, you are," Cass says resuming her glass scoring. "The wildest thing you've ever done is tell a boy you like him through interpretive dance and break a store window. You weren't even being reckless. Total accident. You'll be eighteen soon enough. You don't need my permission to go to a party. Go. Be immature. Be irresponsible. Make bad choices. I've been waiting for you to finally do something interesting for once. You're so boring, I was starting to wonder if you were even my son."

"I'm not boring," I say. I catch Cass smiling. "Are you sure you're not going to be upset your baby isn't spending his special day with you?"

"That's a sickening way to put it. But if it makes it more fun for you, I'll take back my blessing and you can sneak out like you should have started doing a few years ago. It's about damn time you went and raised some hell."

"It's not going to be that kind of party."

"I've only got one condition. Don't get in so much trouble I need to make another statue."

"You're the worst." I cross the room and give her a hug. "I'm lucky you decided to make me."

Cass squeezes me back. "Don't go getting all mushy on me. You're getting overly sentimental in your old age, fuddy-duddy."

As Wanda, Cass, and Uncle Andy sing the final notes of "Happy Birthday," I puff out my cheeks. I focus on them and use my wish for the people across from me, hoping Cupid's arrow hits a bull's-eye for each of them and that my schemes ring true.

I've never been one to rely on wishes alone. I'm not one to sit around hoping what I want will be delivered to me. There were all these trends like putting things out into the universe and the book *The Secret,* and then manifesting. But beyond a want that something drops in your lap out of nowhere, there was no real action plan.

I cut my ice cream cake. As I hand Uncle Andy his slice, I tip the dessert plate so melted ice cream dribbles onto his shirt.

"I'm so sorry," I say, scrambling for napkins that I hand to Cass who is seated beside him.

She takes the napkins, which I managed to smear some hot fudge and pink icing onto with my thumb as I passed them over, and begins rubbing at the spill on Uncle Andy's shirt, another plaid button-up I've advised him against. I've got to get him confidently serving some hot DILF realness.

No matter how much I've told Cass to dab or work in a circular motion from the outside in, she rubs at the spilled ice cream. I knew she would.

Cass throws up her hands. "How did I manage to make it worse?"

"That's going to stain. We need to treat it immediately," I say, pitching my voice a touch higher than normal and speaking quickly to create a sense of urgency with the tiniest hint for potential panic. The last thing anyone wants from this birthday boy is a gay meltdown. I know Cass and Uncle Andy remember my sugar high crashes of yore and the accompanying hysteria only a four-year-old strung out on Pixy Stix and cupcakes can achieve.

"I'll wash it when I get home," Uncle Andy says.

As if she's in on what I've got going, Cass says, "No. Bobby's right. You need to nip a stain in the bud. Take it off and give it to me."

"It's fine. Really."

I couldn't have asked for a better performance from Cass. She begins unbuttoning Uncle Andy's shirt for him. "Don't be silly. I'll run some water through it."

Uncle Andy tries to shoo Cass's hands away and finally catches them in his. He holds them. They stare into each other's eyes before Cass delicately pulls her hands away. I swear, her cheeks go pink.

"I can do it," Uncle Andy says softly. He finishes unbuttoning his shirt before he slides it off his shoulders and hands it to Cass. He's not in a T-shirt today but a white tank undershirt.

I comment, "Beefcake alert! Those are some serious Ronny Cammareri vibes you're giving, Uncle Andy." This is coming together even better than I could have planned.

"Huh?" he asks.

Cass holds the shirt in both hands before running water through it under the tap. "Nicolas Cage's character in *Moonstruck*," Wanda says.

"I love that movie." Cass works dish soap into the spot and rinses. "There, good as new. It just needs to dry." Cass hangs the shirt on the back of a chair. "You should finish your cake and get going soon. Don't take five years to get dressed like you normally do, Bobby."

"Excuse me for wanting to look good," I say.

There's a knock at the front door. Cass answers it and returns to the table with a bouquet of long-stem roses with a card. "For you," she says.

I make a point of furrowing my brow and trying to seem confused as I take the envelope and rip it open. When I pull out the card, two tickets flutter out. Cass picks them up.

"These are for the sold-out Mapplethorpe in the Vines interactive exhibit."

"A friend's dad is head chef at the winery," I say. "She sent me tickets for my birthday." I don't mention that Tricia texted how she scored the vineyard because of her personal connection, and I took that as my opportunity to finagle two tickets to the Mapplethorpe show. Then a quick trip across the street to Mr. Fumagalli got me a bouquet of roses at a low cost. All Mae needed to hear was I was helping out a couple and she arranged for the tickets and flowers to be delivered right after dinner.

I take the tickets from Cass and study them for a second. "They're for tonight," I say. "And even if Wanda and I didn't have that party, it's a twenty-one-plus event. You should take them." I hold out the tickets for Cass. "You've been dying to see how they use his photographs."

"I'll go with you," Uncle Andy offers, as I knew he would.

Cass raises an eyebrow at him. "Mapplethorpe was rather risqué, and the interactive element is supposed to be quite provocative."

Wanda takes the roses from Cass and gets a vase out of our cupboard above the refrigerator.

"I'm sure I can handle it," he replies. "And you'll be able to enjoy the wine without worrying about driving home safely."

I remove the sparkly plastic *Birthday Girl* tiara and feather boa Cass pulled out for me today and leave them on the table. "You'll need to tell me all about it in the morning," I say as I get up to change my outfit for the party.

"Shoot," Uncle Andy says. "I open the store tomorrow."

This is the only wrench my plan has come up against, and I can't have all my efforts go to waste. This night is tailor-made to get Andy and Cass together. Wine. A moonlight vineyard. Suggestive art. The scene is set. They need to take the stage. I stop before I exit the room. "I can do that for you."

Uncle Andy stands and picks up his shirt. "You've never opened on your own before."

"I've helped Gladys open loads. I've got a key. It's the opposite of locking the door and turning on the alarm. Besides, I've got to learn some time and Sunday mornings are a ghost town."

"But aren't you going to be out at that party late?" Uncle Andy asks.

Cass takes Uncle Andy's shirt and helps him slide it on then stands in front of him and does up the buttons, leaving enough undone so his chest and tank still show. "It's Bobby.

Late is eleven o'clock. You can afford to take the occasional break. You don't have to be in that store twenty-four seven."

"All right, Bobby," he says then moves to do more buttons up.

Cass places her hand on top of his. "Leave it. It's a warm night and it looks better that way."

I sashay down the hall. Every piece is falling right into place.

Wanda follows me to my bedroom. "You're shameless. I can't believe they didn't pick up on it."

"I know. I'm good," I say, pulling a mesh shirt embroidered with flowers and bees out of my closet and deciding against it. I take out a super cute bubblegum-pink cropped varsity jacket and short set I wore last Halloween.

"Jacket, yes. Shorts, no," Wanda says.

"I know I had that blip with Truman, and it was a big blip, but I'm back. You saw how that went off. I could help you with chickn_backflip if you let me," I say.

Wanda makes a face.

"At least tell me why you, Wanda Lee, haven't pulled the trigger on the chickn_backflip situation. I'm your BFF."

Wanda sighs. "You're not going to give up. Fine, I'll tell you but no specifics and no follow-up questions. Those are my terms. Take them or leave them."

"Take them," I agree grudgingly.

"It's just gaming so far, nothing romantic, so stop thinking that. But if it's going to go beyond that I need to be sure he's all in."

"Did he give you any reason to believe he could do that?"

"That sounds a lot like a follow-up, but I'll allow it. He says he wants to be around long term, but saying you want something isn't the same as being prepared to actually do it. And I already know you're going to tell me I have to take a chance, but every risk is calculated, and I don't have enough data to do that yet."

"Fair enough," I say.

"No more questions and remember what you promised," Wanda says.

I remember the promise I didn't make very well. Instead of pushing her for more, I hold up the outfit. "Are you sure the shorts are a no? My ass looks great in them."

"Do what you want." Wanda ignores my offer. "But don't come complaining to me when your legs are itching from mosquito bites later."

20

Meet Not Cute

We follow the firelight across the field. I'm glad I listened to Wanda and put on the pair of jeans that were slung over the back of my desk chair. While the shorts are very flattering to my derrière, she was right: I don't want to be providing a Bobby buffet to a bunch of insects.

"Thanks for advising against eyeliner," I say to Wanda. "I would have looked like a raccoon."

Wanda takes the baseball cap off her own head and places it on mine. She considers it before reaching up and turning it backward. She wrinkles her nose and turns the cap forward again but skews it on an angle. "Better," she says. "You're giving off a barely legal jock vibe."

"Eww. Such a gross description. Couldn't you have given me your hat before I spent fifteen minutes styling my hair?"

Wanda teases me about being only a few hours into eighteen as we approach the fires and the figures around them start to take on more distinct shapes. When we get close enough to make out faces, a familiar person greets us.

"Bobby and Wanda. Together as usual," Evie says from where she's positioned herself beside Luke on a log around one of the firepits. "You must be joined at the hip."

A girl I've never met sitting across the fire says, "You can't say stuff like that." She upspeaks when she talks. "It's offensive."

Evie asks, "How?"

"I shouldn't have to explain it to you. Your ableism is not attractive."

As Evie starts arguing with the girl, Luke slips away.

"I didn't know if you were still coming since you didn't text me back," he says.

"I didn't get any texts." I check my phone. It's almost dead and went into battery-saving mode, limiting functionality.

"Did you bring a portable charger?" I ask Wanda.

"It's in the purse you told me not to bring," she replies.

Great. My phone is basically unusable.

"No worries." Wanda holds up her phone. "Mine is at full battery."

Luke jerks his head toward another fire. "Come on. I want you to meet my other roommates." He leads us through the darkness to another group of college kids.

"You already know Jerome and his girlfriend, Mya," Luke says, gesturing to the new couple who barely look up from making out on their blanket in the grass. "And this is Roger. I don't know where Jack got to, but he might have gone back already."

Roger gets up from the group of people he's sitting with to come over to us. He might as well have walked out of a catalogue. His face is perfectly symmetrical, his jawline square, his hair has the right amount of product and volume, and the fact that he must go to the gym daily is apparent. He's holding an obscenely large beer can.

"This is Bobby. And you remember Wanda from camp," Luke says.

"We went to middle school together," Roger says. "Before I went to the private arts high school. Have you been well, Bobby?"

The way he asks reminds me why I never liked Roger. We were the only two out boys in middle school, so everyone thought we should not only be friends, but boyfriends. Except Roger was a colossal snob, constantly referring to himself as a thespian and talking about how many buildings his parents own around town and how much tuition for his arts high school was going to be. I'd bet Roger's family not only owns the house Luke lives in but most of the properties on the block.

"Great," I reply.

"Same. One might even say a dream. *A Midsummer Night's Dream*. You've probably heard I've been cast," Roger wastes no time telling me.

I want to gag but Luke starts giggling.

"He's Bottom," Luke says.

Wanda and Luke burst out in laughter.

Roger rolls his eyes. "You two are so juvenile. Grow up."

"He's playing the ass." Luke wipes at his eyes as he and Wanda try to contain their giggles.

I hold back a grin. "No. Not a full ass. He'll only have the head of one."

"Asshead." Wanda and Luke laugh harder, not trying to cover it up anymore.

Roger's not smiling even a bit. "Such base humor. It isn't that funny."

"No, it is," I say as Luke and Wanda regain their composure. "Shakespeare used base humor in all his plays. He knew it appealed to the masses, and, as much as the aristocracy might not admit it, they probably found it funny too. Being an asshead can only be a completely intentional choice."

Luke and Wanda crack up again.

"I see you know the Bard," Roger says. I can't tell from his tone if it's a compliment or a throwdown.

I plant both my feet firmly and tilt my head. "A little bit. My mom and uncle have been bringing me to Shakespeare in the Park every year since I can remember. The histories aren't really my jam. They're a bit dry."

"I can't get enough of them. I'd kill to play Richard III," Roger says.

I start to laugh but no one else does. "That wasn't meant to be a joke?"

Awkward silence. I open my mouth to explain, but Roger beats me to it.

"I get it. Because Richard murders to get the throne."

Wanda and I share a sidelong glance. She was never a Roger fan either.

"I'm going to say hi to some gaming friends over there," Wanda says, waving toward a nearby fire.

"I'll grab us drinks. Water, Bobby?" Luke asks.

I nod. Luke leaves Roger and I together.

Roger turns so half his face is illuminated. "You two have been spending a lot of time together."

The way Roger delivers his line, I know there's intention behind the words. I tread carefully. "We're becoming friends."

Roger takes a swig from his beer. "I remember when you tried to befriend me."

This time I catch his meaning. "This shouldn't come as news. I never had a thing for you. You're not my type." I know they're fighting words but can't help but add, "At all."

Roger's eyes glint with fire. "Glad you cleared that up. We wouldn't want any misunderstandings." Rogers pauses a beat too long before he says, "Like you being Luke's type either."

I might be caught off guard if Roger weren't still so *Roger*, but this is a battle of words and words are my Thunderdome. Without thinking, I say, "Duh. Luke isn't even into guys."

Roger crosses his arms. "Everyone knows Luke is into everyone."

Everyone? I fumble for something to say.

Roger swoops in when I don't reply immediately. "It's no secret. He doesn't hide he's pan. He said he told you."

I wrack my brains trying to think when Luke might have told me. The only even remote thing he said was about liking content over the cover treatment. But Luke can't think that conversation was clear in conveying a double meaning. Or was that his way of telling me something private? Maybe Wanda was right, and Luke has been feeling me out all along.

Roger pretends to laugh. "Funny how history repeats itself. Like me in middle school, Luke isn't interested."

"You'll make the perfect asshead," I say. I move forward, bumping Roger with my shoulder intentionally as I pass him. His beer slops out the top of the can onto his shirt. Roger seems to think there's something there too or he wouldn't be trying to scare me off. I keep going and don't stop to look back.

Bobby Ashton doesn't scare easily. But I'm not sure what to do with Luke being pansexual. Was he trying to get me to give him the green light all along? Do I even want to? I like Luke and the way he blinks and his hidden smile. But do I *like* him? And now that I know he could like me back, how do I act around him?

I move faster. I need Wanda.

21

Eighteen Candles

I sink onto the log beside Wanda, hands in my lap, as she and a bunch of people I never really spoke to much in high school talk video games. For a self-described introvert, Wanda seems to be having no problems being the center of attention. I want to pull her aside and ask her if she knew about Luke being pan. That's the sort of information that if Wanda thought was sensitive, she'd keep a secret.

"Can we talk?" I whisper to her when the conversation turns to manga. That's not a big area of interest for Wanda.

"What's up?" she asks.

"Not here."

Wanda nods and we go to get up, but Luke slides in and bumps me with his shoulder.

"There you are," he says. "Roger said you left." He unscrews the lid on a bottle of water and hands it to me.

I put it down beside me. Having watched Luke arrive, Wanda pats my hand and returns to the conversation going on around us.

"I'm glad you didn't." Luke pushes a small, wrapped box toward me.

"Someone told me you turned eighteen," Luke says into my ear. "Happy birthday."

"You didn't have to get me anything." I unwrap the box.

Luke throws the paper into the fire. It rests on a red-orange log a moment before the tendrils of flames lick at it and it bursts into a small blaze.

I tip a smooth stone from the box into my hand. It fits perfectly into my palm. I can see something engraved into it in the moonlight. *Baroness von Snatched.*

"It's from the original *Pebbles* tour," Luke tells me. "It's meant to be with you."

I grip the stone tightly. "How did you even find this? I love it."

"The internet is an all-powerful tool."

Luke grins and jerks his head to the side. I nod back and we get up. I slip the stone into my pocket.

Luke and I meander back to the other fire. Jerome is still on the blanket with Mya, but instead of her being astride his body, he has his guitar. He's strumming but I can't pick out one distinct melody or tune. It sounds like he is trying out the beginning of a song and changing his mind partway in.

Roger emerges from the darkness. "Play some vintage Taylor Swift," he tells Jerome.

Jerome settles on one melody and picks up the tempo. Roger steps up onto one of the logs ready to sing. I want him to suck so hard, but Roger sings out "You Belong with Me," and he's legitimately amazing. By the time he hits the chorus, the group around our fire has grown and everyone is singing along with him. In true triple threat fashion, Roger isn't an awful dancer either.

Roger grabs Luke's hand and tries to pull him up to dance. Luke waves one finger at Roger. Roger dances in front of Luke, trying to coerce him into joining, but Luke doesn't move.

Out of the corners of our eyes, Roger and I catch movement. Evie is dancing alone, and she is tragic. She's not in time and she's got no rhythm. She's stiff and her self-consciousness is coming off her in waves. Her smile falters as she keeps motioning with her hands for someone to join her. A couple of people we all went to high school with laugh right at her before they take a few steps away.

I cover my eyes. I know she's my frienemesis, but this sort of public fail isn't something I'd wish even on her.

I look up when I hear hooting as Roger sings out the final chorus. Luke has left my side and is dancing with Evie, matching each tragic, out-of-rhythm move with his own. The people who stepped back from her now join in, bouncing up and down.

Luke returns to sit beside me as Roger starts singing "Late Night Talking," and the people dancing continue to sway and gyrate awkwardly along with Evie. A girl who I assume is also a counselor for the drama camp by the way she hams it up joins Roger and turns the song into a duet.

I lean in so my lips are close to Luke's ear and smell grapefruit and laundry detergent and aftershave and woodburning stoves on winter nights. "That was kind of you."

"Evie's not that bad if you give her a chance."

I roll my eyes. Luke laughs and bumps his body into mine.

The drama counselors take turns singing. A bag of marshmallows and a few sticks get passed around.

"I'm an expert at roasting," I say into Luke's ear, picking up the scents again.

Luke smirks. "Have you been hiding your past as a Boy Scout? All these secrets, Casanova."

I spear the marshmallow through the middle and extend the stick. "You'll see, love Grinch."

By the end of the song, I'm one of the few who hasn't set their marshmallow ablaze. I pull it back and offer it to Luke, knowing the outside is roasted brown and the insides are gooey with a tiny hint of char.

Luke plucks it off and pops it in his mouth. His eyes widen. He opens his mouth into a big, round O, huffing and puffing around it. "Hot. Hot," he mumbles as he fans his open mouth.

I laugh and find myself leaning into him as I do. I straighten up immediately. I wouldn't have thought twice about this before, but now I know Luke likes guys too, it feels like crossing a line.

"My fingers are getting sore. Last song," Jerome says. "Come on, Luke."

Luke shakes his head as he open-mouth chews the marshmallow.

"I've heard you in the shower," Jerome says, picking up the beginning of a song and repeating it. "I'm not giving up until you join me."

"You're a singer? All these secrets," I say into Luke's ear.

Luke swallows. His mouth forms the word *no*. But he stands and moves over to kneel beside Jerome on the edge of the blanket.

"Slow it down," I hear Luke tell him over the crackling of the fire and the strings of the guitar. Luke taps one hand on top of his thigh to keep time. He's not a singer in that he'll never record an album or be a professional, but his voice is deep and grumbling like every line is being unearthed with resistance from deep within him. He sings Dua Lipa's "Break My Heart" in a register pitched low at a slow tempo, so the crowd around the fire stops to listen. I see Roger swigging from another tallboy beer can. In the darkness, the song is mournful and haunting. When Luke finishes, people applaud before they break off into smaller groups to chat again.

Luke gets up.

I walk over to him. "You said you weren't a singer."

Luke smiles. "You're a better roaster than I am a singer."

Evie comes up behind him and taps him on the arm. "Can we talk for a minute?" she asks. "Over there."

"For sure," Luke tells her. To me, he says, "Wait here. I'll be back."

I stand around, searching for Wanda, and make out her silhouette back at the firepit where we left her.

Suddenly laughter makes me turn my head. Roger's standing in a group, everyone straining to watch the phone in his hand.

"Why didn't you serenade us with some Madonna?" Roger starts singing "True Blue" while imitating my flash mob's choreography. "History's repeating itself. You never learned to stay in your own league."

22

Punch-Drunk Loathe

It's as if the ground juts up under me. My legs feel wobbly. Roger and his onlookers' outlines glow red. The fire sends up thick, murky smoke.

The realization hits me that Roger will almost undoubtedly be in classes with the drama and theatre students I convinced to be my dancers. He'll be able to talk to them, get any dirt that wasn't obvious from the video, and really make fun of me. Roger has the ability to spread a video like mine among our peers and make my next few years at Little Elm College a living nightmare.

Roger takes another swig from his tallboy. "And you're still using love antics to get attention."

"I didn't want this sort," I say.

"Your video tells a different story."

Trying to reason with Roger as two adults, I reply, "I'd appreciate it if you stopped showing everyone my video."

"What video?" Luke says from behind me.

Roger's smile takes over his whole face as he looks from me to Luke and back. "He hasn't seen it."

"What video?" Luke repeats.

Evie steps in beside Luke. "He really doesn't know?" she asks Roger.

Roger finishes the tallboy and crunches the can in his fist. "Back off, girl. This ain't your rodeo. And you've never been any less pathetic than Bobby. You've been throwing yourself at Luke too since he arrived. Now is not your moment."

Evie shrinks back from Roger and the firelight.

"Don't speak to her like that," I say, balling my hands into fists.

"I don't need you to defend me," Evie says before she takes off into the darkness.

I look to Luke before I go in the direction Evie left.

I hear Luke say behind me, "How many beers did you have?"

I catch up to Evie and grab her arm.

"Stop," I pant. "Seriously. When did you learn to run so fast?"

Evie spins around. "I saw the way you looked at me back there. Save your pity for someone else."

"I stuck up for you," I say, but I know what she means. I felt bad for her because I look down on Evie too. I've always thought she was pathetic, like a lost puppy, following me around and imitating me. Except now I know what it feels like to be the pitiable one and I don't want to think about Evie like that anymore.

"We're not friends. We haven't been for a long time." Evie crosses her arms.

"Whose fault is that?" I ask. "You made yourself my competition, not me."

Evie moves and circles me like a wild animal. "Because you never learned to share. Everything you wanted, you found a way to get and no one else could even have a piece of it. The book club. Campus Books. The Reading Festival. You can't blame anyone for enjoying your fall from grace. Not when you've always gotten everything so easily."

"I worked my ass off and earned what I got."

Evie stops circling and backs away. "And then you lost it. I guess we should all feel sorry for you. It's all about you, all the time. Isn't it? Go help yourself. I'm not the one who needs it." Evie stomps away.

I expect to feel something after that. Anger. Sadness. Devastation. Relief even that Evie and I finally said all the things bottled up between us. Instead, I'm sticky and clammy, my skin moist and cool. All I feel is tired. It's like the emotional part of me decided it's had enough and booked itself a vacation. And that is a relief.

When I find Wanda laughing with the group I left her with, I lean in and whisper, "I'm ready to go."

"Give me a second to finish up," Wanda says.

"You stay," I say. My classic indoor-kid best friend having a good time at a party is a big, positive step for her. I don't want to ruin her night. "I've hit saturation."

"At least let me call you a cab."

I shake my head.

"Text me when you get home," Wanda says. "We'll talk tomorrow?"

"For sure." I put her baseball cap back onto her head before I leave.

I stare up at the black sky speckled with stars. The moon shines bright behind some clouds barely shifting in front of it.

Cass will be so disappointed. I probably did everything she wouldn't do, and I'll be returning home early, as she anticipated. So much for a wild college party on my eighteenth birthday. I only hope that if anything is happening between Cass and Uncle Andy, I won't be interrupting it.

I get to the edge of the field and am about to begin my walk home when I hear footfalls behind me.

"I've been looking for you," Luke says. "I need to apologize. Roger was . . ."

"An asshead," I suggest.

". . . not himself," Luke says. "I've never seen him drunk before. It's not a good look on him. Jerome and Mya took him home."

"You don't need to apologize for Roger."

"I'm not."

"You didn't do anything. You don't need to be sorry at all."

"But you're upset."

"I'm tired."

"I'll take you home," Luke says.

"It's Little Elm. I can get home on my own."

"Stop being stubborn and let me walk you."

"Stop being stubborn and insisting on taking me home."

"Where would you prefer I take you?" Luke asks.

I throw up my arms in defeat. "Fine. I give in. Take me home."

Luke puts his arm across my shoulder and steers me back toward campus. I tense up under his touch. Is this a platonic arm over the shoulder or something more? The stone in my pocket presses against my thigh.

I stand still. "Wrong direction. I live that way."

"I need my backpack from my locker. The AC is that way. We'll go right after."

I still don't move. "I could be halfway to my place by now."

"If you weren't so stubborn, we'd be halfway to my locker." I open my mouth to protest but Luke says, "Or we could stand here and argue all night about which one of us is more stubborn."

I sigh pointedly but start walking. I keep getting whiffs of Luke's smell, laundry detergent, dad aftershave, and grapefruit shampoo mixing with bonfire. The crickets and other bugs are the only sounds beside the distant voices of college kids goofing off around the firepits.

Luke slides his arm off me as we reach a door set into the side of the building near the pool. There isn't a knob, only a piece of metal bent into a handhold below an industrial-looking lock. Luke takes a set of keys from his shorts pocket and flips through, then inserts one. The sound of the door unlatching is magnified through the quiet night.

Luke pushes the door open. "I'll only be a second," he says. "Whatever you do . . ."

I step in and pull the door shut behind me.

". . . don't shut that door," Luke says a moment too late.

23

Forced Proximity

"No!" Luke exclaims. "No. No. No. This is bad." He rushes to the door and bangs it with his fist.

"What's wrong?" I ask, backing up. My hip pushes against the metal bar and we hear the lock unlatching.

Luke pulls me away from the door. "If you press that handle, you break the emergency mechanism and trigger the fire alarm."

I jump away from it. "Why would you come through this door then?"

"Because turning off the alarm system leaves a record and this door is the only one that's a one-way alarm. Using the key to get in isn't recorded. It's only when you try to leave. Why would you pull the door closed behind you?"

"How was I supposed to know it's some trick door with a thousand rules?" I ask defensively, anger rising in my voice to hide my anxiety.

"One rule. Don't let the door close behind you. One."

"What now? How do we get out?"

"We don't. Not unless you want to alert the fire department."

Not only don't I want that. I can't have it. I pull my jacket around me. Dean Perez warned me about boys and everything else, no more stunts. I got my one strike. There's no second or third. Next one, I'm out.

"There has to be another way out. What do we do?"

Luke sits on the nearest bench beside the pool. The smell of chlorine fills my nostrils.

"There isn't. We wait until someone finds us."

I start pacing. "Finds us? Oh, no. I really can't get into any more trouble."

"More?" Luke asks. "When are you going to tell me what everyone else knows but I don't?"

Like a reflex, I say, "It's nothing."

Luke leans back to rest on his elbows. I can feel his eyes following me as I pace back and forth. He doesn't push me for answers or try to get any more information out of me as seems to be his way. He just watches as I walk a few feet in one direction, then a few feet back.

"You're seriously not going to ask me anything else?"

Luke keeps his eyes on me. "I did. You chose not to answer. I'm not going to pry you open like a stuck jar of pickles."

I stop pacing. "That's such a weird simile to choose."

"Only because you're the pickle jar."

"Eww. That sounds even worse. It's like you're going to turn me upside down and smack me until you can pop me open."

Luke wrinkles his nose. "Why do you make opening a stuck jar of pickles sound like a BDSM scene? You know you can run jars under hot water and use a spoon to break the vacuum? You don't have to spank your pickle jar into submission."

I close my eyes and hold up a hand. "This conversation has gone in a really bizarre direction."

"I know I'll never look at a jar of pickles the same way again."

I roll my eyes. "Get up. Come on. I'm sure we can find a way out."

"There isn't one."

"Humor me." I take off toward the locker rooms.

"Don't bother with the gender-neutral one," Luke says as he catches up. "It can only be accessed from the deck and there's only the one door. And the other locker rooms lock from outside."

"How are you so sure?" I walk into the women's locker room and test the door. It doesn't budge.

"I'm the one who locked them."

I head to the men's locker room in case Luke's wrong. He's not.

"Told you so," he says when I return to the deck.

"Isn't there an office or some sort of maintenance hatch?" I ask.

"The office is down the hallway outside and there's no access to maintenance areas from the deck. You can't have people wandering through all the pumps and chemicals."

"How about windows or those skylights?"

Luke points up. "Even if you could scale the walls, they don't open."

I climb the bleacher steps. "What about that door?" I call.

"Storage."

"Who designed this building?" I ask.

"Want me to text Evie? She gives campus tours. I bet she'd know."

I groan at the mention of Evie. She'd be one of the last people I'd text. Then an idea comes to me. "Wanda. She'll get us out of here."

"How? She doesn't have a key. She'd have to find someone from the college to spring us."

"Right. Don't text her."

"Too late." Almost instantly, Luke's phone dings and vibrates. "She says she'll let your mom know you're not going to be home tonight."

"I told you not to text her," I say, coming down the steps.

Luke lies down on one of the benches. "I didn't listen," he says. "Remind you of anyone?" He closes his eyes and crosses his hands over his chest. "I'm guessing Wanda is another person who you let into your pickle jar?"

I screw up my face. "I'm serious. Put that on your list of phrases to never say to me again."

"Are you one of those people who hates the words *moist* and *wad* too?"

"Not if they come before *cake* or *of cash*," I reply.

"Moist wad of cash," Luke says. "Casanova's pickle jar."

"How do I get you to stop?"

Luke pivots his body and is up, standing in front of me in one fluid motion. We're as close as we were on the day we met at Corner Books. "Give me a good enough reason to." In the moonlight coming through the windows along the tops of the walls, the skin along his cheekbones and nose radiates with that golden undertone.

His eyes hold mine.

I refuse to look away first.

I realize (too late, I admit to myself) Luke never lacked curiosity. Nor was he simply respecting my privacy. He'd been running me under warm water to loosen me up. He was giving me time to trust him.

I take a deep breath and tell Luke everything. About Truman and the unicorn and the fountain. About how I planned this grand gesture to win him over. About the Summer of Bobby and the smashed window and losing my job and nearly losing college too. About the statue and Cass and Corner Books and the Baroness. About Roger and the video. The story spills out like water onto cobblestones. Then it slows to a drip before it stops.

Luke listens. When I'm done, he waits a few seconds, tilting his head to the side, his eyes roaming my face. He steps forward. He pulls me in, closing his arms around me, and he holds me. One one thousand. Two one thousand. Three, four, five, six, seven, eight—I stop counting long before he releases me.

I avoid his eyes and fumble for the start of a sentence before I manage to get out, "What was that for?"

"Because you needed it," Luke replies. "And because I don't think you'll like what I have to say next." He pauses and although I'm not looking at him, I can feel the heat of his eyes on my face. "If this video has so much power over you, you need to confront it. You need to watch it."

I meet his eyes. "How does that make any sense?"

"The video is not the issue. Your fear is. The longer you wait, the more it grows and controls your future actions. Give yourself a birthday gift and don't let anything have that power over you." Luke takes out his phone, unlocks it, and hands it to me. "We can do it together. It won't be as bad as you think."

As I sit down on the bench, I realize I'm shivering. Luke sits beside me, so close he could have his arm across my shoulders in a breath and pull me into him. My fingers hesitate above the phone screen.

"You're the most determined person I know. If you want to end this, you've got everything in you already to do it." Luke puts a hand on my knee. "You do want this to end. Don't you?"

I think about pulling the shades and cloistering myself in the darkened living room. My biles. My Danish disease. The Summer of Bobby. Truman. My humiliation. Luke is right. I could have let it go. I could have moved on. But I didn't.

I push my finger to the screen and access my online storage drive. I find the unedited video. All the footage from the day at the fountain in its entirety. All the stuff that didn't stream.

"If we're going to do this, it needs to be the full version. No one has seen all of it. Not even me."

"Remember," Luke says, "it's only a video. It's all in the past."

Except it's not yet.

I inhale sharply as I press play and watch myself laid out on an inflatable rainbow unicorn raft veering off course.

The small screen is a series of images, each one a different feed from the cameras set up around the courtyard. A green rectangle appears around the screen Wanda was sending out live.

Madonna's voice is tinny on the phone's speakers. The dancers don't immediately miss their cues as I sail under the fountain's curtain of water and emerge, drenched, a few seconds later.

Seeing myself on camera is surreal. I have no control over the mini-Bobbies. I can't scream at them or warn them. I am aware of exactly how someone watching sees me. The wobble of my arm flab. The way the rolls above my hips stick out. The roundness of my cheeks and my extra chin. None of those things are as apparent when I look in a mirror.

A ripple goes through the dancers when I'm not where I should be to lift. One of them moves to grab the raft, presumably to pull me back on track but stops when I begin to paddle.

The raft shoots up with the rubbery squeak of friction against taut plastic before I splash into the fountain.

Truman stands in the shadows of Campus Books' entrance. A figure behind him. Truman turns his head to whisper.

Wanda cuts the Madonna remix and the only sound in the courtyard is the fountain.

Then my voice plays, high, faltering, nervous. I stammer. I don't remember stammering.

Truman's voice is soft. The mics barely pick him up.

The onlookers shift nervously, hands over mouths as they whisper to one another. Evie holds her phone in front of her, recording.

The rose, red in my hands. Truman shakes his head. It's a warning to stop. I don't pay attention. He turns to go.

I stoop and pick up the pebbles. Then the fateful rock. My throw is weak. Still, the stone finds its mark.

In one rectangle my entire body angles as I fall backward. I didn't realize until now, my ass hits the edge of the fountain.

In another rectangle, I watch as Scott and Truman hear the glass crashing. It's Evie who screams at them, "Watch out!"

Scott rushes out of the shadows of Campus Books and shields Truman with his body while the fractures spread like a spiderweb. Then a large section of the window drops, followed by smaller sections, as if in slow motion, giving up their desire to hang on. Pieces of glass spray across the courtyard.

People scatter away from the shards shooting toward them.

I flounder in the water. I slip several times trying to gain my footing and flop, gripping the fountain's edge, spluttering. Two dancers help me.

I touch my head, see the blood, and sway on the spot. I grab the rose, drop to my knees, and hold it out again to Truman. The recording picks up both our voices, mine stilted from catching my breath. Tru's quiet, trying not to be picked up at all. He tells Wanda to cut the stream. The green rectangle turns red then disappears.

Wanda begins turning off the cameras. Sections of the screen go black, before the individual rectangles disappear. The others get larger to occupy more space.

The last camera feed shows Truman leading me over the broken glass, one hand between my shoulders and the other on my elbow as he helps me. Scott gives Truman a handful of paper towels which Truman pushes against my head.

I don't know why Wanda didn't cut the last camera's feed faster. It keeps recording.

"You're hurt," Truman says.

I begin to shiver, one hand pressing the paper towel to my bleeding head.

Evie emerges from Campus Books holding a blanket. Wanda is at my side. The two of them wrap it around me. Evie, Wanda, and Scott linger.

"Give us a minute?" Truman asks.

They step away, off-screen.

Truman rubs my shoulders and arms. "Do you need medical attention?"

I shake my head forcefully. Eyes closed. I remember hoping the water dripping down my face hid my tears. I turn my head away from Tru.

"You're a good kid, Bobby," Truman says softly. "I like you a lot. But not the way you hoped."

He ducks his head, hoping to catch my eyes. "At least look at me, Bobby," he says. "Are you all right?"

"I'm all right," I hear myself whisper, each word forced.

"Let me take you home. We can talk some more on the way."

I shake my head. "Stop being nice to me."

"I'm sorry, Bobby," Truman says. He stops rubbing my back and arms. "You're a great kid. Really. Some other guy would be lucky to have you. I promise."

"But not the one I want." I see myself straighten up and push the blanket off. I shove it back into Truman's arms. "We don't need to talk. There's nothing to say. Just leave me alone."

Truman reaches out for me. I push his hand away. We stand in the wreckage of my plans for the Summer of Bobby and what it means to have me love him.

24

It Had to Be Him?

Luke presses a button on the side of his phone. The screen goes black. He gently removes his phone from my hands.

"Wow," he says. I see him suck his lips in, but the corners of his mouth turn upward. Not in that almost unnoticeable way but in a very easily noticeable way. He bursts out with a full-belly laugh that makes him clutch at his middle as he doubles over. He must see my expression of horror because he laughs twice as hard, tears beading in his eyes.

I smack him in the arm. "It's not funny!"

He wipes his eyes. "It's hilarious."

"My heart got broken." I smack him in the arm again.

"Not as badly as the window. This is what you've been afraid of?"

"That is the worst moment of my life."

Luke wipes at his eyes. "It didn't end up so badly. You've still got your scholarship. You've got a new job. Your mom and friends have your back. The only thing you don't have is this Truman guy. I don't get why he was worth all that effort. You must have spent weeks planning all that."

"It's clear you don't understand." I spent almost a month making plans, finding the dancers and practicing, ordering the unicorn, and hijacking Campus Books' audio system. Then there is Campus Books, the Reading Festival, the sculpture, not to mention my pride.

Luke massages his side. "And I gave you a rock for your birthday."

I shove away from him. "You really are a love Grinch. You're not taking my pain seriously."

"You're taking it too seriously. If you really liked him, why did it need to be this big show?"

"Because telling someone you love them is a climactic moment. It's fireworks on the Fourth of July or running down the aisle of a packed theatre into your lover's arms so he can lift you into the air. It's every feeling you have for that person that's too immense for your body to contain, turned into reality for this one singular event."

Luke shakes his head. "If you're fortunate enough to find the person that can really make you feel that way, everything else should pale in comparison."

"I think I know a bit more about all this than a love Grinch."

"I forgot you were the expert, Casanova. Enlighten me. What makes Truman so special that he deserved a whole production? Because I don't see it."

I shove Luke's shoulder. "You don't even know him."

"I'm pretty sure I know enough."

"He's smart. He was nice to me. He'd tell me what to read so I could talk to him on a higher level. He made me the best version of myself."

Luke has no clue about Truman. How Truman always saved a seat for me beside him at book club. How Truman always made a point to ask what I was reading. How Truman wrote me a recommendation for Little Elm's Big Summer Reading Festival's freshman liaison position and put in a good word with Campus Books' staff. How Truman and I would put away the chairs at the end of book club before I'd walk him back to his dorm and he'd tell me about the stresses, essays, midterms, and the literary journal like I was in college too. How Truman was the perfect, best, most obvious object of my affection.

I open my mouth to tell Luke all this but instead, "He's no worse than Roger" shoots out.

Luke doesn't hesitate to respond. "And you're more than either of them."

"Then why didn't he want me?" I snap.

It's not like I don't know the answer. It's not like I don't know Scott is accomplished and famous and important. Or that Scott looks more like Roger than he looks like me.

I go to bury my face in my hands, but Luke grips my biceps and says with complete surety, "Because Truman is the type of guy who needs you to wear fake glasses so he can see how smart you are. He could never appreciate how you strut into a college party looking like a tricked-out baseball Ken doll. Or how you can take on some drunk drama student over Shakespeare and school him. Or how you can meet a new guy in town and run down the block to give him a book he's too ashamed to buy for himself. You're so much better than any Roger or Truman. You should never feel you have to orchestrate some big spectacle for Truman or anyone else to see your worth."

But I've always been Bobby Ashton who helped people find love. Without that, what would I do? How would I even out the playing field so a guy like me can one day find his own happily ever after? Luke said he didn't trust in love, and with all my pretenses stripped away, I don't know if I ever trusted it either to deliver my Prince Charming if I didn't work for it. Love is for beautiful people in books and movies, not fat, bookish boys who fall into fountains and smash windows.

Luke's face is so close to mine I know he can see my tears forming. I get a whiff of grapefruit through the chlorine surrounding us.

Instead of a dozen good responses I could reply with, the only thing I can think of to say is, "I didn't think you noticed my outfit."

I can feel his breath against my nose as he whispers, "There wasn't a single person there who couldn't help but notice you."

The tears trickle down the side of my nose but with Luke holding my arms I can't wipe them away. I bite my lip, then brush my tongue across it and stare into Luke's eyes. Not for a second do his eyes even flit anywhere else.

The memories of being wrong about Tru's feelings are so fresh, and I know I shouldn't entertain the idea that Luke could have any interest in a guy like me. A guy who plans a declaration of love and nearly injures everyone in the process.

A guy so opposite to Luke in every way. And with or without my fake glasses, I've never had a clear read on Luke.

So, I wait for him to do something. To say something.

But the seconds tick on and neither of us make a move.

His eyes soften, the tension across his brows and lids receding. His grip on my arms relaxes. He lets go of my biceps and straightens.

He surprises me when he asks, "Do you want to go swimming?"

25

Pride and Pool Water

"That's so random." I wipe my eyes. "Where would I even get a swimsuit?"

Luke looks around. "Do you need one?" He bends double to untie his sneakers and kicks the first one off.

"You want to go skinny-dipping?" I ask, not trying to hide the horror in my tone.

"Why not? How many other chances will we get?" Luke kicks off his other sneaker and uses his feet to push off his socks. "We're in a dark, enclosed, private space. No one can see us. It's got to be better than a lake with alligators or leeches."

"There are no alligators anywhere near Little Elm. I'm not sure about leeches, but I doubt it."

Luke pulls off his shirt. He undoes the top button of his shorts, his hands brushing the trail of hair. "If you can't swim . . ."

"I know how to swim."

Luke holds his zipper but doesn't undo it. "You can't be shy. You planned an entire big-budget dance sequence to tell some guy you liked him. This is nothing in comparison."

"Not while naked." I clasp my hands together and slide them down in front of me.

"I would be too."

I know he knows, but I point it out anyway: "I'm fat under my clothes."

Luke runs a hand over the hair on his chest that goes from nipple to nipple. "And I'm hairy. And I've probably got a pimple on my butt."

"You can pop a pimple."

Luke shrugs. "We've both got a general idea of what's going on under each other's clothes."

I keep my hands clasped in front of me. "General isn't specific."

"The water and the darkness can cover up the specifics," he says. "We need something to do. I'm going in. If this really makes you uncomfortable, I can grab my trunks out of my locker."

I take a deep breath and unclasp my hands. I'm locked in a pool with a guy on my eighteenth birthday wanting to skinny-dip. Cass would disown me if I let my insecurities stop me. "Ok. But no looking. We turn around when the other person is getting in or out. Promise?"

"Cross my heart." And he crosses his heart the same as the day we met. Luke lets his shorts drop and kicks them up onto the bench. I try not to look too much at him in just his boxer briefs.

I stand and face the locker room door. Before I have a chance to even remove my shirt, I hear a splash. I look over my shoulder to see Luke's underwear slung over the bench I just got up from and him emerging from the water, pushing his wet hair back off his face.

"Get in," he calls.

I check a few more times that Luke is facing in the other direction as I take off my clothing, fold it into a neat pile on the bench. I'm tempted to fold his too but think it would be weird if he came back to his stuff and found I'd touched his delicates.

No matter how many times I check, he is facing away.

I take off my underwear and toss them on top of my pile of clothing before I tiptoe to the edge of the pool. I sit on the cold tiles and quietly slide in, making sure I'm covered to above my chest before I say, "You can turn around now."

Luke swims over. "No leeches."

"No leeches," I repeat.

"If you put your head under, it's not as cold." Luke disappears, the dappled surface of the water catching moonlight. He reappears seconds later, shaking his head and spraying me.

"Stop! You're getting me wet," I squeal.

He splashes water at me. "You're already wet."

I use my hand to shoot water back at him and soon we're in the middle of a splash fight, spraying each other with as much laughter as water.

"Want to race?" Luke asks when we get tired of roughhousing.

"You'll win."

"I'll give you a head start."

"That won't make a difference." I stare down at the dark outline of my chest and belly jutting forward under the water. "And I don't want my bare butt on display for you, thank you very much. I'm already pushing the boundaries of my comfort being platonically naked in front of you."

"And you thought I was the one hanging with the frat boys?" Luke deepens his voice and dulls his eyes. "Yo, bruh. It's cool, man. No big deal. We're just gonna get platonically naked."

I splash Luke again. "You're so dumb."

"If you don't want to race, how about we have a contest to see who can hold their breath longest?" Without waiting for my reply, he grips my hand in his. He holds them up between us like we're about to arm wrestle. "On the count of three. One. Two." With his free hand he pinches his nose and says in a muffled voice, "Three."

I have just enough time to pinch my nose too before Luke pulls me underwater with him. I kick out my legs to stay down and open my eyes. I can make out Luke's blurry, wavy shadow in front of me. Luke grips tight to my hand and I grip back. A tingle runs up my arm. Bubbles expand in front of our faces before they escape. My cheeks are puffed and my eyes sting from the chlorine, but I keep them open to watch Luke.

I keep moving my legs to keep me underwater. My heart races, beating in my ears so loudly I don't know how Luke isn't managing to hear it. My lungs start to ache, and I feel like I have no choice but to inhale at any second.

I pull Luke up by our joined hands. He surfaces, bumping up against me. I jut my hips back, away from Luke. He doesn't loosen his grip. We both take deep breaths, our chests heaving.

"You win," I say, panting.

"Want to go again? Best two out of three."

"You'd beat me every time." I float closer.

Luke blinks slowly. Water droplets cling to his eyelashes, liquid crystals. A trail of water snakes from his temple down along his jawline and over his neck. The tingling in my arm intensifies when Luke opens his eyes and holds me pinned in his gaze. My breathing isn't slowing. The water feels like it's crackling everywhere it connects with my skin. And I'm aware of how naked, how exposed I am, how we shed the barriers left between us.

I yank my hand from his and dart back, unable to hold on or be near him a moment longer. "I'm ready to get out," I say. "Turn around."

Luke nods once, then swims to the opposite side of the pool and rests his arms on the edge as I climb the ladder. I hold my hands over my junk as I waddle across the deck toward the locker room.

"I'm taking the women's," I call, grabbing my stack of clothing as I pass. "I saw a towel in there earlier."

I get into the shower and am fortunate enough to find some shampoo and conditioner in the built-in caddy. The water is cold, but that's a blessing.

I return to the pool area clothed, using the towel to dry my hair. Luke is still in the water swimming. I watch the shadow of his body move down the length of the pool. He bursts from the depths, spraying water droplets and moonlight from his sun-soaked body. With both hands, he smooths his wet hair off his face and walks through the shallows, up the kiddie steps to emerge into the pool air.

I cover my eyes with my fingers, hoping he didn't catch me watching. I sense him as he comes nearer.

He passes by me and walks toward the men's locker room.

"You were the one who said no peeking, Casanova," he says before he disappears, leaving me no time for a defense. My entire face burns.

Luke returns from the locker room with a towel tied around his waist. He doesn't say anything as he picks up his underwear and slides them and his shorts on under his towel.

"Are you hungry?" he asks once his shirt and shoes are back on.

"Where are we going to get food from?"

Luke doesn't say anything as he heads back to the men's locker room again and returns with candy bars and small bags of chips like the ones you get on Halloween.

"I had some Fuzzy Peaches, but I ate them before the party. I love gummy candies."

I take the bags of chips. "Ketchup? All-dressed? Why do I recognize none of these flavors?"

"Only the finest of junk food for me," Luke says. "Canadian imports from my aunt. She ships me care packages."

"So, you can eat garbage instead of real meals like the true frat boy you are?"

"Totally, bruh." Luke takes back one of the bags of chips and pulls it open. "Platonic snacking, man," he says. He offers me a chip and hums the opening to the happy birthday song.

We pass the bags back and forth between us. If there's only one of a type of chocolate bar or candy I've never tried before, Luke insists I'm the one to eat it. When we're done, he offers me some mouthwash also from his locker.

"Do you have a bodega in there?" I ask, peering around his shoulder.

"I like fresh breath," he says without any further explanation. "We should get some sleep. Hopefully, the cleaning staff will come by at some point tomorrow."

"Tomorrow?" I say, remembering. "I'm supposed to open the store tomorrow. I can't miss work."

Luke shrugs. "It's too late to call anyone. You'll have to phone your uncle or Gladys in the morning and explain. We should probably conserve my battery until then, in case." Luke powers down his phone and tucks it into his pocket.

I silently curse. I can't call Gladys. All the tepidness she's come to treat me with will vanish and I'll never hear the end of how the first and only time I'm trusted to open the store, I louse it up and let everyone down. That means calling Uncle Andy and letting him know he shouldn't have trusted me. As much as I don't want to admit it, that's my best option.

I look around and only see hard aluminum benches. Sleep sounds a lot easier than it looks right now. With all the grace of a fish flopping on dry land, I manage to lie with the narrow seating down the center of my spine.

"My back is going to be so sore in the morning, assuming I manage not to fall off this thing," I say but no one answers.

Luke emerges from the supply room, his arms full. He drops the items he's holding onto the deck and begins moving them around. "We're not sleeping on those," he says as he works.

I tumble off the bench, landing on my knees. Luke has assembled a bunch of flotation devices and life vests into a makeshift bed.

"I've only got the one dry towel left," he says. "We're going to have to get cozy. Do you sleep right or left?"

"I don't know. I have a single."

"Same. You take the side against the wall. I don't want to have to dive in to save you if you roll into the pool."

"Do you really think that's going to happen?" I ask, getting down onto the foam boards that soften the hard floor a little bit.

"I'm not the accident-prone one," Luke says.

I want to argue but instead I push Luke lightly as he settles in beside me and adjusts a lifejacket between his arm and head.

"I'd keep your little jacket thing on," he says as he tosses the towel over both our torsos. "Night, Casanova."

"Night, Luke," I say as I make myself comfortable.

We lie together, a few inches between our backs. A low humming sound comes from the pool, either a pump or filter. Luke's freshly washed hair gives off the grapefruit smell strongly. The heat off his body radiates into the space between us and warms my back. The sound of his breathing deepens and becomes heavy.

The thoughts of being caught and getting into more trouble fill my head. Dean Perez. Gladys. Corner Books. Even Cass chastising me for being out all night.

But my worries are nothing compared to how tired I am. I fall asleep and only wake up when I feel a chill up the front of my body. Luke's back is pressed against mine. The towel is only half on him. It's slipped off me completely.

Groggily, I roll over, wanting to warm my chest and arms. I slide a hand in my pocket and feel something hard and round. I pull out the stone but with it comes the penny Wanda gave me. Blinking sleep from my eyes, I push myself up on one elbow.

"What the hell," I mumble and throw the coin. It plunks into the waters. My wish for a safe return.

I pull the towel up over Luke's shoulders and then my own before I tuck my arms between my body and Luke's and drift back to sleep.

I turn my head into my lifejacket pillow, trying to block the morning light incessantly beating against my lids. I'm not ready to be awake and my eyes don't want to open.

Someone's arm is over me, hugging me, a hand on my soft belly. Without thinking, I clutch the hand, lacing my fingers through.

"Bobby," I hear someone whisper into my ear, their breath tickling my lobe and neck.

I groan and cover my face with my arm.

"You've got to wake up. Someone's coming."

Luke leans over me, his mouth by my ear.

"What time is it?" I ask, feeling suddenly very alert.

"I haven't turned my phone on. I heard keys jingling. Someone's going to open that door." Luke points. "Get ready to slip past them into the hallway. Head right and then left and leave out the main entrance. Hurry."

"What about you?" I ask, getting to my feet.

"Don't worry about me. I don't have any strikes."

"But if you get caught . . ."

"I can deal with the consequences. If you're stopped, whatever you do, don't give them your real name. Tell them you're Casanova or some actor named Roger."

I want to laugh but instead I quietly take my position. I press myself against the wall beside the door Luke pointed to. He lies down, facing away from the door, positioning himself to look like he's asleep.

Keys in the lock. The door swings open and a janitorial cart pushes in followed by a guy wearing headphones. He lowers his headphones and scratches his head as he sees Luke laid out on the floor.

I slip behind him.

I stop myself from running, worried about making too much noise and hurry, following Luke's directions. Once I'm outside the building, clouds blow in, and the wind picks up. The sky darkens. Rain can't be too far behind.

I have no idea what time it is or if I've missed opening Corner Books, but maybe, if the penny from last night worked, then both Luke and I will have good luck.

26

And the Art of Motorcycle Maintenance

Corner Books has people standing outside it when I get there, their umbrellas up. The rain is sprinkling, not knowing whether it wants to start or move along.

"I'm sorry. I'm late," I call as I pass the crowd and fish out my wallet where I stored Corner Books' key. My Summer of Bobby list comes with it. I shove it back into my pocket beside the stone.

"Bobby, sweetie," Cindy says, stepping out from the group. "You look . . . not yourself. What's going on?"

"I'm late," I say, fumbling with the key and dropping it.

Cindy picks it up. "The store doesn't open for another ten minutes." She presses the key into my hand. "Breathe."

I take a deep breath.

"That's good," Cindy says. "This is my meditation class. We just had a session on sitting with grief. Breathing is central to staying balanced. But caffeine can't hurt. Take my macchiato. It's caramel and I shouldn't be drinking so much sugar first thing in the day anyway." Cindy pushes her paper coffee cup into my grip. "Get yourself inside. Fix your hair. Drink the coffee. Pop a mint when you're done. Everyone will wait to meet the Book Whisperer. By the way, cute outfit."

I slide the key into the door's lock, then turn off the alarm before I go to the back room and the tiny employee washroom. I wish I had a Mary Poppins locker like Luke's because I could probably use a comb and some deodorant. I wet my hair and use my fingers to style it, taking sips of Cindy's drink which is more sweet syrup than it is coffee.

I pop one of the mints Gladys keeps behind the counter. It tastes medicinal and I want to spit it out, but it has to be better than my bad breath. I sip the coffee around it and the two seem to mellow each other out. I turn on the old POS system and plug my phone into the charger I keep hidden from Gladys to avoid her lectures on personal phone use at one's workplace.

Even though not being late gives me a momentary sense of relief, I can't seem to calm down. Instead, I wonder about Luke and what's happening to him. What if he loses his job? How will he cover his expenses? What happens to Mr. Martinez and the other seniors?

And what about last night between Luke and me? I don't think I'm reaching in concluding there were moments. But what did they mean? Did he feel it too?

After, I welcome Cindy's group in. I'm grateful I told Uncle Andy to keep his eyes out for a coat rack and umbrella stand, which he found on clearance in a consignment store down the block. The raincoats and umbrellas drip onto the boot tray, which doesn't fit the décor but Gladys insisted on and is now proving its worth in terms of functionality.

Cindy must sense I need help, because she keeps introducing me to one member of her meditation group at a time, engaging the rest in small talk while I work my Book Whisperer skills. Some of them I already know. I didn't realize how many people in Little Elm were grieving, and with each person being different from the next one, I'm kept on my toes.

For one woman I recommend a sci-fi action novel with a strong kick-butt feminist heroine. A different woman takes home a series by Susan Juby featuring a Buddhist butler amateur detective. For one guy I recommend a picture book about a dog that he fights me on taking until I tell him the dog is never in danger of dying and the ending is happy for man and man's best friend alike.

The rain must be to blame because more customers keep steadily coming in. Patience starts to run thin among them as they seem to have heard of the Book Whisperer and need my book magic. But magic doesn't happen instantly. I don't know what book someone needs until I can figure that person out. It's a slow process and the speed of our cash register doesn't help.

"Would you mind holding on a minute," I say to a woman buying several pricey photography books. "I need to call the owner. We weren't expecting so much traffic on a Sunday morning."

My first call rings through to voicemail. I hang up without leaving a message and hit redial. My cell phone finally powers on and its screen lights up. It goes crazy with missed text notices. I finish cashing out the woman with the photography books, thanking her for her patience. I ignore my texts and dial Uncle Andy with my cell. He picks up this time.

"Bobby?" he asks. He sounds like I woke him up, his voice deep and groggy.

"Can you come down to Corner Books?" I ask.

"What's going on?" I can hear him waking up.

"It's a big rush. There's a lot of customers. They all want personal recommendations . . ." My voice trails off as I hear something in the background of the call. Someone is singing. A woman. "Hold on a minute. A customer needs me," I say so I can listen carefully.

I recognize the song. Annie Lennox, "Walking on Broken Glass." I give it a second longer to be sure. When the singer repeats *walking on* a third time, I know it's Cass. I don't know where they are or what they did, but I know if Uncle Andy is only waking up now because I phoned him, he spent the night with her.

"Actually," I say into my phone. "I'm good. Don't come in. Do whatever it is you're doing."

"If you need help . . ."

"I don't," I say in my happy yet confident tone. "Gladys is on her way. I was overreacting. You know me. I always blow things out of proportion. Enjoy your Sunday off."

"If Gladys is coming in, I guess it's under control."

"She is. It is," I say. "You're going to be wowed when you check today's sales."

I hang up. I put down my cell phone and pick up Corner Books' handset. I brace myself as I dial the number taped onto the desk.

"Gladys?" I say when she answers. "It's, uhm, Robert. I need your help."

☙

Two customers are insisting they're next for the Book Whisperer. I've never had two women argue over my attention. I am certain of two things. One, two people fighting over you is not as sexy as books or TV lead you to believe. It's awful and uncomfortable and there's nothing for me to do but wish I were somewhere else. Two, I am most certainly and gratefully gay.

"I don't know which one of you got here first," I say when they ask me to weigh in.

"What is this nonsense?" Gladys's harsh tone cuts across Corner Books from where she stands at the entrance.

She removes the see-through plastic bonnet from her permed hair and hangs it up with her raincoat and umbrella.

"Let's settle this chaos," she says. "Those wishing to make a purchase or place an order, form an orderly line at the register. Those who want Robert's assistance, form a separate, equally orderly line against the wall and wait your turn. Preferably silently."

She walks over to the two bickering women. "If you two can't resolve this as adults, you can go to the back of the line or leave."

Both women open their mouths to argue, but the look Gladys gives them is short of baring teeth and snarling.

"Yes, ma'am," they mumble.

"Brace yourself," Gladys says to me quietly. "Here we go."

In a matter of minutes, Gladys manages to clear the line of customers waiting to make purchases. If they're frustrated with the wait, no one dares say so. You can hear Gladys booming "Next!" throughout the store and the old register's cash drawer opening and slamming shut over and over.

The Book Whisperer recommendations aren't quite as expedient, but Cindy lingers despite Gladys's giving her the hairy eyeball. She chitchats with those waiting, laying it on thick about the life-changing books they're about to buy. I get the feeling some of the people waiting for me aren't expecting to take home a good read so much as a miracle. No pressure, right?

I finally help the last customers in my line and Gladys has cashed them out.

"You need to learn how to shut down conversation," Gladys says to me.

"What a team you two make!" Cindy cheers. "I don't want to sound like a Debbie Downer, but I really thought everything was going downhill at one point."

The door's bell rings and a gangly guy I recognize from high school with long hair and acne comes in. He was a few grades younger than me so we don't know each other well, but we give each other a head bob of recognition just the same.

"Someone ordered delivery?" he asks.

"Over here. Hurry up. And don't slouch," Gladys commands.

He straightens up as he approaches the register. Gladys inspects the contents of the paper bag he slides across the counter before she pays him.

"No tip necessary," he says, handing Gladys back her change.

She counts her money before she extends two one-dollar bills toward him. "You'll take this and don't let me catch you slumped over like that anymore. You're quite tall. Own it. Do you understand me?"

He nods. "Thank you, ma'am," he says, then, spine straight, he leaves.

"Robert, get us two more chairs. Cindy, I ordered you a sandwich. Don't get too excited, it's vegetarian. I can't keep track of what everyone eats or doesn't nowadays."

Gladys passes out napkins, sandwiches, and hot-pink, icy-cold cream sodas. She makes a point of mentioning how the drinks match my "odd choice of apparel." We eat, Cindy chattering away, apparently not worn out for topics of conversation from the earlier rush.

When we're done, Cindy leaves for afternoon cocktails with friends.

"Find that woman a book on how to slow down," Gladys says. "She isn't at all what I thought of her when we first met. Neither are you."

I feel the sandwich turn into a lump inside me. "You were right about me. I couldn't handle today."

Gladys slurps her straw, noisily sucking up the last of her cream soda. "No. You couldn't."

I sigh. "I wanted to give Uncle Andy a morning off." At least the Uncle Andy and Cass part of my plan worked out better than my first opening.

"You did."

"But it cost you your day off."

"It did."

"You don't have to agree with every negative I say."

Gladys dabs at her lips with her paper napkin. "They're facts. They're neither negative nor positive. They are what they are."

"That doesn't exactly make me feel better."

"I didn't intend to make you feel better. How about some more facts?" Gladys stands and collects the glass bottles for recycling. "You tried to open the store by yourself. It got out of hand. You had enough sense in that skull of yours to realize it and you called in reinforcements. Does that sound correct?"

I nod. It's a concise summary.

Gladys starts moving the chairs back where they belong. I get up to help her.

"I'm certain I'm the last person you wanted to be calling. It isn't demonstrating inadequacy to put aside your ego and recognize your limitations. You'd do well to remember that in the future. You did well today, Bobby."

I spin around. "Did I just hear you call me Bobby?" I ask.

Gladys harrumphs. "How would I know what you heard, Robert? Now get these floors mopped and vacuumed. Let's run the sales reports for the day before Andrew arrives. You'll both be pleasantly surprised by our numbers."

We both turn our heads at the sound of an engine chugging. A motorcycle with a sidecar pulls to a stop in front of the store. The woman with the shaved head, leather vest, and tattoos from the graphic novel book club takes off her helmet, picks up a package wrapped in paper, and walks into the store.

I catch Gladys patting her hair as the woman approaches the register.

"You forgot these when you left brunch so abruptly," the motorcycle woman says, holding the package out to Gladys. "I hope it wasn't anything I said or did."

Gladys snatches what is unmistakably a bouquet of flowers. "Don't be ridiculous. I told you we'd have to take a rain check."

It takes all I can not to burst out in a cheer. I found out Gladys's secret! Gladys and the motorcycle book, she was trying to impress this woman.

The woman tilts her head down toward her shoulder and grips her arm with her other hand before she risks looking up at Gladys and giving a small smile. "Last I checked, it's still raining."

Gladys delivers her signature scowl. "I suppose it is. This is my place of business, you are aware. I conduct myself professionally."

I nearly choke at what Gladys considers professionalism. I cover it by clearing my throat.

"The motorcycle is getting soaked out there. Maybe you could go cover it, Gladys?" I suggest.

"Yes, Gladys. Cover it. The sidecar will be full as a bathtub in no time."

My eyebrows furrow. "I meant you," I say and point to Corner Books' Gladys.

"Gladys"—Gladys motions to the woman—"meet Robert. He's a bit of a nuisance, but he's grown on me. To be clear, because I know you're slow to pick things up, I am named Gladys as is my companion."

"Companion?" the second Gladys asks. "Don't turn the charm on high. I won't know what to do with myself."

Gladys frowns at the second Gladys, but there's no malice in it. "Don't get cheeky."

"Uncle Andy will be here soon," I say. "You should go. I've taken up enough of your day."

Gladys opens the package and smells the flowers inside. "If he's on his way, I suppose an early dinner wouldn't be out of line."

"It would be my pleasure," the second Gladys says. She steps ahead to hold open the door for Gladys.

As Gladys passes me, I notice a used book in the dollar bin by the register. I snatch it up and hold it out for Gladys.

She peers at it through her thick lenses. "*How to Win Friends and Influence People*," she reads. Gladys tosses the book back to me, then fastens the snap of her plastic rain bonnet securely under her chin. "Oh, young, naive Robert. Save your Book Whisperer garbage for some loser who doesn't have everything I've got going on." Gladys joins the second Gladys standing by the door and says to her, "Be a doll, will you, and help me with my slicker?"

27

Texts from Not Quite Exes

I'm about to check my phone for texts from Luke after the Gladyses pull away, but the bell on the door rings again. The guy puts down his umbrella and pushes the hood back on his raincoat. Truman.

"We're about to close," I say, knowing that running away and ignoring Truman is not an option. Besides, I was able to watch the video. I can talk to Truman.

"Your sign says you're still open," he says, shaking his umbrella and sending water droplets onto the floor.

I walk past him and flip the sign hanging in the window to closed. "We're closed now."

Truman slides past me, peering around at the store. "This place cleaned up well. And you seem to be doing ok. Everyone's talking about this Book Whisperer guy who works here and knows just the right read to solve all your problems. What do you recommend?"

"You've got the Reading Festival, the literary journal, Campus Books, book club, and famous boyfriend Scott Horatio. I don't think you've got any problems the Book Whisperer could help with."

Truman pulls two books from the shelves, *Great Expectations* and *Love's Labour's Lost*. I don't think he even intends the irony of the titles; he just chose the only two he saw with fake leather binding and gold embossing on their spines. He keeps scanning the shelves.

"I miss you at book club. You won't answer my calls or read my texts. Do you really hate me that much?"

"It would be easier if I did. I made it clear how I felt, and you made it clear you don't feel the same."

"I didn't mean for you to get hurt." Truman puts the two books down on top of the shelf.

I remember what Luke said about me being determined and not allowing anything to control me and decide to lay out the truth to Tru. "Be honest. You knew I liked you the whole time. And I thought if I just read the right books or was smart enough or wore the right clothes or told you in some big way or if I was less extra or loud or fat then eventually, I'd be worthy of you. And you knew how I felt. And you liked me mooning after you. And you knew no matter what I did, for whatever reason, it would never be enough."

"Fine. I suspected. But you be honest too. You never really wanted me. You wanted a boyfriend. Any boyfriend. Your grand gesture was about you having some big romance like you read about in one of your books. I just happened to be the guy you cast in the role opposite you."

I close my eyes and swallow hard, not willing to cry in front of Truman again. "Thanks," I say.

"For what?"

"Making it easier to get over you. I'm not mad at you. I don't think you're a bad guy. But it's taken me this long to get even this far. We're closed, Truman. I need to ask you to leave."

"Bobby," Truman says, almost a whisper.

"Maybe one day I'll be the kind of guy you'll want. But I probably never will be. Right now, I'm just trying to be the kind who doesn't hate himself whenever he thinks about you. I really need you to go."

And he does.

28

Lazy Lions

With Truman out of the store, I send a text to Luke to find out what happened after I made my break for it. I don't mention Truman in my texts. I need to know Luke isn't in trouble first.

I mop. No reply. I vacuum. No reply. I lock the door. No reply. I print out the daily sales report and place it on Uncle Andy's desk. No reply. I wipe down the counter, the keyboard, the door handles, the windows. Still no reply.

The back door creaks open and I hear Uncle Andy humming as he enters. He's in the same shirt and pants he wore last night.

Seeing me, his cheeks flush. "You're still here," he says. "I thought you'd have left."

"Still closing."

Uncle Andy avoids looking at me. He moves things around the back room, trying to keep busy. It's like he's guilty. Maybe if I'd spent the night with my not-related nephew's mom, I'd have mixed feelings too. But for all I know, Uncle Andy could have spent the night on our couch or engaged in something else neutral like platonic nudity.

I hand Uncle Andy the day's sales.

"These are fantastic," he says, scanning the bottom line.

"As good as Mapplethorpe?" I ask.

His cheeks are flushed when he says, "It was a good show."

"I'm all done here. Unless there's something else that needs doing."

"Looks like you've got everything covered. Good work today."

"Awesome," I say. "It's still raining badly and it's pretty dark out. Could you give me a ride home?"

Uncle Andy hesitates. "Your mom's got the sculpture, and I'm sure after your wild night out . . ."

"It's coming down hard," I interrupt.

He finally looks at me and sighs. His keys jingle as he takes them from his pocket.

I keep checking my phone as we drive. Still no reply. I fill Uncle Andy in about Gladys coming to the rescue but don't spill the beans about the second Gladys even though it would mean winning our bet.

We pull into the driveway, and I go to get out, but Uncle Andy isn't budging.

"Aren't you coming in?" I ask. "We've got all those leftovers from my birthday."

He runs his hand along the dashboard, then wipes the dust off on his pant leg. "I'm sure your mom doesn't want to be entertaining me again so soon."

"I wouldn't be so sure." I point to the porch where Cass is coming down the steps, an umbrella in each hand.

She crosses to the passenger side to hand me an umbrella then waits by the driver's door for Uncle Andy.

"Hi," she says as he steps under her umbrella.

"Hi," he answers.

"You're getting wet." She slides an arm behind his back and pulls him close to her, walking him up the steps.

Over dinner, Cass makes me recount the story of getting locked in the pool. I don't mention the part about skinny-dipping or sleeping next to Luke.

"I'm no expert, but how many moments do you boys need before one of you makes a move?" Uncle Andy asks.

"You're definitely no expert," Cass replies. "It's hard enough picking up the signals when you know someone's sexuality. Bobby isn't exactly spot-on where a guy's interest is concerned. No offense," Cass adds as an afterthought. "My son's a lot like me. Fearless. When he likes someone, he whips it out and lays it on the table. We're go-getters. Hunters. Like lions."

"Male lions don't hunt," I say. "Only the lionesses."

"Exactly!" Cass agrees as if I've proven her point. I'm certain I did not. "The lions lounge around and wait for the females to take down the prey and deliver it to them. People like Bobby and me, we don't sit around waiting for those lazy lions to get their acts together. We're busy taking down gazelles and wildebeests and zebras. We're not afraid of a bloodbath to bring home the goods. If his intuition is telling him not to make the kill, he should pay attention."

Uncle Andy and I look at each other, each of us raising an eyebrow.

"That's a confusing and complicated analogy," Uncle Andy says.

"I think you lost the thread and the audience," I add.

Cass heaves a sigh. "If anyone's to blame for inaction, it's Luke, not my son. It's an attractive quality when a person knows what they want and they're willing to go after it."

Uncle Andy's chair scrapes as he stands and gets up from the table. He leaves the house with only one look back at Cass.

"What did I say?" Cass asks as we hurry after him.

He pulls something from the backseat before striding back up the path. He takes the steps two at a time onto the porch, soaked through from the rain, and thrusts the item in his grip at Cass, a bottle of red wine.

"I had a good time with you last night and unless I'm mistaken, you did too," he says.

Cass takes the bottle with both hands. "I did."

"That was your favorite from last night. I can bring over a bottle anytime you want." Uncle Andy's nostrils are flared, and his eyes burn into Cass's. The summer night feels cool compared to the heat radiating between them. They stare at each other, breathing heavily. "I can be a hunter too."

"I'm going to spend the night at Wanda's." Before either can protest, I slip on my shoes and rush up the stairs.

Once I'm in Wanda's bedroom, I say, "Do me a favor? Keep the volume on your computer turned up loud."

"I don't want to disrupt your mom," Wanda says.

"I wouldn't worry about that. Crank it."

The next morning, my phone is lit with messages from Uncle Andy. I rub my eyes, and it takes me a second to remember I'm in Wanda's bedroom. Her shower is running.

Uncle Andy: *We'll drive to work together.*

Uncle Andy: *Wanda too.*

I do a happy dance. The blanket I was curled up under slips to the floor.

I yawn and stretch. In front of me, a bar along the bottom of one of Wanda's computer screens flashes. I check I can still hear the water running before I sit in her chair and hover the cursor over the flashing bar. A miniature preview of the window enlarges enough that I can see it's a DM with chickn_backflip. I squint and can make out the last few messages. Mainly, Wanda gloating about kicking butt during their gaming session last night. The last message from chickn_backflip stands out.

Have a great day at work.

While it may seem innocent enough, he sent an emoji right after. The kissing and winking smiley face with the little heart.

It's all I need to confirm that the little online-battling, ogre-slaying, zombie-beheading minx has been destroying hearts this entire time! She's got this guy wrapped around her trigger finger sending her emojis like that. Everyone knows the winky-smiley-kissy face translates to deeply, madly in love if not totally obsessed. It really speaks to Wanda's lack of experience with love that while in the midst of some passionate online tryst, she sits back and lets me spend the evening blathering on about being trapped in the pool with Luke and how I'd done what fate couldn't by getting Cass and Uncle Andy together after decades.

All along I could have been helping her secure things with her online gentleman caller instead of telling her, "Behind you! Gut him!" I'm really going to have to keep a closer eye on Wanda to find a way to add my expertise to this chickn_backflip situation. I'll be understated like an unobtrusive backseat driver. A hint here or a suggestion there. A casual, calm word of advice. It's not right that my own bestie is the only one who doesn't benefit from my knack for romance.

I take the Summer of Bobby list from my pocket and add a new item: *Help Wanda*. I tuck it back in next to the Baroness's stone.

I stand up to go downstairs and grab a quick shower and change of clothes before we leave when my phone lights up with another text. Across the notifications on my lock screen is Luke's name. I unlock my phone.

Luke: *Fell asleep. Everything cool. Explain later. See you after camp.*

My worry about Luke and the fate of his job lifts from me. He wouldn't be texting to meet after camp if he had gotten fired. I remember the penny meant for a safe return. Maybe it brought us both the luck we needed.

Eager to know what happened with the cleaner, I go to reply but stop myself before I hit send. Whether Wanda knows it or not, she's played it right by taking a shower at the most opportune moment during a text convo. Keeping a guy waiting is a tried-and-true strategy to ensure a man's interest. No one wants to seem like they're desperately waiting for a suitor. It gives the other party all the power.

I leave my text to Luke unsent for now and text Wanda instead to meet Uncle Andy and me downstairs.

THE SUMMER OF BOBBY

(AKA Bobby Ashton's Plan for the Perfect Summer Before College)

☑ Summer job: Corner Books

☑ Play nice with Gladys

☑ Become a star employee

☑ Spruce up Corner Books' image

☑ Hope Evie tanks Big Summer Reading Festival

♡ ~~Land the Perfect Boyfriend: TRUMAN~~

♡ LUKE???

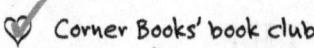 Corner Books' book club

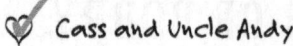 Cass and Uncle Andy

♡ Help Wanda

29

A Fine Bromance

Uncle Andy and Gladys are in great moods. Gladys's good mood still means calling me Robert. And making me mop the floor after yesterday's rain even though I've done it twice. And painstakingly giving me instructions on the proper way to mop. But it feels a bit more like harsh constructive criticism than Gladys's being critical.

After lunch, I text Luke back.

Me: *Sure. Want to go for hot dogs?*

Luke: *Processed meat products and your celebrity discount? Do you even need to ask?*

I almost reply *I'm not a celebrity* but leave it.

Luke texts again. A sign not responding immediately was a sage move.

Luke: *I'll even treat since it's on Mr. Papadopoulos. Order whatever you want and as much as you want.*

With the start of the college term only a few weeks away and reading lists getting posted online, the afternoon flies by with phone calls and keeners dropping by to grab used copies of textbooks.

"Things picked up around here all of a sudden," I say when the store empties out.

Uncle Andy slides a box of paper bags under the counter. "We get a break when the festival gets going. Everyone swarms to Campus Books, the *Official Bookseller of Little Elm's Big Summer Reading Festival*."

"That doesn't seem fair," I say. "We display their posters and hand out their schedules. Why don't we have a place at the festival?"

"It's their festival. It's their rules. I can't complain. They've always left us the used book market. Things pick up again the first couple of weeks of term. We could really use an extra pair of hands then, but you'll be in classes."

Gladys jabs a finger in my direction while staring down Uncle Andy. "I've finally got this one skimming along at a satisfactory level. I'm not training another employee that is certain to be a downgrade from Robert."

I lean over the counter and bat my eyelashes at Gladys. "That may be the nicest thing you've ever said to me in all our time together."

"Don't be fresh." She swats me away with a Casey McQuiston book.

I smile to myself knowing Luke wouldn't be able to get through *Red, White & Royal Blue* (novel or film).

"You should grab your own set of course books while we still have stock. And before you make some comment about how I'm softening toward you, think twice. It's a sound, logical course of action and it guarantees us a sale," Gladys says.

As I access my required reading lists, Gladys puts herself in charge of selecting the best copy of each title I need and stacking them in a box with big rubber bands around the books for each class with a piece of paper listing the course and its code.

"It sucks," I say out loud to no one in particular. "Campus Books wouldn't even know how to handle used book sales. How many students came in here today alone? We deserve a presence there too."

"Would you be thinking that way if you were still at Campus Books?" Uncle Andy asks.

I wince.

"It's ok," he says. "I appreciate the loyalty you've developed for Corner Books."

I smile, but it's weak and fades quickly. "Corner Books was always loyal to me. I shouldn't have forgotten so easily." I shuffle my toe on the carpet. I hope Uncle Andy gets the subtext and by "Corner Books," knows I mean him. "Are you going to see Cass tonight?"

He smirks. "Your mom needs to work."

"You heard her about lions."

"It's easier to miss someone when they're not underfoot and us older lions and lionesses don't bounce back quite as quickly," he says. "And the young lions need to sleep in their own beds. You can't spend every night at Wanda's."

"I'm happy for you two," I say quietly so Gladys doesn't overhear.

"I'm happy for all of us." Uncle Andy clears his throat. "Gladys and I will handle closing. You've got plans with the pool boy."

※

Luke is already seated in a booth at Elm Dogs reading over the menu. When I slide in, Mr. Papadopoulos appears at the tableside and plucks the menus into his hands.

"I didn't realize *you* were coming," Mr. Papadopoulos says. "You won't be needing these. I'll have the kitchen send out this year's festival specials."

"That's really not necessary," I say, blushing already and hoping he doesn't try to kiss me on both cheeks again.

Mr. Papadopoulos makes a tutting noise before going into the back.

"Don't," I say to Luke, catching his grin.

"Whatever you say, Casanova." Luke drums his thumbs on the tabletop. "I didn't know if I was supposed to invite Wanda, but she has some big competition she's participating in with chickn_backflip."

I knew about the stream. Wanda had been talking about it and it sounded a lot like a book blog tour where a bunch of streamers joined up in hopes of attracting each other's followers. "You know anything about him?" I ask.

Luke shakes his head. "Not really. Some of the other counselors were teasing her about how much time they're spending together. That is, until she decapitated their characters in front of the campers and used their heads to decorate her fortress."

"Sounds like her." I wait a second before I say, "Spill. The cleaner. What happened? I'm dying to know."

Luke runs his hand through his hair. "The vapid frat boy thing came in handy." Luke clears his throat. "*Ah, man. I'm so glad you're here. I don't know what happened. I locked myself in. You saved my ass, bro. I don't know how to thank you.*"

I laugh. "That can't have worked."

"He told me we've all been there. I even saw him around today and he told me not to lock myself in tonight."

"That was anticlimactic."

"What were you expecting? A showdown?"

I hold up my hands in a shrug. "I thought you were going to lose your job."

"That's melodramatic. It's nice you worried about me, but it's all good. I did want to talk to you more about that night. I shouldn't have gotten angry at you for closing the door."

"You were kind of a jerk about it," I say. "But only kind of. I shouldn't have pulled it shut."

Luke's drumming speeds up. "I got used to people coming and going from my life with all the divorces, but I never want you to be one of them. I don't want there to be any weirdness between us. It was already sort of awkward after everything with Roger. He's my roommate, and I wouldn't want to lose a friend like you over something silly."

"A friend?" I ask. I let myself half hope Uncle Andy was right about there being something with Luke. Now that I know Luke is into guys, I wondered if I didn't read enough into the bench or the rock or the night in the pool.

But wouldn't Luke have made a move if he was truly interested? Wouldn't I, if I had been sure? I don't want this to be another Truman situation where I'm the only one who feels it, and I create delusions of some sweeping romance that will never be reciprocated.

"We are friends. Aren't we?" Luke asks.

I force myself to smile, even though the half of me that was hopeful is deflating like a sad, rainbow unicorn. "Of course. Why wouldn't we be?"

"I probably sound like I'm six years old asking you that." He stops drumming and searches my face.

I look at the spot on the table that's been worn smooth.

"I don't know a lot of people in Little Elm," he continues. "And I don't want to lose a friend. I was worried I pushed you too far or things got misconstrued. I never want to make you uncomfortable, Casanova."

I force my smile even harder, making it broader than before. "You don't. You were a perfect gentleman when you weren't being a love Grinch. No worries."

"A perfect gentleman," Luke repeats, still watching me.

I meet his look and hold it.

"Friends?" I ask.

Luke nods. "Friends."

I force my smile as bright as I can, seeing Mr. Papadopoulos loading his arms with plates and heading in our direction. "Cool. Because I'm not normally friends with frat boys who get locked in pools overnight. I hang with a cooler crowd if you haven't noticed."

Luke scoffs. "I'm not cool enough for you?"

"Jury's still out."

But on the topic of where Luke and I stand, the verdict is in. Friends.

30

A Head for Business

"Anything by Julie Murphy is a sure bet," I say to a pair of customers as the bell above Corner Books' door tinkles and Evie walks in.

Evie loiters by the tables near the entrance, perusing new releases while I serve the duo, a woman with short blue hair and a guy with luxuriously cascading hair who told me they record a podcast. They decide to buy Julie and Sierra Simone's steamy series of Christmas romances at my suggestion.

"I find they pair well with ample amounts of Mariah to set a festive mood," I say, keeping Evie in my peripheral view as she meanders about.

When the duo leaves, Evie keeps glancing from the cover of the book she's holding to me and back again.

I cross my arms and stand by the register. "You made it clear you don't need my help," I call across the store.

Evie puts down the book. "I suppose I deserve that."

Gladys pokes her head out of the back room where she said she's checking stock for a call-in customer, but I suspect she's having a work-unrelated conversation with the second Gladys. She remains in the doorway, watching.

I don't answer Evie.

Evie says, "I told Luke you wouldn't make this easy."

I narrow my eyes. "What should I be making easy? And why would you be talking to Luke about me?"

"He's the one who suggested I speak to you. I need some additional resources for the festival. He thought you might have them." Evie suddenly becomes very interested in inspecting the fingernails on her left hand.

"Little Elm College has been putting it on for years. They should have this thing down to a science," I say.

"But I don't. I'm in over my head." Evie lets her breath out in a long exhale. "We need volunteers and more moderators. And Campus Books missed ordering copies of about half the presenters' books. And I know what I said and there's bad blood between us, but I need someone to make sure the festival doesn't flop." It all flows out of her in one steady stream. When she's done, she stands there watching me.

My Summer of Bobby list said I hoped the festival would go down in flames. Another item to check off. "I've got my hands full at the moment arranging a book club for the seniors from the assisted living center. Excuse me, but none of this sounds like a Bobby problem."

"I wouldn't be here if I wasn't desperate." Tears bead up in Evie's eyes. "I told Luke you wouldn't help me. This year's festival is going to bomb hard. We both know they should have kept you. The fountain wasn't a fail. It was an example of how you're one of the only people in this town who can envision something of this magnitude."

I feel someone's hand on my arm.

Gladys stands beside me. "I'll call you back." She clicks the phone off and says softly, "It takes a lot to go to the last person you'd want to ask and ask them for their help."

I open my mouth to argue but Gladys squeezes my arm.

"Whatever you answer, remember that." She releases my arm.

The Big Summer Reading Festival was supposed to be mine. I was supposed to be the freshman liaison. I had all the plans made and ready to go. It was going to be truly fabulous. Spectacular even. An event Little Elm would talk about for years to come. And then they dropped me without a second thought.

Except it was never really mine to start with. It's *Little Elm's* Big Summer Reading Festival. Not Evie Bosendorfer's or Bobby Ashton's. It doesn't belong to me, but to our entire town. Without it, I doubt Little Elm would even be on the map. The festival brings in a lot of money, money that keeps residents able to pay their rent and bills throughout the year. It's important on a macro scale.

But none of that means I'm not going to strike an advantageous deal for the promise of all my work. Wanda, with all her new interest in monetizing business opportunities, is about to be proud of me.

"If I agree to help, what's in it for me?" I ask.

Evie shifts uncomfortably. "What do you want? Your job back?"

"No," I say quickly. I even see Gladys perk up in surprise as she listens. "I've got a job and I like it here. I'm not bailing on Corner Books."

"I don't exactly have a lot of power if you're thinking of extorting me. I can give you recognition, but that's about it."

I shake my head. "I don't need that. I've had enough of being the center of attention. I'll help you get the festival back on track. I can get the volunteers and moderators and even the missing books. I want a booth in exchange."

"A booth?"

"A booth," I repeat. "It's about time Corner Books was invited to the Reading Festival."

Evie shakes her head. "That's not possible. All available space is reserved. Besides, Campus Books won't like it."

I pull up an aerial map of the festival on my phone. "It's possible and Campus Books is going to like a failed festival even less. Shove Corner Books in at the end of an aisle. Pull tables out of a classroom or building if you have to. If you want me, you'll find a way."

"I guess Corner Books is getting a booth." Evie holds out her hand for me.

I shake on it. "Confirm our presence officially first and get us added to the website. Then text me and we'll get a plan going. My number hasn't changed."

"I'll thank you when this is all done," Evie says.

"Make no mistake, you'll worship at my feet."

Evie leaves and Gladys hands me the store's phone. "You drive a hard bargain. Give your uncle a call. He'll need the two of us to help get Corner Books ready for its first Big Summer Reading Festival." As she walks away, she adds, "And Robert? You were amazing."

I reply, "I'm not unaware of the fact."

THE SUMMER OF BOBBY

(AKA Bobby Ashton's Plan for the Perfect Summer Before College)

♥ Summer job: Corner Books

♥ Play nice with Gladys

♥ Become a star employee

♥ Spruce up Corner Books' image

♡ ~~Hope Evie tanks Big Summer Reading Festival~~

♡ Make Little Elm's Big Summer Reading Festival SICKENING

♡ ~~Land the Perfect Boyfriend: TRUMAN~~

♡ ~~LUKE???~~

 Corner Books' book club

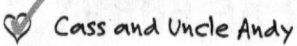 Cass and Uncle Andy

♡ Help Wanda

32

Not Grand, Average-Sized Gesture

It takes two days for Evie to confirm Corner Books' spot at the Reading Festival. I stop between customers long enough to double-check we were added to the website before sending back an email asking for a list of presenters, titles, publishers, and ISBNs. I attach a link to my planning documents, telling her to get acquainted because this evening, we start the real work.

The celebration between Gladys, Uncle Andy, and me dies quickly as we all realize how much preparation and organization this is going to take.

"I'll handle it," I assure them. "This is what I'm best at."

I see Uncle Andy open his mouth, probably to tell me *we'll* handle it, but Gladys swats at him and says, "And steal all the glory? I don't think so. We work together and reap the spoils together. There won't be another word on the matter."

"Yes, ma'am," Uncle Andy and I say in unison.

I pull out my Summer of Bobby list. Somehow, things got salvaged. I drop it on top of my tote bag when a group of customers comes in.

Once they've been served, Gladys suggests I busy myself dusting the shelves.

"I dusted last week. Shouldn't I start the planning?" I ask. Dusting isn't really a task for the person who negotiated Corner Books a spot in the town's biggest literary event of the year.

"You can plan at the same time. The polish repels future dust." She hands me a rag and a canister of lemon Pledge.

I head to the back corner. If I have to start somewhere, it might as well be among the romances. I run my finger along the spines of the novels, indulging in my usual thrill. My finger bumps forward on a section of the shelf. These books' spines are sticking out more than the others. A book sticking out isn't that unusual. Books, like people, come in all dimensions. But these ones are part of a romance series from the same author and the same publisher. They should line up exactly. I try to push them in. There's resistance.

I yank a handful of paperbacks off the shelf. Yup. Right against the bricks of the back wall is a book. A jolt runs through my hand.

I pull out a novel written by the same author Luke was reading when I met him in this spot. I can tell it's an old release. It must have gotten pushed behind the others and forgotten. The pages are yellowed, and the cover is dinged up. I place the other books back in their spots. They now line up perfectly. The hidden book, *The Flesh and the Devil*, comes with me to the register.

I put it down on the counter. I gave the first *Devil* to Luke. The other is sitting in front of me.

The old Bobby would have seen this as a sign from the universe on how some people are meant to be together. I'd have jumped into action . . . and set myself up for failure. The irony of a devil tempting the new Bobby back to his old ways doesn't get past me unnoticed. If the tree in the middle of Eden had been chopped down and used to make books, I wouldn't have stood a chance. But this isn't forbidden fruit. It's an old book. That's it. Merely a coincidence at best. And Luke established we're friends. Nothing more.

Gladys looks up. "Where did that ratty old thing appear from?"

"It must have gotten lost in the shelves."

She scans it, then turns it over and begins typing into the ancient cash machine. "It's not in the system. Why don't you keep it? With its condition and age, I doubt we could charge more than ten cents anyway."

"Sure," I say. "Throw it on top of my stuff."

Gladys peers at me through the thick lenses of her glasses. "You can't have finished dusting already."

Evie arrives at Corner Books as we're closing. She greets Gladys but gives a wide berth as she skirts around the older woman.

I hear the telltale chug of the second Gladys's motorcycle pulling up to the curb.

The OG Gladys barks, "Make sure to lock this door. You can't have riffraff running in off the street."

"Since when are there riffraff in Little Elm?" Evie asks once the Gladyses have driven away.

"Beats me," I say. I point to three chairs I set up by the windows for us. "Should we get started?"

We cross the store and take our seats, each of us pulling out a clipboard and pen. Not to brag, but the stack of paper on mine is much thicker than Evie's. My eyes glance to the extra chair.

"He's not coming," Evie says.

"Who isn't?"

"Luke."

"I didn't expect him," I lie before I change the subject. "Corner Books already had the majority of the presenters' missing books in our inventory. Uncle Andy called in favors for rush deliveries on the others and Mae from the post office is doing some behind-the-scenes magic to help them get here even sooner.

"Next," I say, barreling on, "the volunteers. I've got a three-pronged plan. One, Little Elm College's day camps wrap at the end of next week. Those counselors could make great volunteers, especially for setup and cleanup. I suggest we recruit as many as we can. Two, I've already invited Mr. Martinez and Mr. Shah and the other seniors to do shifts manning the info booths. We're giving them green room access for their time. I already let the caterers know to consult with the dietitian at the residence. Three, I've called and texted people I've helped around Little Elm and customers who seem like a good fit for the extra spots. The responses have been enthusiastic. We should have more volunteers than we can use."

"You did all this in one afternoon?" Evie asks as I finish and assign each of us actions.

I nod. "It's no big deal. A couple of days and the festival prep will be back on track."

Evie fiddles with the clasp on her clutch and looks as if she's about to say something. She shakes her head and stops fidgeting.

"I owe you an apology," she says. "You stood up for me with Roger even though I was happy he was going to show everyone that video of you."

"You were nearly giddy with glee," I agree. "I get why. I sucked at being a friend to you."

"It took two people to make that friendship toxic," Evie says. We walk to the door, but she stops before she leaves. "I don't know if we're going to be friends again, but I don't want to be enemies either. I deleted the footage I took from the day at the fountain. I wanted you to know."

"Thanks, but I don't think it could do more damage than the existing video I already put into circulation myself." I open the door for her.

Evie gestures to a car outside. "My dad's here." She stops again and stares at the third chair before she leaves. "Not everyone is better as friends."

I tilt my head.

Evie gets into the waiting car without looking back.

I go to the register to gather my things. *The Flesh and the Devil* sits on top of my tote, wrapped in brown paper and tied with string like Gladys does for special orders. Not once has she succumbed to my pressure and launched into a *The Sound of Music* sing-along medley. I really don't understand where she gets her resolve from.

I turn the book over in my hands, the wrapping making it look special. I remind myself it isn't a sign, only a coincidence. It's just a book.

I sling my tote over my shoulder. Once the alarm is set and the doors checked and rechecked, I stand outside and hold the package. Teresa Denys only published the two books, and they must have sat happily together in Corner Books for years.

With the brown-paper-wrapped book swinging in my grip, I start moving through Little Elm with the confidence of Julie Andrews's portrayal of a nun-turned-governess marching along the tree-lined avenues of Austria.

It may be only a book, but it belongs with its companion.

32

You Can't Lose Something You Never Had

I stand on the sidewalk outside Luke's house, staring up. The confident nun inside me must have worn herself out from the walk because I don't seem able to move another step forward.

Lights turn on in a room on the ground floor. Probably because it's a rental house, no one thought to hang curtains to block someone from peering right inside.

Luke steps into the frame made by the window. Roger joins him. I can't hear what they're saying but I don't need to.

Luke steps closer to Roger, almost no space left between them. They stare into each other's eyes. Roger plays coy, turning his head away, then back, gazing up at Luke.

As they speak, Luke links both his arms around Roger's neck.

Roger pushes against Luke's chest but makes no real effort to move away. He reaches up and brushes Luke's hair back, letting his hand linger as his fingertips trail down Luke's cheek and jaw.

Luke leans in, his lips draw nearer to Roger's.

Then Luke stops.

His lips move. I don't need to hear him to be able to make out the shape of the three words he says to Roger, encircled in his arms.

I've watched and rewatched them said over and over at the climax of every movie I love.

I grip the book harder, my other hand covering my mouth and jaw, squeezing my fingertips in. I clench my eyes shut. My heart beats deep in my ears, throbbing and drowning out all the other noises of Little Elm. An ache bleeds through me and fills, so dark and heavy and deep. It sits there, pressing and crushing me from the inside.

I know Luke and I established we are only friends. We agreed. Friends isn't so awful.

But seeing Roger in Luke's arms, seeing Luke profess his feelings, it hurts in a way I never knew it could. I wrap my arms around myself, suddenly cold in the summer-night air.

Wanda knew from the second she met Luke. Uncle Andy knew too after my birthday. Luke could have liked me. But I chose not to see it. I denied it. I played it safe. There were no big plans. No grand gestures. There were only books and a bench and a night in a pool.

I start to leave and trip over the uneven sidewalk, falling face down and toppling over several metal trash cans. Garbage explodes everywhere. The book shoots away from me. My palms and knees scrape. I pick myself up. My gut bulges, the waistband of my shorts cutting in. I pull out my tucked-in shirt to hide as much as I can.

The door to the front of the rental house opens and light from inside pours over me.

Luke's and Roger's shadows stretch out tall, long, lean in front of them. My shadow blobs into a puddle at my feet.

As Luke comes closer, he says, "You're bleeding."

Roger leans his muscular frame against the railing and crosses his arms and ankles.

"I tripped," I mumble.

"Come inside. We'll get you cleaned up."

"It's not that bad. I'm fine."

"He said he's fine," Roger says gently, placing a hand on Luke's shoulder. "Did you come here for a reason?"

"No," I say. My eyes dart along the sidewalk.

Roger notices the package and hops down the steps, retrieving it before I have a chance to move. "What's this?"

"A book." I pick myself up.

Roger starts to untie the string. Luke stops him. He takes the book and holds it out to me.

I shake my head. "It was for you."

Luke rips the corner of the paper and sees the title.

"She only wrote the two," I add quickly. "They've spent all that time together. They should stay together."

"You didn't have to come all this way," Luke says. "I could have gotten it from you next time we hung out."

I clear my throat. "I wasn't sure when that would be. The festival is keeping me busy."

"I guess I'm to blame for that." Luke takes another step down. "Stay here. I'll get you a wet paper towel for your scrapes."

"I don't need one," I say, but Luke has already gone back into the house, leaving Roger and me alone.

Roger places one hand on his hips and sways them ever so slightly as he bridges the distance between us.

"I drank too much the other night," he says. "Despite the video, I was the one who looked bad, not you."

"Is that an apology?"

"An explanation." He pauses. "But I am sorry. I know I've given you no reason to believe me."

Luke returns and goes to press the paper towel to my cut.

I take the wet wad from his hand. "I can do it." I dab at the blood and wince.

"You should come inside," Roger says.

I shake my head. "I have plans."

"Always a scheme." Luke grins at me.

I dab at my palms with the wet paper towel. They sting worse. "What else would go awry for mice and men?"

Roger puts his hand on Luke's shoulder again. "He's referencing Burns's 'To a Mouse.' I used to recite it as one of my audition pieces. My Scottish brogue once got me the role of Macbeth. One day it might land me Shrek."

Luke and Roger stand in front of me looking like they walked out of a movie. Luke with his skin laced with gold and Roger with his Hollywood appeal. A power couple on the edge of greatness. They make sense together. They look perfect side by side. They look like a couple I could have matched together. I should be happy for Luke.

"I'll see you both another time," I say and start down the block.

"Let me walk you," Luke offers.

"No. Thanks. I'm fine."

Roger says in a hushed tone, "Let him go."

The universe did give me a message. The two books are the same. They belong together. Anyone can see it. But a hefty tome like *War and Peace* can't sit on the same shelf. It doesn't belong. It's all wrong.

33

Broke Backward Statue

"You can't just freeze out Luke," Wanda says as we lift a heavy plate of glass encased by a metal rim into Uncle Andy's truck.

"Easy," Cass instructs. "The structural integrity was already compromised when the glass was initially damaged. Wrap them in those blankets like they're newborns."

"You don't say," Uncle Andy says, wiping his brow.

I give him a look that tells him to cut it out. Cass has no sense of humor when she's stressed.

I say to Wanda, "I answered all his texts."

"He showed me. You were polite. And grammatically correct. Not replying would be better than using passive-aggressive punctuation." Wanda grunts as we lift another of the plates into the truck. Fortunately, a lot more camp counselors are already at the library, where the statue is to be assembled.

"He's with Roger," I say. "I have to respect that. That means no drama or confrontation or profession of love. It's what Dean Perez told me to do anyway."

"He should be with you."

I lift my end of the plate onto the truck first. "Well, he's not." I cross to Wanda's side to help.

"You can't just ignore your feelings."

"People do it all the time. It's a valid course of action. Besides, it's all I could think of." I don't tell Wanda that I can't ignore the dark ache that fills me. I don't tell her I've been exhausting myself to try to avoid thinking about Luke. I don't tell her I wake up from dreams of conversations I have with him where I try to convince him I'm the right person for him and then can't get myself back to sleep. I don't say any of those things because I don't know how else to get through all this, and if I fall apart like I did with Truman, nothing will get done. Not the statue. Not Corner Books' booth. Not the festival. I've got no time or desire to indulge emotions I wish I didn't have. With mere days to go till the festival, I've got too much work, and if I learned anything from the situation with Luke, it's not to let my emotions control me.

"Maybe you should let Bobby drive your truck," Cass tells Uncle Andy when the last of the plates are loaded in. "He drives with the brake. He's annoyingly safe."

"Hey!" I call across the driveway.

"I know how important this is," Uncle Andy says. "I'll treat my driving as carefully as I do you. You're my shotgun, Cass."

She throws up her hands. "Fantastic! Even Bobby moves faster than you. We won't arrive until next century."

I get into Cass's car that I'll be driving with Wanda, so I miss Uncle Andy's reply if there is one.

Wanda slides into the passenger seat. "He can't be with Roger. No one likes Roger. Everyone likes you."

"Not everyone." I start the engine and back down the driveway.

"I should have pushed you two together when I met him, but I thought Little Elm's resident meddling romantic would have it in the bag."

I check my blind spot before I change lanes. "I'm mending my wicked ways. Give me some credit. I didn't get involved with chickn_backflip."

"Because I told you it isn't like that and to butt out. How was setting up Cass and Andy mending your ways?"

"It does count." I try to change the subject. "How are things going with your mystery man?"

"We decided we're going to meet."

"Things are getting serious. When?"

"We didn't establish anything concrete. That's all you're getting. I'll be taking no further questions at this time."

Not setting a date to meet is a serious red flag, but I hold my tongue as we slow down in front of the library.

Evie is organizing the volunteers into teams.

"Are Roger and Luke here?" I ask.

Evie points. "Over there."

"I'm in a different group, right?"

"Like you requested." Evie flips through pages on her clipboard. "Everyone knows what they're doing?" she calls.

"Transport vehicles finish arriving any second. Get ready, people! It's go time!" What Evie hasn't developed in organizational nitpickiness, she makes up for with the authoritarian attitude of an overlord.

As soon as Uncle Andy slows to a stop, Cass is out of the truck and at Evie's side.

"I can't stress enough the pieces need to stay in order. Everything is labeled."

"I hear you," Evie says. "Top priority after safety."

As the teams begin unloading the plates, Cass hovers to give instructions to whomever is nearest. She needn't because it's all being handled flawlessly. I keep glancing around, making sure Luke and I don't intersect.

That is until Roger decides to lift the same end of a glass plate as me. Uncle Andy and Wanda grab the other end and we're in motion as a unit before I can back away.

"I hate apologizing," Roger whispers, "and I've already done it once to you. But if you're ticked off at Luke because of something I did, I'll say it again. I'm sorry."

"Neither of you did anything," I say. "The festival is in a few days. I'm inordinately busy."

"He's inordinately upset about you," Roger grunts as we carry the plate up the steps of the library, walking backward. "He's a nightmare to live with."

I don't need a reminder Luke and Roger live in the same house. The whole thing is bad enough as is. "There's nothing for him to be upset about," I say, wishing we could put down the plate so I could get away from Roger.

"My sentiments exactly," Roger says. "I can't believe he's falling for your drama queen routine."

I turn my head to give Roger a dirty look, but in doing so I don't lift my foot high enough on the stairs. My heel catches. I stumble and pull Wanda and Uncle Andy off balance. Roger, sensing me about to fall, steps aside, leaving the weight of the glass plate all on me. Wanda and Uncle Andy overcompensate. We lurch and I topple through the open library doors into the foyer, crashing backward into a stack of plates for the statue. There is a sickening crunch as I collide, then a crack, the corner of the plate in my hands hitting the ground with me.

Everyone stops.

Uncle Andy is the first to reach me.

"Are you ok, Bobby?" he asks, kneeling.

Wanda kneels on my other side.

"I think so," I reply.

They slide the glass plate off my legs.

Cass walks around the stack of cracked glass plates. "Breaking that damn window once wasn't enough for you?"

"Cass," Uncle Andy says, helping me to my feet. "He didn't trip on purpose."

"Back off, Andy," Cass warns.

"Don't you see he's exhausted? He's been working every waking hour to make the statue and the festival a success. He should be at home resting, not lifting a heavy statue."

"I told you to back off. You don't need to get involved with everything in our lives. And there's only a statue because of his screw-up."

The flames ignite in Uncle Andy's eyes as he stares at Cass, but this time it's not passion. "I know you're stressed out, but I'd be careful what you say next."

"I mean it. Butt out."

"Don't be like this, Cass."

"Like what?"

"You pull me close one second and shove me away the second things don't go as planned. You did it in high school. You're doing it again now. People aren't yo-yos."

"Don't start that again. You didn't show up."

"You didn't wait. I've always shown up for you."

"Who asked you to?" Cass asks. "It's my job to take care of me and my kid, not yours. You're not his father."

I get up and step between them. "Don't fight."

"Don't worry. I'm done fighting." Uncle Andy pulls out his keys. "I'm done being the guy you want when no one else sticks around. You don't want me showing up for you? Fine. I won't be your last resort anymore." Uncle Andy walks out of the library.

"Do something," I say to Cass. "Yell at him. Go after him. Anything."

Cass balls her hands into fists. "I've got a broken statue to deal with."

I look at the glass plate with the cracks running through it. I toss the car keys to my mother who snatches them out of the air, and I jog after Uncle Andy.

"Wait," I call. "She didn't mean it."

Uncle Andy sighs and jerks his head to the passenger seat. We both get into the vehicle.

"But I did," he says. "Get in. I'll drive you home."

"I'm sure I can smooth things out once you both calm down."

"It's not your job to fix everyone." The bite in Uncle Andy's tone is gone. "Your mom told me to be a lion. We would have done better to leave the cage shut."

We drive in silence. I rack my brain, looking for solutions. For the statue. For Uncle Andy and Cass. For Luke and me.

After Uncle Andy drops me off, I continue to look for answers. I lie in bed until I hear Cass unlock the front door.

Cass stops at my bedroom. "That got ugly."

"How's the statue?"

She sighs and sits down beside me. "I might be able to fix it, but I need more time." She pats my thigh. "The biggest mistake I ever made," Cass says, "took me nine months to turn into the best thing that ever happened to me. I don't have nine months. I don't have nine days. The unveiling is Saturday night." She stands to leave. "I'm sorry I lost my temper."

I sit up in bed. Cass almost never apologizes. If she's saying sorry, someone else deserves one too so things can begin being mended.

"What about Uncle Andy?" I ask. "How much more time do you need?"

"It's not your job to fix us." Her tone is a lot like Uncle Andy's. "Get to sleep. Tomorrow morning is damage control," she says as she leaves my bedroom.

I grab my phone and set my alarm for extra early. It might not be my job, but there might be one way I can buy more time.

34

Beggin' Like Beckham

Wanda and I stand outside the office doors.

"I can do this alone," I say to her.

"I know, but what kind of best friend would I be if I couldn't figure out what you were planning? You need someone in your corner, so what's the plan?"

"Beg." I push open the doors and step inside Dean Perez's outer office.

"This place is swank," Wanda says, looking around at the gleaming wood.

Michael glances up from his screens momentarily. His fingers are a blur as he continues to type at rapid speed. "Bobby Ashton. Dean Perez is not expecting you."

"I know," I say. "But I really need to see him."

"Do you game?" Wanda asks, eyes transfixed on Michael. "You could join my quest any day."

"No," Michael says, smiling. "If you want to tell me what this is regarding, I can set up an appointment. I'm sure you understand the dean is rather busy at this time of year."

"Send them in, Michael," says Dean Perez from the door to his office, his phone in his hand. "And fix this ludicrous device again." He plunks the phone down on the edge of the desk.

"Dean Perez will see you now." Michael sighs. "And there goes today's schedule."

"You I have a vague memory of," Dean Perez says as I take the same seat as last time. "But I don't believe we've met," he says to Wanda. "Although there's a good chance I've forgotten. I'm terrible at placing names and faces. You are?"

"Wanda Lee." Wanda holds out her hand.

"That doesn't ring a bell. Who are you?"

"I'm Bobby's best friend."

Dean Perez continues to stare at Wanda.

"I live upstairs from him," she continues. "I'm enrolled as a freshman for the fall semester." Wanda's voice raises at the end of her sentences as if she's asking questions.

"I suppose that answers who you are. I should have asked why you're here."

Wanda gives me a sidelong glance. I should have warned her Dean Perez is offbeat.

"She came for moral support," I say.

"Ok, gotcha." He picks up his Rubik's Cube. "No offense, but you're like an emotional support animal. Except, human, of course." He absentmindedly starts twisting the toy.

We both know what the dean said is offensive and dehumanizing, but one look at each other trying not to laugh has Wanda and me giggling.

Wanda composes herself before I do. "You know there are proven techniques to solve those."

"I'm not actively trying to solve it. I believe if I twist the pieces around enough, eventually it will work itself out." Dean Perez keeps rotating the cube. "I've found it to be a very stress-relieving approach. For example, I knew the replacement Bobby wasn't going to be good for the Reading Festival. Lo and behold, I hear the original Bobby is back. The other girl is rather stress-inducing. Smug sort of thing. Is that why you're here? The festival?"

"Not exactly," I say, taking the tiniest pleasure in being compared to Evie in this way. "There's been a small setback with the statue."

"That sounds stressful," Dean Perez remarks as he keeps twisting the pieces of the cube.

"There was an accident with the glass."

"Another one? Most unfortunate. I hope Cass is figuring out a solution. As a fan of her work, I can say she's rather brilliant."

"She is. But we need more time. Is there any way we could get an extension?"

Dean Perez puts the Rubik's Cube down in front of him and holds his hands, palms together, in front of him. "This isn't an essay. The piece was bequeathed to the university to be unveiled during the closing of the festival."

"Couldn't we just do it in another week? Before Shakespeare in the Park?"

Dean Perez shakes his head. "Absolutely not. We've already made arrangements and advertised. It's on the programming schedule. The entire town has signs and banners and posters." Dean Perez picks up the cube again and begins rapidly twirling the pieces in his hands. "I'm sorry, Bobby. There can't be a delay. I must be firm."

"But the statue may not be stable. It's glass. I'm sure the university doesn't want the liability of someone getting hurt."

"Your mother will figure it out," Dean Perez says. He holds up the cube. "See. One side is completely red. That's one-sixth solved. Things have a way of working themselves out."

"But Dean Perez . . ."

He stands and motions us toward the door. "Thank you for stopping in. I'm delighted you're working on the Reading Festival again, Mr. Ashton."

Dean Perez walks us to his office door and says, "I do hope you'll both remind me of who you are again next time we meet. My bad memory is a real problem. You see, I meet so many interesting people in this job and I find it difficult to retain them all. Speaking of"—Dean Perez shakes my hand—"do give your mother my warmest regards. I'll never forget meeting *the* Cass Ashton. She's really something special. Such a unique woman." With that, Dean Perez closes his office door with us outside it.

"He's the one who runs this place?"

Michael looks up from his computer with a smirk as the intercom crackles to life.

"Michael, did you get that blasted phone working?"

35

One for a Return

The final days leading up to the festival are too full for me to develop any more best-laid schemes. After working late every day, I spend evenings on campus to go over things with Evie before heading home to handle Watch Me Unravel or text the volunteers, and, as has happened almost every night, fall asleep in Wanda's room to the sounds of artillery being fired.

Gladys, Uncle Andy, and I work to check and double-check what we will be bringing to the festival, then get it packed up, ready to go. Gladys rivals me with her organization, resulting in the most detailed and neatly labeled boxes I've ever encountered.

"I've got to keep focus," Uncle Andy says whenever I bring up Cass, even in the most subtle and indirect manner.

"I need to work on the statue. It's keeping you in college," Cass replies when I make any mention of Corner Books or Uncle Andy. "It's going to come down to the wire."

I feel guilty trying to tell Cass what to do with Uncle Andy, considering I've essentially ghosted Luke. My polite and grammatically correct answers have turned into one-word replies, mostly *yes* or *no*.

Wanda gets up from her gaming chair and stretches. "We both better get some sleep. Tomorrow's the festival."

"I only have a few more things to respond to," I say, switching between my laptop and phone.

"By the time I'm done in the bathroom, we're both turning off all electronics for the night."

"Sure," I yawn, typing as fast as I can.

Tomorrow will either be a disaster or work out successfully, a lot like Dean Perez and his Rubik's Cube.

I turn off my laptop and phone, place them on the corner of Wanda's desk, and notice the bar on the bottom of her screen flashing.

I lean forward and click open the game she was playing, a futuristic space adventure. There's a message from chickn_backflip.

Hope tomorrow is great for you and your friend, it reads.

I know I shouldn't, but I can't help myself. At least one person I know deserves a happy ending and Wanda's the last man standing. She's almost family, after all, but since she doesn't share any genetics with Cass or me, Wanda can't have the same skill at lousing things up with guys as we do. Wanda's putting herself out there more. She must be overdue for romance.

I listen to make sure I can hear water running before I sit down in Wanda's chair and type: *Maybe I'll see you there?*

chickn_backflip sends a reply: *Is that you saying you're ready to meet?*

My first instinct is to answer, "Duh!" But Wanda wouldn't do that. She'd play it cool.

I type, *It's a public event. Say hi if you're around.*

I see chickn_backflip typing but the water stops running in the bathroom. I log out of the game. It goes back to its loading screen, erasing the messaging history.

When Wanda enters, I stand and stretch. "I'm going to sleep in my own bed tonight. I'll see you tomorrow."

"No more electronics," Wanda warns, shutting her computer down. "Promise?"

"They're already turned off." I head downstairs.

My sleep is restless and I'm up before my alarm, which I set extra early so I could get to Corner Books to do my own checks before Gladys and Uncle Andy arrive.

I'm the first customer in the coffee shop down the block and it's nice to see Mya is working and hear her and Jerome are still going strong. I order one of the new, overpriced, deluxe beverages. My only instructions to her, "Extra caffeine and lots of sugar." After a couple of sips I can feel the buzz.

As I enter Corner Books and relock the door, I get a text.

Luke: *Are you going to give me the cold shoulder IRL too?*

I look up from my screen to see him standing on the other side of the door, holding his phone.

I open the door. Luke steps inside and follows me to the stacks of boxes that are going to the festival.

"You don't answer my texts anymore?" Luke asks.

"I answered."

"Barely."

I wave at all the boxes. "I've been swamped." I swap my coffee for my clipboard with my pages of checklists.

Luke places his hand over my papers. "We hang out all summer. You say we're friends. Then you won't even look my way. I think I deserve to know what I did."

Excuses form, but they never take shape. Instead, I say, "You didn't do anything. That's what you did."

He wrinkles his brow. "I don't know what that means."

I wet my lips and swallow. "The night I fell outside your house, I saw you holding Roger."

Luke's brow furrows, thinking. "That wasn't what it looked like."

"You had your arms around him. You told him you loved him."

"I didn't."

"I saw you."

"If you'd let me explain."

"I don't need an explanation."

Luke takes his hand off my clipboard. "I never know where I stand with you. You've been sending me mixed signals from the moment we met."

"Want to talk about mixed signals, love Grinch? How about you never told me you were into guys."

"I told you the second time we spoke."

"You weren't clear. I thought you were talking about reading."

"You read everything," he says. "You should have read between the lines."

We're both silent.

Finally, Luke says, "What was I? Another person for you to manipulate? A piece in one of your plans?"

"I help people find love."

"You play with them. You can't stop yourself. I don't even think you know you're doing it."

"Like you're any better with your bench, or the stone, or the skinny-dipping. At least mine are innocent mistakes. I try to do something good."

Luke shakes his head. "Tell that to your collateral damage. Like Andy. Or Cass. Or Truman."

I smack my clipboard down on the nearest stack of boxes. "I'm not the one who was playing house with my roommate."

Luke slings his backpack off. "You don't even know what you saw."

"I know exactly what I saw."

Luke unzips his backpack and pulls out three books. The three I gave him. He holds them out to me.

"Tell the Book Whisperer I'd like to make a return."

When I don't reach out to take the books, Luke puts them down on the counter. He pulls a folded piece of paper from his pocket and smooths it out on top of the stack, then turns and leaves.

My list for my perfect summer with Luke's name crossed off.

36

Truman Holiday

The bell tinkles and I turn, expecting to see Luke's returned.

Instead, a guy with pale skin and broad shoulders who looks like he's in his late thirties sticks his head in. Both his arms are tattooed in full sleeves with a flower design going up his neck.

"I saw the lights. Are you open? I could really use a recommendation," he says.

I quickly wipe at my eyes and blink several times. "We're closed today because we'll be at Little Elm's Big Reading Festival. But come in. I'm sure I can help you. I've got a gift for what people should read."

He enters the store. "I'm trying to reconnect with someone. I meet her in a few hours."

Past lovers reigniting a flame. "Having history with someone is hard," I say. "I rarely say this, but I'm not sure a book is your best bet."

The guy begins backing away. "You're probably right. I should go."

"I only meant there isn't a lot of time for you to read."

He shakes his head. "It's probably a mistake I came back at all. I've made a lot of mistakes. I'm sure she won't really want to see me."

"So have I. Don't worry. We've got short books." I lead him to the children's section and see a copy of *Where the Wild Things Are* poking out in a display of children's classics. I think this will do in a pinch. I hand it to him. "We all need someone to forgive us and keep dinner warm."

"I read this as a kid. I don't understand." He takes the book and flips through the first couple of pages.

"You will," I say. "Read it again carefully."

The guy slips a twenty-dollar bill into my hand.

"This is way too much for a paperback," I say. "This is mostly a used bookstore."

"Thanks for the help." Without a look back, he's gone.

Alone with my thoughts, I wipe at my eyes again. I can't. Not today. I've got lists of tasks to accomplish. Things to do. The day is full. Crying over a guy isn't on the agenda. There's no room left in my schedule.

I grab my clipboard and a tear falls. It stains the page, smudging the ink, before I wipe the back of my forearm across my eyes. I get a tissue from behind the counter and give my nose a good, hard blow.

"I told you to always keep this door locked," Gladys says, the bell tinkling as she enters.

Uncle Andy follows behind her, looking tired. His usual plaid shirt and khaki pants are wrinkled.

"Let's get this over with," he grumbles.

"Get yourself a coffee first," Gladys instructs him. "Bobby, you get the dolly. I'll get my cart."

I stick to the plan. Load the boxes into the truck. Drive to Little Elm College, the three of us squished into the front seat of Uncle Andy's truck. Park in the vendors' lot. Set up Corner Books' booth.

Do not let yourself think about this morning. Do not obsess. Do not cry. Do not fall apart.

But when we get to our table, there's a surprise. There's a second booth decorated like Lucy's therapy stand from the *Peanuts* cartoons. Someone painted across the top, *Bibliographic Help - 5 cents* and *The Book Whisperer is IN*, below.

"It was Gladys's idea," Uncle Andy says. "I thought it was overkill."

"You loved it two weeks ago. Who put a bee in your bonnet?" Gladys snipes back.

"Unload the boxes. I'm going to find another coffee." Uncle Andy stomps away, leaving Gladys and I with the setup.

He returns when we're nearly finished as are the booths and stages around us.

"I see you didn't bother to think of us," Gladys comments. "That's unusual for you."

Uncle Andy grunts, plunking his coffee down onto the table with enough force the folding legs wobble and some liquid sloshes out the plastic lid.

"Is everything ok?" I ask him quietly.

"Peachy," he mumbles. "This has been a lot of work already."

Gladys gets right up into Uncle Andy's face. "I don't know what's gotten into you lately, young man," she says, "but you can change that attitude immediately. A lot of effort went into getting Corner Books here and you'll be grateful and pleasant even if you need to fake it."

Uncle Andy starts to say something, but Gladys isn't done.

"And before you sass me, Andrew," she warns, "I suggest you think twice. You think you've seen the worst of me; you still haven't seen me on one of my bad days."

"Sorry, ma'am," replies Uncle Andy.

Gladys nearly pushes me into my seat behind the Book Whisperer stand.

People pass and ask, "Do I give the five cents to you?"

"That's only a joke. Tell me, what do you like to read?"

Books are flying from Corner Books' tables. We are sold out of used textbooks and giving out flyers for students to stop in after the festival by the time Evie frantically comes up behind me.

"Mayday! Mayday!" she calls. "Truman is AWOL. He's nowhere to be found and he's not answering his phone. He's the host of the main stage. There isn't a backup. What do we do?"

"We'll find him," I say. "Truman is one of the most reliable people I know."

"Get off your hiney and go get him," Gladys says. She walks around to the front of my booth and turns the little sign from *IN* to *OUT*.

I see Wanda working the AV setup of one of the stages as I pass in my hunt for Truman.

"Do whatever else you need. I know where to look," I tell Evie.

I have the perfect advantage. After memorizing his schedule when I liked him, I then spent months keeping my distance from Truman. I know exactly where to find him.

37

Friend Zone

After his apartment and the literary journal offices show no signs of him, I check for Truman in his next usual spot, between the buildings where English classes are held. I can smell the lingering scent of his clove cigarettes before I see him.

Truman, one foot resting on the brick wall of the building, watches me as I enter the walkway and head in his direction. "You're going in the wrong direction. Shouldn't you be running from me?"

"When did you develop a sense of humor?" I ask, leaning on the wall beside him, our shoulders touching.

"I've always been hilarious."

"Not because you mean to be," I say, finding it freakishly easy to talk to him after our last encounter. "The first time we met, you told me the first rule of book club is we all talk about book club."

"That was funny."

"It really wasn't. But I liked how dorky and serious you were. The brooding older college guy thing really fed my age-gap romance fantasies."

"I'm only a senior. I'm not so much older than you."

"Old enough, daddy. Are you going to tell me what's stressing you out or do you want me to guess?"

"How do you know I'm stressed?"

"You're kind of obvious. We should never play poker. I know all your tells."

"Are you sure you want the guy who broke your heart unloading on you?"

I laugh.

Truman raises an eyebrow at me.

"See, you aren't intentionally funny," I say, knowing he didn't get it. "What's up?"

He shakes his head. "Everything. I'm done here at the end of this year. I don't know what I'm going to do. I've got no job. No prospects. It's all ending. I guess I could go to grad school, but do I even want to? And when I'm around Scott and his friends, all I am is his college boyfriend. They've all accomplished things. Now I'm supposed to get up on a stage and interview all these authors who not only knew what their dreams were but followed them? I'm a hack. I haven't done anything. I'm a nobody."

I take Tru's hand like I used to when we'd walk together after cleaning up from book club. I lace my fingers between his. "You put yourself through college. You became editor of the literary journal. You're head of book club. You helped put on this festival. You're not a nobody, because they don't know who you are yet."

"You always saw the best in me to a fault."

"Because you let me. You should let more people see it."

"I know this is a messed-up thing to say considering our history, but I really do regret not being able to take the rose from you," Truman says. "I wasn't fair to you. I never deserved you liking me."

I squeeze his hand. "You were right not to. We're better like this."

We step away from the wall and Truman pulls me into a hug. When he doesn't let go, I raise my arms up his back and rest my head on his shoulder.

"Do you think we'll ever be friends again?" he asks.

"Only if you get funnier."

His body shakes as he lets out a laugh. "Thanks for coming to find me."

Hugging like this, I'm surprised the only thing I feel is comfortable. There's no longing. No desire. No heat. No passion. No sorrow. No loss.

Luke stands at the end of the alleyway watching us.

I push back from Truman. In the second it takes me, Luke is gone.

"Is something wrong?" Tru asks me.

"You've got to get on stage, and I've got to talk to someone," I say. I give Truman a push in one direction. I take off in the other.

"Stop," I call after Luke after catching sight of him in the distance when I exit the alley. "Cut me a break. I'm fat and it's hot and I hate running."

Luke turns. "Was that your plan all along? To get him back? Or do you just rebound quickly?"

"It wasn't what it looked like. We're friends."

"Same as Roger and I rehearsing wasn't what it looked like? Or same as you and I were friends?"

I wrinkle my brow. "Wait. Go back to the rehearsing."

"Why? It doesn't matter now. You're with Truman."

"I'm not. I never was. I came running after you."

"I don't want to play games, Bobby," he says. "I don't want to be with someone I'm always trading accusations with. I don't want to have to wonder if you giving me a book or closing a pool door or hugging some guy from your past is all part of one of your schemes." He runs his hand through his hair, turning back and forth as if he's trying to decide whether to walk away or not.

"You were never one of my plans," I say.

"Why not?" he asks. "If you really liked me, why didn't you plan for me?"

"Because once I figured it out, I thought I was too late."

A car horn honks. We both jump and look in the direction of a modified hatchback. The guy who gave me the twenty dollars this morning is waving out the window.

"Hey, book boy!" he calls. "Do you know where I can park?"

I swallow and blink a few times before I answer, "A left out of this lot and follow the signs."

He gives me a double thumbs-up. "Wish me luck. I'm about to meet my daughter."

"Daughter?" I ask out loud.

He's pulling away when I catch site of his bumper stickers, *I'd Rather Be Raiding* and an upside-down chicken with some curved lines coming out of it that make it looks like it's somersaulting.

"Oh crap," I say, my hands flying to my mouth. "chickn_backflip. We need to find Wanda, immediately. That's her dad."

38

When Lt_GlittrBomb Met chickn_backflip

"I thought he was her boyfriend," I explain as Luke and I race through the crowds.

"You're really unbelievable," Luke calls back.

"Lecture me later. Why isn't she on tech? Where is she?"

Luke points beyond the stage to a line of elm trees. Wanda is standing beneath them with her father. He gives her the copy of *Where the Wild Things Are*. Relief replaces the adrenaline that was fueling me a second ago when Wanda smiles and takes the book.

"It's ok," I say. "She looks happy." But I'm talking to myself. I turn and see Luke in the distance, walking away from me.

I take a deep breath and swallow down the fear building inside me despite my momentary relief. I join Wanda and her dad under the trees.

"My parents, your other grandparents, moved us," I hear him explaining as I approach. "They thought your mom was trouble. I found real trouble. But I paid my debts and cleaned up my act. I swear." He notices me. "That's the book guy."

"I figured," Wanda says, the smile dropping from her face.

I gulp down the fear again. "I thought you two were dating."

Wanda's dad looks from her to me. "That's nasty," he says.

"I warned you to mind your own business," Wanda growls.

"But you're happy to meet him. It worked out. Right?" I ask.

Wanda smacks me with her purse. "Just because things work out doesn't give you free license to mess with people's personal business. Especially not when they make it clear they don't want your help. You don't get rewarded for your bad behavior. What if this had gone horribly wrong? What if my mom had been here?"

Wanda's dad straightens and runs a hand over his hair. "Your mom's around?"

I know I shouldn't, but I can't help but ask, "Do I sense some residual feelings, Mr. Backflip?"

Wanda smacks me with her purse again. "Stop it." She raises her purse again. "We're not blindsiding my mom with her high school boyfriend."

"And baby daddy," I add.

Wanda lifts her purse. "I'm warning you."

I screw up my face waiting for her to hit me. "But long-lost loves, Wanda. That's a top-shelf romance trope." When I don't feel the purse, I hazard opening an eye.

Wanda's dad has his arm around her. "Yeah. They are," he says.

"This doesn't make things between us ok," Wanda says. "Tomorrow, you and I are having a reckoning."

"Come on, Wanda," her dad says. "Forgive him. He meant well. And from one badass to another, being a tough cookie doesn't get you anywhere good."

Wanda rolls her eyes. "Boys! So clueless. You don't feed the monster."

❧

There are very few books to bring back to Corner Books at the end of the day, which is good because we're all exhausted.

The three of us make quick work of loading the few boxes into the rear of Uncle Andy's truck and then back into the store.

The familiar chug of a motorcycle engine comes from outside. The second Gladys waves.

"That's my ride to the unveiling. Looks like we'll have just enough time to make it there after all."

"You'll have to fill me in tomorrow," Uncle Andy grumbles.

"You can't *not* be there," I say.

"I don't go where I'm not wanted."

Gladys pokes me with one of her crooked fingers and whispers, "Let me handle this." Rounding on Uncle Andy, she says, "Andrew, stop your nonsense this instant."

"I was pleasant to customers all day. You can stop bullying me now. I'm not going," he replies.

"If you don't want to go to your oldest friend's unveiling, that's your business. Although I think you're making a mistake, it's yours to make."

"Thank you, Gladys." Uncle Andy opens a box and begins unloading its content.

"But you're denying her only son the opportunity to see his mother unveil her final statue. It's a once-in-a-lifetime event." She lets her statement hang for a couple of seconds before she adds, "Oh, well. I'm off."

"You can call a cab, Bobby," Uncle Andy offers. "I'll cover the cost."

"By the time it arrives, the ceremony will be nearly over. Ta. See you Monday, boys."

Uncle Andy groans as he retrieves his keys from behind the counter. "Get in my truck."

Thank you, I mouth to Gladys through the glass of the front door.

I'm not certain because of the sun reflecting off her glasses, but I think I see her wink at me before she joins the second Gladys and they pull away from the curb.

We get into Uncle Andy's truck but I'm too busy gripping the handhold of the door and digging my feet into the floor from Uncle Andy's erratic driving to try to make conversation. He swings around corners and other vehicles like a stunt driver. He slams on the brakes as he pulls into a parking lot.

"Come with me?" I ask.

Uncle Andy stares out the windshield.

I don't open my door. "I shouldn't have gotten in the middle of you two."

Uncle Andy shakes his head. "We didn't do anything we didn't want to. We'd been following our trajectory for a long time."

"Do you regret it?"

Uncle Andy takes a deep breath. "The only regret I have is not doing it sooner."

I reach under me and pull a used copy of *Uncle Mame* from my back pocket. I put it on the seat between us.

"Cass didn't speak for me." I open the door and slide out.

The driver's door slams, and Uncle Andy is at my side, gripping my shoulder. "You're a good kid, you know. Do you know if she managed to fix it?"

"I don't. I guess we find out tonight." And I guess I find out if I keep my scholarship.

I reach up and squeeze Uncle Andy's hand before we walk into the library foyer. The room is packed. The central area is curtained off, the sculpture hidden behind draped fabric. I see Cindy waving at me, but we can't make it to her through the crowd. Farther in I recognize Mr. Martinez and Mr. Shah seated with the other seniors. There's Mae and Trisha and people from both Campus and Corner Books' book clubs.

Uncle Andy and I squeeze in, getting pressed forward by the people coming in behind us. There are whispered greetings nearby. Some call me Bobby and, some, the Book Whisperer.

Dean Perez is already partway through his speech.

"Where some might have seen tragedy in the loss of the etched window, I saw promise. I knew this was a piece of Little Elm College's legacy I could bestow back to its future generations," Dean Perez says. "Without further delay, the incomparable Cass Ashton, out of retirement."

Cass looks around the full room as she stands up. She's in an old pair of paint-smeared coveralls, her hair tied up with a bandanna and work boots on her feet. She adjusts the mic and there's the squeal of feedback. She scans the crowd, squinting into the audience.

"Woo!" I hear from me beside me. Uncle Andy raises his hands above his head and begins to clap. "Woo! Cass!"

I whistle and begin to clap too. The rest of the room joins in until everyone is hooting and applauding.

Cass takes a deep breath and says into the mic, "I will keep this brief. This statue almost didn't happen. There were a lot of accidents that lined up for it to come into existence. A sculptor had to get pregnant and give up her art. A boy had to break a window and his own heart. Then a misstep broke the statue and improved the design. A lot of unplanned coincidences had to happen to bring everything together. Drop the curtains, please."

The sheets around the statue drop. Attached to the frosted glass base are what appear to be clear glass padlocks in the shapes of hearts. The plates of glass are stacked into two shapes. The sculptures appear suspended on impossibly small foundations. But it doesn't look like anything. A loud click like gears turning fills the quiet room. The plates twist.

"I call it *Lovers Locked*," Cass says.

Murmurings begin among the crowd.

"What is it?" someone asks nearby. Soon, that sentiment is being echoed through the viewers.

Cass stands at the mic and smiles. She gives a nod. More clicking of gears silences the room, and the plates begin to move, spinning on their axes. As if by magic, two lovers appear, made of layers of glass. They each rest on tiptoe, their other leg stretched out behind them as if they're running toward each other, palms almost pressed together, lips almost touching. It's hard to tell whether the statues are male or female. I know Cass did that on purpose. The crowd gasps before the room fills with *ooh*s and *ahh*s.

"Once a day, the statue will shift into this form, because like the statue, life and love are kinetic and mutable and defy the odds that oppose them." She scans the crowd, searching but doesn't seem to find who she's looking for. "The rest of the time, it's in flux. Now, I invite you all to be a part of this artwork by attaching your own lover's locks to the base of the statue. Bring a padlock and lock it on." The crowd begins to chatter but Cass holds up both hands for silence. "One more thing. I said the last accident improved the statue."

The room dims as lights in the base of the statue come to life. The lovers illuminate. The glass sparkles and beams of light refract over the crowd, walls, and ceiling in dancing rainbows.

The audience erupts into cheers once again.

"It's magnificent," the mic picks up Dean Perez saying as he pumps my mom's hand up and down in his own. "As I knew it would be."

I turn my head, looking for Uncle Andy, but he's no longer at my side. I catch sight of Luke who is staring right back at me. He turns his eyes toward the statue.

Uncle Andy has pushed his way through the crowd toward Cass and Dean Perez.

"Cass," he calls to her. "Cass!"

She spots him and waves security away as he mounts the steps to join her.

Dean Perez removes the mic from the stand and slides behind Cass.

"We've been spinning around trying to find each other for enough years now," Uncle Andy says. The mic catches him and plays his words through the speakers. "I don't think I can spend one more day waiting to be with you."

"It's about time we changed that," Cass answers.

The cheering of the crowd for the statue is nothing compared to the sound they make as Cass steps toward Uncle Andy, and he takes her in his arms. They kiss and it happens with such rapidity and ferocity, I can't tell who kissed whom first.

"Absolutely lovely," a bald man in a black suit says beside me. He dabs at the corners of his eyes with a red handkerchief. "A happily ever after still gets me every time."

I squint at him. I feel like I've seen him somewhere before. "Have we met?"

He smiles. "Have we?" He points above the sculpture where rainbows have dappled the ceiling. "How she thought to turn the planes of glass into prisms is a stroke of brilliance."

"Or a lucky mistake," I say, remembering how I cracked the plates during the moving.

"Life is full of those, isn't it?"

Suddenly my mind clicks into place like Cass's statue. I do know him. All I needed was to add hair and makeup. "You are. Aren't you?"

The man raises a finger to his lips. "Shh." He opens his coat. It's lined with red leopard-print satin. From his inside pocket he takes a slim red metal case and slips a business card out.

"I heard about a young man who simply adores romance novels and works in a quaint little book shop downtown. I almost had the pleasure of meeting him. Perchance we could correct that with the release of my next book. I feel inspired to tell more of the story I began in *Pebbles* and the president of Little Elm's Baroness fan club should help plan the launch."

He holds out the card. I take it disbelievingly.

"I'd be honored," I say, tucking the card into my pocket safely and fumbling through my brain for something to say. "I have so many ideas."

"Excellent. I expect an email within the week. *Lovers Locked*. Wouldn't that make for an interesting title?"

He slips through the people marveling at the statue. I can't believe I met one of my personal heroes. I bounce up and down and turn my head to find someone I know to tell. I first look to where Luke was. I search the room, the joy I felt at meeting the Baroness deflating. Luke is nowhere in sight.

39

Pebbles Tossed at a Window

I text Uncle Andy and Cass that I'm heading home.

But the only person I really want to text is Luke. I want to tell him about the Baroness. I want to finish our conversation. I want to make things right.

But after freezing him out and his finding my list and everything between us today, I'm probably the last person he'd want to hear from. I wouldn't even read texts from me if I were him.

Halfway across the parking lot, someone calls my name. Tru waves from the passenger seat of a car full of his college friends. "We're going out. Join us."

"Another time," I say.

I keep walking, my feet aching and legs sore from the long day. At least they won't feel any worse when I get home.

I kick off my shoes once I'm in the door and strip off my clothing on the way to shower. I get in before it warms and enjoy the cool water washing over my body. I grab the shampoo and scrub, then the body wash, getting every last inch of me, every roll, every crevice, until I feel human again.

I slip on a pair of slides and cross the living room in an old pair of pajama pants and a ratty T-shirt. I make myself comfortable on the chaise longue pushed up against the windows and pick up the nearest book to unwind with, but the words on the page won't stay in focus. It slips from my hand and I fall asleep.

⸙

Something repeatedly striking the window wakes me.

I sit up and rub my eyes before going to the window.

Luke stands in my backyard, arm pulled back. I realize he's throwing pebbles.

I grab the silk robe I left draped over the back of the chaise longue and toss it on as I open the door and step onto the porch.

"I was wondering if I had to break some glass to get you to come outside," he says.

I stand at the railing. "What are you doing here?"

Luke glows golden and silver standing in the moonlight on my lawn. "I couldn't sleep. I kept going over all the things I need to say to you."

"You came to tell me off some more?"

"No," he says. "Well. Maybe. I'm not sure yet."

I yawn. "Can it wait until tomorrow afternoon then?"

"No." Luke continues to stand there.

"If you're not going to say anything else," I finally tell him, "I'm going to go back inside." I pull the robe around me and step toward the door.

"I never read past the first chapter of the book you loaned me," he blurts out.

My hand rests on the doorknob. "Because you didn't like it?"

"Because I need to know they end up together. Do they?"

I nod. "Of course they do."

Before I finish the sentence, Luke sprints across the grass and leaps onto the edge of the porch, swinging his legs over the railing.

I stifle a gasp. "Why did you do that?"

"I don't know. I get around you and I don't know what it is, reason and logic stop working. And when I'm not around you, I can't stop thinking about you. You drive me crazy, and you argue with me and frustrate me, and challenge me, and I don't know what to do with myself anymore. I don't care if I was one of your plans." He steps closer to me, his breathing heavy. I can smell his sweat mixing with the grapefruit and aftershave and laundry detergent. "And I don't care if I wasn't."

"You were just what happened."

"I like your crazy schemes. And I like your meddling and your good intentions. And I like that you'll work to make the most unrealistic dreams attainable not just for yourself but everyone around you." He brushes his hair back with both hands. "You know I don't believe in grand gestures. But if I have to, I'll keep throwing pebbles at your window.

I'll smash every window in Little Elm or whatever you decide is enough until there's a sign or gesture big and unmistakable enough to make you understand how I feel about you. I don't care if it's all a manipulation. Manipulate me. Tell me what I've got to do, Casanova. I'll do it."

"This," I say, our eyes locking together and a current traveling between them. "Just this."

Luke grips the back of my neck and yanks me toward him. His lips press to mine, urging them open. They willingly part to accept him. He holds me against him in the kiss as his other hand moves up my body, urgently groping, as if warring between savoring every inch and wanting to race on.

I cover his hand with mine to stop him, knowing he'll feel every bulge and that no amount of clothing or dark water can ever hide my body from his touch.

But lightning crackles through our every touch and ripples through the night air around us. And if my insecurities were clothing, I'd strip them off and let them ignite in a blaze at our feet, because now that I'm in Luke's arms, the only emotion to control us is desire actualized.

I grip his hand.

His fingers dig in and travel over my flesh.

And I know I'm helpless to stop him because I don't ever want this to stop. I press his hand to my chest. He pushes me against the wall with his body, pinning me in place, kissing me over and over, his stubble leaving my skin raw and alert and alive.

We come up for air. I hold his hips against me, part of me afraid he'll pull away. But he rests his forehead against mine, panting. I can feel the warmth of his breath on my lips still wet from his mouth.

"Casanova?" he asks, his hand moving down my back.

"Luke?"

"That night in the pool, I peeked too. And you should know whoever designed your cover," his hand slides farther down and squeezes, "did a really good job. Ten out of ten, would recommend."

I smack him in the chest with my palm as I laugh. "You're so weird. Add that to the list of things never to say to me again, love Grinch."

He kisses up my neck and nips at my earlobe. I'm unable to contain a moan.

"Pickle jar," he whispers into my ear.

I hit him softly again before I yank him by the front of the shirt into the house.

EPILOGUE
Play It Again, Bobby

"Your dad and mom seem to be getting along well," I say to Wanda as we follow our little group through the field toward the stage under the elms. Fairy lights are draped overhead, giving a sense of magic to the summer evening.

"You're going to stay out of it," she warns. Even though she's forgiven me for my chickn_backflip blunder, I know she's expecting me to pull some stunt to help her parents rekindle their relationship.

But I can tell from the way Wanda's parents look at each other that my help isn't required. The kindling is raring to go.

"You don't need to worry. I finally learned my lesson," I say. "No more getting involved in other people's love lives. No one needs me to make a mess of things for them. They're capable of doing it themselves."

"It helps you've got a love life of your own to keep you busy." Luke falls into step beside us and slides his arm behind me, his hand resting above my hip. He points with his other hand. "Cass and Andy are over there."

Evie rushes by, stopping only long enough to say into a walkie talkie, "All actors are to gather backstage in five minutes exactly. Showtime in ten."

"I guess I better get going. What do you think of my costume?" Roger asks, standing from where he was crouched talking to Jerome and Mya.

"You make a great ass," Luke says. "Even without the head."

"The cast party is at our place. You should come too, Bobby," Roger says. "It would be good to see you there."

"We'll see," Luke says, pulling me tighter against him. He whispers in my ear, "We don't have to. But now that we're together, he really wants you to like him."

I laugh. "I'll keep him working for it awhile longer."

Cass looks up from Uncle Andy's phone screen. "We got a great spot thanks to the Gladyses."

Gladys and the second Gladys are seated on a bench behind where Cass, Andy, and Wanda's mom and dad have laid out blankets on the lawn for all of us. As we sit, Gladys pokes Luke in the back.

"You're tall," she says.

"I am," Luke agrees.

"Don't go being all tall and block my view of the performance."

The second Gladys takes Gladys's hand in hers. "He can't help his height."

The OG Gladys harrumphs and cranes her neck.

Luke settles down, legs crossed at the ankles in front of him, leaning back on his elbows. I rest my head on his shoulder, one hand placed on his chest over his heart. A spark tingles through me.

Wanda sits in front of us, behind our respective sets of parents. She peers over Uncle Andy and Cass's shoulders at their phone screens.

"What's with the real estate listings? You're not moving. Are you?" Wanda asks.

I shake my head. "We're all happy living in our own places. They're trying to find Cass a studio. She's officially out of retirement. We're still cleaning glass slivers out of the hardwood."

The setting sun turns the sky fuchsia and magenta. Hints of lavender creep in.

"Cindy!" I call out to her as she walks by in a group all dressed in yoga gear.

"Looking good, Bobby," she says with a wink at Luke and me.

One of the women with Cindy looks over her shoulder and then stops to kneel beside me.

"Aren't you the Book Whisperer?" she asks.

"Not anymore," I say, sitting up. "I only handle event planning for Corner Books now."

She tilts her head to the side. "I'm having guy troubles. I could really use one of your recommendations."

I shake my head. "I'm done with that sort of thing."

Luke leans close. "Come on, Casanova. For old time's sake." He laces his fingers through mine and holds my hand. "You know you want to."

ACKNOWLEDGMENTS

Writing acknowledgments is the absolute worst. It's like walking on, walking on, walking on broken glass. But the need to express my gratitude to all those below is more compelling than my loathing. Acknowledgments, you know what you did.

My heartfelt thanks go out to the following:

John Cusick, Mary Kole, Julie Murphy, and Bittersweet Books for coming up with Bobby and Little Elm and trusting me with them. It is a gift to have brought your idea to fruition. I hope I've done you proud.

To TJ Ohler. You told me you'd felt very seen by this story when first we met. The more I've come to know you, the greater weight this holds. Thank you for *taking it*, *taking me*, and pushing the story to evolve. And you looked fabulous every step of the way.

To the team at Zando Projects for giving this book a home and the tremendous amount of work you have done and continue to do: Molly Stern, Sarah Schneider, Kayla White, Andrew Rein, Nathalie Ramirez, Anna Hall, Amelia Olsen, Natalie Ullman, Chloe Texier-Rose, and Emily Morris, as well as freelancers Rachel Kowal and Sara Thwaite.

To Chris Kwon for giving me a plus-size guy on the cover of one of my novels.

To Amy Tompkins and the team at Transatlantic. Amy, the more I get to know you, the more I am sure our work together is its own love story.

To my friends and family who heard a lot about "the Julie project" in vague details for a long time. You know what you did and have my love for it.

ABOUT THE AUTHOR

PAUL COCCIA, the author of Glitterature, writes mainly for young readers with award-winning titles including *Cub* and *On the Line*, coauthored with Eric Walters. Paul has a specialist degree in English literature from the University of Toronto and an MFA in creative writing from the University of British Columbia. He is often found baking in his Toronto home, joined by his nephew, three dogs, and parrot. Paul loves classic romance novels and when the couple gets together in romantic comedies, despite being more of a Luke than a Bobby.